"It's important that I tell you this."

Luke paused before he spoke again. He saw a lone tear fall over her lashes and catch the moonlight as it made its way down her cheek.

"I couldn't let you know how I felt, because it would ruin everything. I knew that you could love me, maybe even in a romantic way, but I didn't want you to. I wanted something better for you."

Kristen started to say something, but he placed his finger gently against her lips to silence her.

"I wanted for you . . . to be more than I was, more than you could be with me . . . I wanted you to have a shot at everything you deserved, without me to drag you down. And the only way to do that was to stand back and let you grow away from me."

Kristen's breath caught in her throat.

"Don't you know," she asked in a hoarse whisper, "that *everything* I am, I am because of you?"

ABOUT THE AUTHOR

Tracy Hughes is a pseudonym for prolific romance novelist Terri Herrington. Winner of the 1987 RWA Golden Medallion Award, she's written books that have drawn rave reviews from critics and fans alike. Her fourth Superromance, *White Lies & Alibis*, is set in Florida, where the author lives with her husband and two young daughters.

Books by Tracy Hughes

HARLEQUIN SUPERROMANCE

304–ABOVE THE CLOUDS
342–JO
381–EMERALD WINDOWS

Don't miss any of our special offers. Write to us at the following address for information on our newest releases.

Harlequin Reader Service
901 Fuhrmann Blvd., P.O. Box 1397, Buffalo, NY 14240
Canadian address: P.O. Box 603,
Fort Erie, Ont. L2A 5X3

White Lies & Alibis

TRACY HUGHES

Harlequin Books

TORONTO • NEW YORK • LONDON
AMSTERDAM • PARIS • SYDNEY • HAMBURG
STOCKHOLM • ATHENS • TOKYO • MILAN

Published April 1990

ISBN 0-373-70399-6

ACKNOWLEDGMENTS
Special thanks to attorney J.Q. Davis
of Bethard and Davis in Coushatta, Louisiana,
for helping me with the legal details in this book.
Also, thanks to Pam Hart
for sharing her criminal justice expertise with me
and making sure my story rang true.

CHAPTER ONE

THE WAIL OF THE SIREN behind him drew Luke Wade's eyes to his rearview mirror, and in the midday sunlight he could see that the car warning him to pull over was not a squad car, but an unmarked Pontiac with a flashing light on the dash.

"Damn it," he muttered, pulling the cigarette out of his mouth and quelling the urge to toss it out the open window, as he usually did. Instead, he stubbed it out in the ashtray and negotiated an exit from I-20, onto an Atlanta, Georgia street that was almost as busy. The car followed him, its siren still blaring.

"Bozos don't have enough murders around here to keep them busy," he told some nonexistent passenger, "so they spend their time chasing people for speeding. Why me?"

Luke found a shoulder about a mile from the interstate and pulled off the road, watching the car follow him to a halt. Not disguising his irritation, he got out and pulled his billfold from a back pocket that had faded into a perpetual rectangle in the shape of his wallet.

"What was I doing?" he asked as the officers approached. "Sixty in a fifty-five zone? Maybe you ought to just book me and lock me up."

Not finding Luke's suggestion amusing, the plain-clothes officer took his license, read it quickly, then handed it to his partner. "We're with the Bureau of Alcohol, Tobacco and Firearms," the man said, flashing his badge at Luke.

Luke's vexation turned to confusion, and frowning, he read the badge. "The ATF?" he asked. "Since when do you guys chase people down for speeding?"

"We have a warrant to search your car," the officer said, ignoring Luke's question. He handed Luke the warrant, and reluctantly, Luke took it and searched for some error.

"Open the trunk for us, please."

Luke closed his hand tighter around his keys and made no effort to move toward the trunk. "What the hell for?" he asked.

"We're investigating a recent theft at the ammunitions plant," the agent said. "We had an anonymous tip this morning that we could find what we were looking for in your trunk. Open it."

"Anonymous tip?" Luke repeated, incredulous. "Hey, wait a minute." He took a step backward as a familiar sense of injustice he hadn't felt in years constricted his lungs, and he swallowed to combat the sudden dryness in his throat. "I didn't have anything to do with that theft. I *prevent* thefts, I don't commit them. I installed their security system—"

Two more unmarked cars pulled in behind the first, their arrival stopping Luke midsentence and making it more than obvious that this situation was becoming serious. Realizing that he had no choice, he raised his hands to illustrate his cooperation. "All right, I'll open it," he said. "I have nothing to hide."

Drawing in a deep breath, he went to his trunk as two more ATF officials approached his car. His key clicked in the lock, and the trunk opened slowly.

The expletive he might have muttered got lodged in his throat, along with his very heart, as Luke's eyes caught sight of the crate of plastic explosives that hadn't been there earlier in the day.

"Those aren't mine!" Luke said, not daring to move a muscle. "Someone's setting me up!"

"You're under arrest," one of the officers behind him said, and suddenly, he felt handcuffs being snapped on his wrists and expert hands frisking him for a nonexistent weapon.

But hours earlier, the explosives hadn't existed, either. Not until someone—some malicious soul he couldn't name to save his life—had decided to pin the crime on him.

"You have the right to remain silent," a harsh, jaded voice behind him was saying. "Anything you say can and will be held against you in a court of law. You have the right to an attorney...."

Attorney, Luke thought desperately. He needed an attorney. Someone he could trust. Someone who trusted him.

Kristen...

He couldn't call her now, after eleven years. Not when her life was going well... not when she'd probably forgotten all about him.

But as the ATF officials escorted him to their car, he realized that once again he'd been left without a choice.

Kristen Jordan was the only person he was sure he could count on. And he needed her now more than he ever had.

IT HAD BEEN A LONG DAY, and an excruciating month. The kind of month that didn't seem to have existed on any calendar, a blurry four-week span of depositions and last-minute hunts for precedents, lots of cold coffee and stale sandwiches, and late-night kisses from her sleepy daughter who'd been tucked in by a sitter.

Kristen Jordan kicked off her pumps beneath her small desk in the corner of the office she shared with two other junior associates of the law firm Broussard, Street and Devereaux, and closed her eyes, imagining how she would curl up on the sofa with Courtney tonight and catch up on all the six-year-old's daily events she'd missed over the past few weeks. Details like the funny items Courtney's friends had brought to show-and-tell, and how Charlie Murphy's glasses had fallen in the toilet when he bent over to tie his shoe. They'd make popcorn and watch Courtney's favorite program on television, the one about the little girl who had two fathers. Sometimes, since the divorce and with Eric's busy social calendar, Kristen wondered if Courtney felt that was two more than she had.

Wearily, she began sorting the papers she needed to take home tonight to work on after Courtney was in bed, and then transferred them to her briefcase. When she was almost done, the office door opened, and she looked up to see the firm's partners filing in, wry smiles teasing their faces as they filled the tiny office.

Quickly, she felt with her feet for her shoes, and slipped into them.

"What's going on?" Kristen asked, beginning to catch the contagious smiles. "Is this a lynch mob?"

Robert Broussard, the firm's senior partner, took her hand and brought her to her feet. Suddenly Kristen felt on stage, and self-consciously, her hand strayed to her hair, where soft, baby-blond wisps had slipped out of her chignon. "We thought you deserved a little something for all the work you put in on the Hamilton case the past few weeks," Robert said. "John says in no uncertain terms that he couldn't have won the case without you."

"Oh, that's silly," Kristen objected. "He tried the case. I just hung around in the background."

"Modesty becomes you," the older man said in lavish approval. "But we happen to know that some of the things you dug up might have been overlooked by the rest of us. And at Broussard, Street and Devereux, we like to reward hard work. Would you come this way, please?"

Feeling like a little girl being led into her first surprise party, Kristen allowed herself to be drawn out of the small room and up the hall, where the offices of partners and associates were located. As they passed by, secretaries smiled in amused conspiracy, and a few muttered mysterious congratulations for some accomplishment Kristen didn't understand. They led her into an office that had once been occupied by a friend of hers, a young fledgling attorney who had been let go for taking too many *pro bono* cases the previous year. They had yet to replace him.

She stepped in, looked around, waiting for her "re-ward." "What?" she asked.

"Your new office," Robert said, beaming with pride. "To go with your new promotion, from junior associate to associate. And if you play your cards right, Kristen, it's our contention that you have everything it takes to be a full partner in this firm sometime in the next few years."

Kristen's smile faded poignantly, and she covered her mouth with her hands as she turned back to the desk in the center of the office, seeing the room in a new light. "Mine?" she whispered, shifting her pow-der-blue eyes back to the partners. "Just because we won the Hamilton case?"

"That and two years' worth of other cases you've worked on," Robert said. "We're proud of you, Kristen, and we look forward to grooming you to be one of us."

Kristen took a deep breath and leaned back on the desk, feeling the smooth finish of polished oak, un-like the plywood veneer desk she'd used in the other office. "I . . . I don't know what to say."

"Say you'll accept."

"Of course I'll accept!" she said. "I'm not crazy!"

The phone on the desk buzzed over the low roar of laughter, and she didn't respond at first.

"Kristen, it's your phone," Laura Ashton, one of the partners, said. "We've already instructed Amy to channel all of your calls here."

"Oh." Feeling silly, Kristen grabbed the phone and put it to her ear, unable to temper her grin or the ela-tion in her voice. "Kristen Jordan."

"Hi, babe." The voice, rough and gravelly and intimately familiar, sent a shiver scampering down her spine. "How ya doin'? It's me, Luke."

Kristen's heart jolted. She caught a sharp breath and forgot the people standing around her.

"Luke?" Her expression faded into a tender half smile, and instantly, she saw his face in her mind, his day-old stubble against a lazy tan, his hair windblown and groomed with neglect, a cigarette hanging defiantly from his mouth and eyes the color of expensive whiskey—a perfect mix of exquisite depth and irreverent decadence—smiling as they always had when he spoke to her. "Luke... how are you?"

"I've been better."

The words were uttered with a dull note of sobriety, and suddenly she sensed that there was something wrong, that he hadn't called her after eleven years just to say hello. It was the same stilted tone he'd used that day he told her he'd joined the army, and made the halfhearted promise to write her while he was away.

"I need your help, kiddo."

The others in the office began to stir, whispering about the look on her face when they told her the good news, and the color of wallpaper they'd suggest, and the chair that squeaked when she went around her desk to sit down. Kristen was oblivious as she dipped her head down, so that the stray wisps of hair tickled her face. "Luke, what is it?" she asked.

A long pause followed, but Kristen waited patiently until he found the words. "I'm in jail," he said, "and I could use a good lawyer."

MOMENTS LATER, Kristen was pulling out of the parking garage that sheltered her car, considering what Luke had gotten himself into this time. Theft at an ammunitions plant. That put him in the jurisdiction of the United States Attorney's office. It meant major trouble, unlike the minor scrapes Luke had had with the law years ago. A shiver of despair coursed through her, and she wondered how solid the case was against him, and if she was experienced enough to get him off. Absolute conviction in his innocence and faith in his character might not be enough to combat such serious charges.

She came to a red light and propped her head in her hand, nervously massaging her weary temples. Luke Wade was a lot of things, she thought, and he'd *done* a lot of things. But he wasn't a thief, and he didn't belong in jail. The fact that he was there, however, didn't surprise her at all. Luke was never where he belonged, because he didn't really belong anywhere.

She inhaled deeply and pressed the accelerator, checked her watch and mentally cursed the rush-hour traffic. Then, trying to calm down, she reminded herself that Luke had waited eleven years to contact her. Eleven more minutes certainly wouldn't change anything.

"I need your help, kiddo."

She smiled at the words he had used, the words that were, in reality, far from funny. But with the memory came a nostalgic rush, dragging her back twenty-one years, to the first time she had helped Luke Wade when she was nine and he was thirteen, right after his parents died and he went to live with his aunt and uncle. The fact that they were her aunt and uncle, too, though she and Luke were only related by marriage, gave them something in common despite the difference in their ages.

"I need your help, kiddo. You know Aunt Margaret better than I do. Is her bite as bad as her bark?"

Kristen remembered feeling awestruck that the thirteen-year-old boy had sought her out for help. "Well, I don't know," she'd said. "She's never really been mad at me before."

"Yeah, well, she's always mad at me," he said. "And last night I sort of sneaked out, and now she's on the warpath. Do me a favor and tell her we were over here talking, will you? It'd sure help me out."

Kristen remembered how syrupy sweet Aunt Margaret, her uncle's wife, had been when she intervened for Luke. "She's okay," she'd told him later. "I never heard her yell at her other kids when they were still home."

"Yeah, well, according to her, they're perfect and never needed yelling at," Luke said. "Everybody knows I'm not. If it weren't for my parents' will, she wouldn't even be stuck with me."

Until that time, Kristen had never given much thought to the fact that her aunt and uncle might have taken in the orphaned Luke more out of obligation and duty than love and concern. Even at the young age of nine, Kristen had distinctly felt Luke's pain at that knowledge, and the loneliness he wore like a leather jacket with some obscene phrase on the back.

But it wasn't that loneliness she saw in his eyes that had made her love him even then. It was the amber depth of his eyes, and the smile that seemed exclusively hers when he flashed it her way, and the way he walked, and talked, and laughed. And it was the way he had protected her and nurtured her, filling the void her father had left when he died.

But Luke had never known just how much he meant to her, and how much his absence from her life had hurt her. He had never known how she had cried on the day he enlisted in the army when she was nineteen. He had no way of knowing that she'd thought of him, in some context, every day of her life since, even when she was in love with and married to another, even when her daughter became a new channel for her love, even when he'd become some phantom of her past whom she might never see again.

She reached the United States Marshal's office where Luke was being held, and found a parking place. Her hand trembled as she reached for her briefcase, then opened the car door. As an afterthought, she glanced in the mirror, smoothed back her hair and breathed a shaky sigh. It wouldn't do to feign sophistication with a man who'd watched her grow up, she thought. But Luke had done even more than that. In many ways, Luke had taught her *how* to grow up. And now he needed her again.

Summoning all her resolve, and all the inside knowledge of the legal system she'd learned over the past two years with Broussard, Street and Devereux, Kristen went inside and secured copies of Luke's arrest report, along with his record dating back to his teenage years. It showed other arrests: for disturbing the peace, for drunk and disorderly conduct and once for marijuana possession. A passenger in Luke's car had been caught holding a joint after they were pulled over for speeding, but the incident was on Luke's record nonetheless. She took her time reviewing the reports, telling herself that her anxiety wasn't that of a twelve-year-old girl nursing her first crush, but of a thirty-year-old lawyer ready to defend a friend before God and a grand jury.

Then, when she had gleaned all the information she needed, Kristen followed the officer down the stairs to the "cages," where both common and uncommon criminals were locked. Quietly, she passed one cell at a time, anxiously glancing in each. Finally, she saw him, standing in a cell with his back to her, gazing soberly out the bar-striped window, with one leg propped on the aged bench beside him. The T-shirt he wore was stretched across his taut muscles, defining his strength and reminding her that this man—who wasn't quite her cousin and had never been her lover—would get through this with or without her. No matter how much life managed to trip him up, Luke always landed on his feet.

The guard behind her rattled his keys and jabbed one into the cell door with a clank, and Luke turned around. Their eyes met—richest amethyst embracing softest cobalt—and Kristen's pulse jolted. No, it hadn't just been her imagination for the past eleven years that his eyes were the color of molten gold, or that his hair had the satiny sheen of rich, melted chocolate. But was it her imagination that the hint of a smile shimmered in those eyes and tugged at those full lips she had never known intimately?

"Kristy." The nickname, so exclusively his, was a reverent whisper, barely audible, except for its soft echo in the almost empty room. He caught his breath, held it a second as his eyes swept over her like a warm ocean tide, then released it in a rush. "How ya doin', babe?"

"Good." Kristen dropped her gaze, unable to maintain eye contact when a million conflicting emotions battled in her heart—loss, abandonment, heartache, confusion. Luke had always read her too clearly; she couldn't allow that now.

She stood up straight and tightened her grip on the leather handle of her briefcase, her nails biting into her palms. Kristen tried not to look so shaken as she went through the open door. The guard hovered at the entrance, waiting for her to tell him it was all right to leave her there. The gesture seemed absurd, she thought. She was a lawyer, after all, and met with clients in their cells every day. But those clients had never made her throat flood with emotion, or her hands tremble. Those clients had never looked at her with eyes that knew who she really was ... who she'd been before. . . .

She dragged her eyes from Luke's steady gaze and nodded toward the guard, indicating that it was all right to lock her in with Luke. Reluctantly, the guard closed the door with a resounding clash, and Kristen's eyes gravitated to Luke again. A sad, nostalgic smile came to her face, and she had trouble finding her voice. "You haven't changed at all, Luke," she whispered.

If indeed there was a smile hovering somewhere on his handsome face, it died at her words. He glanced around him at the dreary, oppressive surroundings, and lifted one shoulder in a lopsided shrug. "No," he agreed. "I still keep managing to wind up on the wrong side of these bars, don't I?"

Kristen sighed heavily and glanced at the concrete floor. Some other prisoner had signed his name there in permanent ink, as if he wanted to record the visit for posterity. Some people clung to notoriety, she thought. Others couldn't shake it no matter what they did. She looked directly at Luke, no longer trying to hide what was in her heart. "I didn't mean it that way," she said. "It's just been so long since I've seen you. I've missed you."

That smile skittered back across his lips, and danced like starlight in his eyes. "But you've become someone important," he said, as if the time they'd been apart had some bearing on her achievements. "I told you you could be a lawyer if you tried."

The pride in his statement deflated her hopes. It was the kind of pride a big brother had for a sister... or a cousin for a cousin. It had always been that way. Grateful, in a way, that Luke had effectively reminded her exactly what their relationship was, what it had to be, she managed to find her professional facade. *Time to get tough,* a voice inside warned. *Time to do your job.* That was the only reason he had called her, after all.

"Tell me what happened, Luke," she said.

He crossed his arms and cocked his head then, and she could imagine the defenses rising up around him like walls, the way they used to with others...but never with her. She was his lawyer now, she reflected, not necessarily his friend. "You have the arrest report," he said. "You tell me."

Kristen knew then that Luke wouldn't cooperate in the normal lawyer-client fashion. If he'd wanted that, he would have called someone else, someone more experienced in criminal litigation. He needed something more. She hoped she could still give it to him.

She lowered herself to the cot. "Yes, I've read the report," she said. "But what *really* happened? The bottom line?"

Luke began to pace across the floor, rubbing the back of his neck, leaving it red. "You'll never believe this," he said. "Not in a million years."

The slightest hint of a smile touched Kristen's lips. Hadn't she heard that before, when he'd gotten arrested for brawling in a bar with an irate boyfriend? Luke had sworn he'd just been "minding his own business," when a girl had "practically torn his clothes off." The funny thing was, Kristen had never once doubted his story. She knew firsthand the effect he had on women. "Try me," she said.

Luke stopped his pacing and faced her directly. He raked splayed fingers through his hair. "All I know is I'm driving down the street today, and the cops pull me over with a warrant to search my car. Next thing I know, they're unloading this crate full of RDX out of my trunk and slapping cuffs on my wrists."

Kristen leaned forward, setting her elbows on her knees. "What exactly is RDX?" she asked.

"It's a plastic explosive. We used it in the Army to assemble bombs. When you mix it with certain plasticizers and waxes, it's stable enough to handle pretty roughly and withstand heat and cold." He shook his head and looked back up at the crumbling ceiling.

"Hell, with my background I'm the perfect scapegoat." He shot her a look over his shoulder. "And did they tell you that my partner and I just installed a massive security system in that plant, and that it was so complex that not even an employee there could have walked out with so much as a paper clip?''

Kristen got to her feet and went to stand beside him. He turned around and leaned back against the wall, his eyes dull with frustration, but rejecting defeat. ''It doesn't look good,'' Kristen admitted. Standing so close, she could smell the faint scent of after-shave—the same brand he used to wear, a brand that used to get him into so much trouble. ''They did some checking on you and your partner. They know that you both served in the ordnance corps of the army.''

''Right,'' Luke said, throwing up his hands and slapping them on his jeans-clad thighs. ''The government teaches me how to assemble a bomb, so I'm the natural suspect when explosives are stolen. Beats the hell out of real detective work, doesn't it?'' He began to pace again.

''I guess they suspect Hank, too,'' he went on. ''We're partners. He has the same background I do, give or take a few smears. They'll probably be dragging him in any minute now.''

Kristen shook her head. She'd already asked the marshal about Luke's partner. ''They searched his car before yours. He was clean.''

''Well, thank God for that,'' Luke said. ''The man has enough problems. His wife's in the hospital, and he sure as hell doesn't need to be locked up right now.''

''Neither do you,'' Kristen said.

The words seemed to remind Luke that he had an ally. He turned around, slid his hands into his pockets, quietly looking for signs of the trust she'd once had in him.

''I'm going to get you out of here,'' she said.

Luke visibly relaxed and a look of reluctant—even tentative—gratitude was in his eyes. Slowly, he narrowed the distance between them and took her hand, turned it palm up and gazed at the lines there as if he read her future as clearly as he remembered her past. "I knew I could count on you, Kristy."

She swallowed hard and willed her heart to stop racing. He'd hardly ever touched her before. When they were younger, it was as if any physical contact at all would destroy the magic of the friendship they'd built, and so they'd kept their distance. But all the logic in the world hadn't kept Kristen from fantasizing about the way his hands would feel against her skin, or the taste of his lips, or the texture of his hair.... Now, the gesture brought back a barrage of fantasies she thought she had buried long ago. "Your bond hearing is at ten tomorrow," she said, her voice rasping. "I tried to get it for today, but the magistrate's schedule was full. Once we get you out of here, we'll start working on your defense. Maybe we can figure out who's done this to you before it goes any further."

Luke let her hand go. His gaze locked into hers, making her feel stripped and defenseless...comfortably so....

Fighting the sensations combating her good sense, Kristen went to her briefcase and lifted it, aware that Luke's eyes lingered on her as she did. She turned back to him, and fought the fear that things would never be the same, that things would never be different.

Knowing he could see the wistfulness in her eyes, as he probably always had when she was a kid, she wrenched her gaze away again and called for someone to let her out. The wait seemed eternal as they stood quietly, at home in each other's presence, and nonetheless, awkward. It wasn't until the sheriff appeared that she was able to speak again. "I'll see you in court tomorrow, Luke."

"Yeah," he said. "I'll see ya."

"I'll see ya." The words evoked a bitter memory, one Kristen still didn't quite understand or accept. He'd said them years ago, before he'd joined the Army and disappeared from her life. And that was the last time she'd seen him until today.

She looked away when the guard opened the door. Tears welled in her eyes, and she didn't want Luke to see. Was she on the edge of crying because they were saying goodbye for the day, she asked herself? Or because they weren't?

That was it, she thought. Luke never said goodbye. He just faded away, the way he'd begun to fade from her life long before he'd joined the service. Would he fade away again, after she'd managed to clear his name?

Rubbing the bridge of her nose with a fingertip, a gesture designed to hide the emotion in her eyes, she started to leave.

"Kristy?" The word stopped her, forced her to turn back. A look of poignant sadness was on his face, as well.

"You never asked me if I did it," he said.

Kristen swallowed the lump in her throat, and realized she'd broken one of the first rules of a defense attorney. Balefully, she wondered how many more she would break before this was finished. "I don't have to ask," she said simply. "I know you, Luke. Remember?"

Luke seemed as touched as she by the reminder. No one else had ever had the patience to dig deeply enough to truly know him. A sad smile softened the lines of his lips. "How could I forget?" he asked.

Kristen tried to return that smile, but failed. Mutely, she left him standing there alone, and went to begin her work.

ALL GROWN-UP, Luke thought that night as he lay on his back on the hard cot, buried in the deepest shadows of the cell. Kristen had grown up and out of his life, and to this day, he didn't know if he could accept that. There was something special about her innocence back then, her naïveté, her blind trust in the goodness that only she could find inside him. What if time had soured her, and taught her the dirty truths he had tried to shelter her from? What if her faith in him didn't run as deeply anymore?

He closed his eyes and imagined her the way she had looked today, standing before him in that tight skirt and that loose blazer, with her baby-fine hair twisted up in a chignon. She still had a waist he could have encircled with his hands—if he'd ever succumbed to the weakness that persuaded him—and her figure was still that of a nineteen-year-old. Her body still made him break out in a fine sweat, made his heart charge and skid, made his throat go dry. And that special Kristen scent—the scent he had never in his life associated with any other woman, though he'd searched long and hard—if that scent hadn't pushed him over the edge, then those wide eyes, which looked at him with adoration and tenderness, almost had.

The thing was, she had never known how much she moved him. But it wasn't right, his feeling that way about her. She didn't need someone like him palpitating for her. Kristen deserved better.

He turned over on the cot, buried his face in the pillow and tried to push her out of his mind. He had to think, he told himself. Had to figure out who could have set him up this way, and why anyone would hate him enough. Explosives stashed in his trunk, a break-in at the ammunitions plant right after he'd installed its security system, an anonymous tip... it just didn't make sense. He'd made a lot of people angry in his life, but he didn't really have any enemies. At least none that he knew of.

Maybe Kristen would come up with something, he thought soberly, then chastised himself that his thoughts had returned to her. He got up from the cot and strode on bare feet across the concrete floor to the barred window. The view of a dark parking lot and a brick building on the other side snuffed any vision a prisoner here might have... but there was nothing to suppress the ones he had of her. What was she doing tonight? he wondered. Was she working on his case? Was she watching television? Was she lying in bed, in the dark, thinking....

The fantasy led to a more pronounced one, and his mind flirted with the image of her lying on a rumpled bed in a white, filmy gown, her hair spread across the pillow like an angel's wings. Something in his stomach pulled at him, but he couldn't escape the image. What would it feel like to hold her against him, to bury his face in her hair? Her skin would be like satin, he was certain, and her hair would feel like long feathers tickling through his fingers.

He turned from the window, aware of how hot it had suddenly become in the cell. And then he realized the heat was coming from within him.

He fell back onto the cot, wrestling with the pillow, and cursed himself. It was starting up again, all the yearning and wishing for something he would never—could never—have. She'd done well without him, and was on her way to the top. She'd married and had a child. And even now that she was divorced, she had a life that had nothing to do with him . . . attributed nothing to him. It had never been easy to stay out of her life. But he had no regrets.

When he was out of this mess, he wouldn't see her again, he told himself. He'd just blur back into her past again, and move ahead as best he could. He wouldn't get in her way anymore.

He closed his eyes, and wondered what her daughter looked like. Did the child resemble her father? He wondered if the little girl saw her daddy, now that Kristen and he were divorced. Did *Kristen* still see him?

He wondered what had led to their divorce, and something twisted in his stomach. He hoped Kristen's ex hadn't hurt her . . . not only in the physical sense. He couldn't bear to think of Kristen with a broken heart.

What had caused the sadness he'd seen in her eyes when she left him today? he wondered dismally. Did she have scars that hadn't healed? Had she learned all the lessons he'd never wanted her to learn, or was there still something she needed sheltering from? He didn't know, and wasn't sure he ever would. All he knew for certain was that he still had the need to protect her.

From life, from pain and, yes, even from himself.

CHAPTER TWO

I HAVE TO PROTECT HER...protect her...protect her....
The words twisted over and over in the depths of Hank Gentry's dream, turning like a knife lodged in his heart. He jumped, shaking himself from his shallow, stolen sleep. Opening his eyes, he saw the dusty streaks of moonlight cutting between the blinds in the sterile hospital room. *Oh, hell,* he thought, sitting straight up in the chair he'd slept in more than in his own bed lately. *I fell asleep again.*

His bloodshot eyes flashed to the small woman on the bed, a limp figure buried in sheets and tubes beneath a light that was as dim and fading as her life. *Sherry's still breathing,* he noted with relief. *Thank God.*

Hank got out of his chair, stiff muscles rebelling with the effort, and went to his wife's side. Her hair had almost completely fallen out, but what was still there he stroked gently. Her skin was grayer than it had been the last time she suffered her leukemia treatment, he thought. And she was much weaker. He could feel her drifting away, pulling into herself, preparing to surrender to death, but he wasn't ready to let her go.

She's going to bounce back, he told himself. *She always has before.*

He turned away from her bed and ran both hands through his blond hair. It was badly in need of a cut. Quietly, he stepped to the window, peered out between the blinds. Streetlights lit the parking lot outside like Chinese lanterns at a lawn party, reminding him that life existed outside this room...that other people did.

Images of his two-year-old twin sons flashed through his mind, and he wondered what time Sherry's mother had gotten them to bed tonight.

"They keep asking for Daddy," Nancy had told him on the phone earlier. "I guess they're getting used to Sherry not being here, but it's hard to explain why they can't see you...."

Hank had bitterly mumbled that she should just tell them the truth: that they couldn't always have what they wanted in life. But the moment he uttered the words, he'd hated himself and apologized. The situation was too complicated for their young minds to understand. Hell, it was too complicated for *him*. Instead, he'd made some promise that he'd come home for a few hours tomorrow, and pick up all the scribbled pictures they'd made for him to bring to Sherry.

Promises, he thought miserably. How would he ever keep all of them? He'd promised Sherry he would cherish her "till death do us part," but he'd be damned if he'd let her out of his life without a struggle. He'd promised the kids she would come home soon, but she was getting worse instead of better. And he'd promised Luke that he'd be back at work— *Oh, no,* he thought suddenly. *I forgot about Luke.*

He looked at his watch, saw that it was past eight. Was Luke still in jail? Had he waited for Hank to bail him out? Or would he have finally gotten past that unyielding stubbornness of his and called Kristen Jordan?

He probably had, Hank reassured himself. She had probably gotten him off on a technicality, even made them drop the charges. Luke was always lucky that way.

At least Hank hoped that was the case.

I let him down, he thought, despite his flimsy hopes. *He's my best friend, and I let him down.*

Sherry moved beneath the sheets, and Hank spun around. Her eyes fluttered open, their pale glaze blurring the clarity he always sought there. But behind that glaze, there was still vitality. She glanced around the room, met his eyes, and the slightest smile lifted the corners of dry, cracking lips. "Perk up, Gentry," she whispered. "You look like hell."

He tried to smile, but he knew that waking up meant she would have to face another battle with pain. And that was something he just couldn't joke his way around. At least, not without effort. "You're no beauty queen tonight, yourself," he said with a grin, stroking her face with callused fingers. "I'll be glad when I can look at you without all these tubes."

She managed to laugh weakly and took his hand in hers. She was cold, he noted. She was always cold lately. He pulled her covers up and tried to warm her hand in the heat of his.

"Did I dream about Luke being in jail?" she asked in a voice barely stronger than a whisper. "Or did you tell me that?"

Hank wished he hadn't told her, but it was hard to be selective about facts when she yearned to know everything that went on, and never stopped persuading Hank to fill her in. News about friends and family was a lifeline, he told himself. It kept her fighting. "Yep, it's true. Ol' Luke's in the slammer. But don't worry. It's all a mistake. He'll get it straightened out tomorrow."

"Aren't you gonna bail him out?" she asked. "You know he won't call his aunt...."

Hank let go of her hand, as if through touch Sherry could sense his guilt. Wearily, he rubbed his three-days' growth of beard. "He has that lawyer friend, Kristen. She'll get him out."

"Are you sure?"

"I'm sure," Hank said with a reassuring smile, but even as he spoke, he knew he wasn't sure at all. There was every possibility that no one had come for Luke. But he couldn't help that now. Sherry had a battle to fight, and he'd be damned if he'd abandon her. Not even for Luke. Today, he told himself, she wouldn't have to fight alone. Luke would have to wait, because Sherry needed him more.

Hank knew Luke would understand. That, after all, was what friends were for.

SOMETHING'S WRONG. The realization seeped into five-going-on-six-year-old Courtney Jordan's mind in stages as she sat across the table from her mother, negotiating the spaghetti noodles that refused to stay wound on her fork. She had first noticed her mother's mood at her grandmother's, when Kristen had come to pick her up late. Her mom hadn't asked if she'd brought any papers home from school, which she hadn't; or if she'd gotten in the talent show, which she had; or even if Thompson P. Harris had pulled her hair again on the bus ride home, which he had.

Courtney jabbed a forkful of noodles into her mouth and trimmed the excess ones with her front tooth, wiggly though it was. The gaping hole left by the next tooth, which had finally come out last week, made the task much harder. What was the use of being old enough to lose a tooth, she asked herself, if you couldn't even eat spaghetti without getting it all over your face? And what was the use of having an interesting day, when no one even asked about it?

It was something about that Luke man, she told herself. She'd heard her mother talking to her grandmother earlier, but hadn't paid that much attention. Now she wished she had. Taking a deep breath, she set down her fork and settled her round blue eyes on Kristen.

"What's the matter, Mommy?" she asked.

Kristen looked up from her plate, which had hardly been touched. "Nothing, pumpkin," she said. "I was just thinking about a case I'm working on."

Courtney's big eyes took on an authoritative expression, and she set her little elbows on the table and leaned forward toward her mother. "Grandma says you need to learn to leave your work at the office."

Kristen's smile grew more genuine, Courtney saw with satisfaction.

"You know what?" Kristen said. "Grandma's right."

"And you haven't eaten enough," Courtney observed wryly. "You don't eat enough to kill a bird."

Kristen wrestled with the smile on her face. "I think that's 'enough to keep a bird *alive.*'"

"No, it's not," Courtney argued, pointing to the full plate. "You've hardly taken a bite."

Kristen gave up on correcting the child, and shoved a forkful into her mouth. "Satisfied?" she asked.

Courtney nodded. "You're thinking about that Luke man, aren't you?" she asked with her mouth full of escaping noodles.

Kristen almost choked on her food, satisfying Courtney tremendously. Reactions were her favorite things. "How do you know about 'that Luke man'?"

Courtney leaned back in her chair and stretched her arms over her head. "I heard you telling Grandma that you saw him today. It made you sad, like when you see Daddy."

More reaction. Courtney dropped her arms and watched, amused, as Kristen washed down her food with a gulp of tea, and focused her astonished eyes on her daughter. "It didn't make me sad to see Luke, honey. And what in the world makes you think I get sad when I see your father?"

Courtney shrugged as if she hadn't given the subject much thought, but she had. Every time her father came to visit, he left her mother with that strained, tight look on her face. Just once, she wished he'd say something nice to her, something to make her smile, something that wouldn't make Courtney feel as if she had to choose sides. But her dad never said nice things. Just clever things that weren't very smart. And that always left Courtney a little sad, too.

"Just...when you're around him, you look mad. You don't laugh or smile much."

Kristen got that look again, and Courtney realized vaguely that sometimes just *thinking* of her father made her mother mad.

"It's just that your father and I don't get along that well sometimes. We rub each other the wrong way. But he's still my friend," Kristen added feebly.

"Is Luke your friend?" Courtney asked.

Kristen glanced back down at her food, and Courtney knew this was one of those subjects that her mother "would rather not talk about." That, of course, made her all the more curious.

"Yes, he's my friend," Kristen said. "Once, he was my very best friend." Her eyes settled, unseeing, on the salt shaker at the center of the table, and Courtney knew she'd lost her mother again to whatever—*whoever*—it was on her mind that was stealing her away.

"See?" Courtney pointed out quietly. "He makes you sad, too."

Kristen wilted and shoved her plate away, and Courtney knew her mother was surrendering, preparing to tell all. "Courtney, I'm not sad because I saw Luke. I haven't seen him in a long time, and I've missed him. *That* made me sad."

"Did you love him?" Courtney prodded, her round eyes fully absorbing every nuance of her mother's expression.

Kristen leaned back in her chair and expelled a long breath, helpless to deny the truth. Courtney waited, sensing secrets in her mother—memories, heartaches. But then she saw sweet thoughts, sweet memories that brought a gentle smile to her mother's lips, and more important, to her eyes. "Yeah, I loved him."

The admission jolted the child somewhat, but Courtney quickly recovered, and came back with the most logical question, in her mind. "Why didn't you marry him?"

Kristen laughed softly and began to cut the noodles on Courtney's plate with the side of her fork. "Well, he never asked me, for one thing."

"How come you didn't ask *him*?" Courtney inquired, as if the solution were incredibly simple.

Kristen propped her chin in her palm and smiled at her daughter. "You don't understand, pumpkin. It wasn't that kind of love. Luke was sort of my cousin, and he lived across the street from me when I was growing up." She struggled for an easy explanation, but the more she tried, the more complicated it all seemed.

Courtney squirmed until she was kneeling on the chair, and reached for the Parmesan cheese across the table. "I know who he was. He was Aunt Margaret's son," she said. "I saw him in a picture album at Grandma's."

Kristen shook her head. "No, that isn't exactly right." She leaned her elbows on the table and considered how best to describe what...who...Luke really was. "Luke's parents died in a car accident when he was thirteen, so he had to go live with his mother's sister...Aunt Margaret. Aunt Margaret was married to my Uncle Ed, your grandmother's brother."

"Grandma had a brother?" Courtney cut in, visions dancing in her head of her grandmother as a little girl with a hulking bodyguard who knocked down anyone who dared insult her. "Was he older or younger?"

"Older," Kristen said.

Courtney's eyes glazed over, and she stared off into space, still picturing the scene. He probably wore a baseball cap and worked on cars. He probably taught his sister how to win at Go Fish. He probably built her a tire swing in her backyard. "I wish I had a big brother," she said wistfully. "Amber Wilkins has a big brother, and one time he beat up a boy who tripped her in the school lunchroom. If I had a brother, I bet Thompson P. Harris wouldn't bother me anymore."

Kristen stared dully at her daughter, exasperated at the fickleness of a five-going-on-six-year-old mind.

Unfortunately, Kristen's thoughts couldn't be diverted so easily. And later that night, after she put Courtney to bed, she found thoughts of Luke creeping up on her, twisting her heart, making her ache like a heartsick kid once again. Every memory, every event in her past, every "first," had something to do with Luke Wade. Through each milestone, Luke had been there to either comfort, guide or protect her. And acting in each capacity, he'd dug his place deeper—and more permanently—into her heart.

You tell that little jerk that if he ever lays a hand on you again, I'll break his legs.

Kristen had been only twelve when he uttered that threat, but in her heart she had fully believed Luke meant every word.

It had been after a family reunion at the park when one of the cocky friends of a distant cousin cornered her in a picnic shelter and tried to kiss her against her will.

"He was just showing off," Kristen said. "He made sure his friends were watching."

Luke's face had reddened like a sunset sky as he sat on the picnic table with his white-knuckled hands clutching the wood. "Yeah, well, *I'll* make sure his friends are watching, too."

Kristen had forgotten that it was her first kiss—her idea or not—and instead had felt a giddy excitement at the possibility that her sixteen-year-old idol was the least bit jealous. "I took care of myself," she said. "He's still wearing my handprint on his face."

At that, Luke had stared at her for a moment, anger still hardening his features, and finally an amused smile softened his expression. "Good for you," he said. "But that won't always work. When we get home, I'll teach you a few surefire ways to make a boy leave you alone." He grinned wickedly then, and added, "I learned them the hard way."

The allusion to his reputation with the high school girls he had dated had sobered Kristen somewhat, reminding her that she was only someone Luke looked out for, not someone he was attracted to. He hadn't been jealous at all.

She had peered at him with eyes that hadn't yet seen a makeup brush, eyes that were too big and luminous and made her look even younger than she was. "I'd rather you taught me how to make the right boys notice me," she said defiantly.

Luke had inclined his head in mild flirtation. It was the boldest he'd ever gotten with her. "You don't need any tricks for that, babe. You had that licked a long time ago."

Now, as she sat in her quiet house, with her child tucked into bed and Luke's arrest report and records sitting on the table in front of her, Kristen realized that despite his lack of interest in her as a female, he had always proved he cared about her as a friend. In his way, he had loved her . . . she never doubted that. But it had never been the right kind of love, and had never been enough for her.

It might not be enough even now, she thought. But Luke's love was priceless and precious, in whatever form it was offered. She would take what she could get from him, and return whatever he would accept.

And if it was the last thing she did, she would get this latest smear wiped from his record. Luke was a lot of things, but he was not a criminal. She knew that with every fiber of her being. The trick would be convincing the magistrate tomorrow.

THE LAW FIRM of Broussard, Street and Devereux was humming to life when Kristen pushed through the glass doors on the fourteenth floor of the Delta Life Building the next morning. Secretaries were already typing with efficiency, phones were ringing and being answered, messengers were coming and going with depositions, statements and documents in hand. Lawyers and paralegals clustered in the coffee room, around the water cooler and in the doorways of their colleagues' offices.

Too distracted to interact with the others, Kristen hurried past the shelves of the massive law library the firm boasted, to the office she'd been awarded yesterday. *Funny,* she thought, looking around at the room that spoke so eloquently for the progress she was making in becoming a respected member of the firm. She had hardly thought about her promotion at all last night, for she was too preoccupied with Luke.

She sat down behind her desk, quickly scanned her messages and decided that none was pressing enough to distract her from Luke's case. She had to concentrate. There was no room for a slipup now. Every loophole needed to be covered. She wanted him out of jail this morning, where she could see him in the light of day, experience his smile again, bask in the freedom of spirit she hoped he still possessed....

To work, Kristen reminded herself. She had to stop thinking of the man and concentrate on the case. She had to get him out of jail because he was innocent— not to fill the void he'd left in her heart.

There was a knock on the door, and John Norsworthy, her mentor and a full partner in the firm, stuck his head in. His youthfully styled, gray-sprinkled hair was perfectly groomed, though fatigue lines beneath his eyes revealed his middle-age. "Congratulations, Jordan," he said. "Sorry I wasn't here when they gave you the office, but I was in court."

Kristen smiled and looked around her, seeing the office almost for the first time that morning. "Thank you for putting in a word for me," she said, knowing that she'd still be crouched in a corner of the junior associates' office if he hadn't gone to bat for her. "I couldn't have done it without you."

"Well, I could say the same thing," he said, sloughing off the gratitude. "Listen, could I see you in my office for a minute? I need your help on the Genpack case."

Kristen gestured to the documentation on her desk. "Could it wait? I took a case last night, and I have to be in court in an hour."

"A case?" John stepped farther into the office, holding his coffee cup in his hand as if it were an elder's staff. He wasn't wearing his coat, Kristen noted, and his tie was loose—unusual for a man who valued his professional image more than his law degree. It was obvious he'd been absorbed in his work all night, for he only allowed himself to look the least bit casual when he was pressured for time. "What case?"

"U.S. v. Wade," Kristen said, motioning to the arrest report on her desk.

As if it were his privilege to sift through her work—for usually her work was also *his* work—he picked up the report and flipped through it, expertly scanning the key facts that would contribute to his opinion. "God, Kristen. This is a real loser. What would make you take a case like this?"

Kristen bristled, but reminded herself that he was her superior. "He's innocent," she said. "I've known Luke Wade most of my life. He asked me to represent him."

John shook his head and tossed the report onto her desk, as if it were trash. "Take my advice," he said. "Don't waste your time on that one. It's a lost cause."

"A lost cause?" she asked, trying to keep her voice even. "Why?"

"Why?" He half laughed, as if the question was ludicrous. "The guy has a record. He had perfect access to the explosives, and he was found with them. And his history in the Army is proof that he knew what to do with the stuff once he got it. The man's guilty.''

"Now, wait a minute, John,'' she said, her tone professional though fumes of rage drifted up inside her. Setting her hands on her desk, she got slowly to her feet. "That so-called proof you're talking about is circumstantial, and as for his record, I don't think disturbing the peace and disorderly conduct are 'proof' that he's capable of stealing explosives. And the marijuana charge wasn't his fault. His friend was carrying it—''

"But the record shows that *he* was,'' John pointed out, "and regardless of the behind-the-scenes knowledge you may have, what's on paper is all you have to work with.''

John sighed condescendingly and rubbed the small of his back. "Kristen, listen to me. My record is better than anybody's in this firm. I win cases. One reason I do that is that I don't waste my time on losers, and I have a certain standard for the clients I agree to represent.''

"Well, I happen to have more faith in my abilities as an attorney than to just take on easy cases,'' she retorted. "And as for my standards, Luke fits them just fine. I'm taking the case, and I'm going to win it. Luke Wade is not going to prison.''

John shook his head. "The prosecutors will have a hell of a case against him. Be aware of that.''

"I am aware of that,'' she said. "And *I'll* have a tight case, too, not to mention my absolute conviction that the man is innocent. You taught me everything I know about criminal defense, remember? I don't intend to lose.''

John gave a shrug then, a gesture he rarely used, bottomed his coffee and tossed the empty cup into her wastebasket. "All right," he said wearily. "Do what you have to. Just don't let your history with this guy blur your judgment. You've come too far."

Kristen swallowed back her wrath and sat down again. "My judgment is fine."

John paused a moment, watching her critically. "I've invested a lot of time in your development as an attorney, Kristen, because I see you going a long way in your career. One instance of bad judgment can mar a career for life. Remember that, okay?"

Kristen nodded with a degree of respect that she couldn't deny, yet she felt resentment. "I'll keep that in mind," she said.

The door closed behind him, and Kristen dropped her face into her palms. What if he was right, she thought, about the D.A. having such a tight case against Luke that even she couldn't help him? What if she lacked enough experience? What if the judge wouldn't release him on bond? What if she let Luke down?

"Don't let me down, okay?" Luke's voice, gravelly and warm, played over in her mind like a lyric from the past.

He had said those words to her before her first date when she'd just turned fifteen, and she remembered thinking then, as she thought now, that she'd jump the Grand Canyon to keep from letting him down. *"Don't let me down...."*

He'd leaned against her mother's car in her driveway, the wind whipping through hair that was defiantly long, though Aunt Margaret had never stopped trying to force him to cut it. "Boys can't always be trusted, Kristen," he'd warned her, dragging on a cigarette and squinting through the smoke with grave eyes. "Some of them'll push you as far as you'll let them."

"The voice of experience again?" she'd asked with amusement.

Luke hadn't found the observation funny at that time, and she could have sworn she saw a shadow of sadness lurking in his eyes. "No kidding, babe," he said. "I want you to promise me that you won't put up with any crap."

Kristen laughed and tossed her baby-blond hair over her shoulder, wishing that, just once, he'd see her as a young woman *he* could want, and not as someone for whom he felt responsible. "You act like I'm dating an ex-con."

Luke dropped his cigarette then and ground it out with his foot. "Hey, we don't know that much about this guy. I just don't want you taking any chances."

Kristen had finally promised to guard her virtue with her life, but that hadn't been good enough for Luke. Before he left her, he'd slid a dime out of his tight pocket. "Put that in your shoe," he said, "and use it to call me if you get into trouble."

"Yeah, sure," Kristen had teased. "As if the infamous Luke Wade is really going to be home on a Saturday night. The town would just have to close down without you, and the broken hearts...well, I can't even stand to think about it."

Luke's mirthless expression held the foundation of a promise. "I'm not going anywhere tonight," he had said.

Kristen remembered the exhilarating feeling she'd had just knowing that Luke was at home...waiting...on the off chance that she would need him that night. It had distracted her from the date, igniting a burning sensation in her heart, making her want to hurry home and tell Luke she was fine, but that it wasn't the football player she really wanted to be with.... Except that telling him that would have forced up a wall between them. Of that she had been certain.

"Don't let me down," he had said. And she hadn't.

She checked her watch now, and decided to get to the courthouse early, so she wouldn't feel rushed and fragmented when the hearing began. Kristen gathered up her papers and stacked them in her briefcase. It was up to her, she thought. She had to get Luke out. She had to get him back into her life. She had to protect him as he had always protected her.

She owed it to him, after all. But more than that, she thought, with an understanding she hadn't had at fifteen, Kristen owed it to herself.

CHAPTER THREE

LUKE SLID HIS HANDS into the pockets of the jeans he'd worn since yesterday, and paced across the tiny conference room where he waited for Kristen. The heels of his shoes echoed on the cold tile floor. Damn, he should have called someone to bring him a change of clothes, he thought. But who? Hank had probably been at the hospital with Sherry all night in yet another battle with her leukemia, and no one else knew he was here.

At least they hadn't known until the paper came out that morning, with the report that he had been arrested in conjunction with a theft at the ammunitions plant. Just what he needed. A media conviction before he'd even been indicted. Already, he could see six months of work flying out the window. Who would hire him and Hank to install a security system when he was being accused of this?

But the knife twisted even deeper, and he thought of his Aunt Margaret's reaction, the I-told-you-so's he knew were probably racing through her mind right about now. *"No son of mine would have wound up in a mess like this,"* she'd told him more than once. She'd always known he would bring disgrace and embarrassment into her family, ever since the day he'd been thrust upon her like an inheritance no one quite knew what to do with. For years, the attitude had been subtle—no more than a feeling—a feeling that Aunt Margaret had hidden her silver just in case her sister's orphaned son decided to help himself.

He could see her now, running around her house pulling down the shades, hiding her car in the garage, unplugging her phones lest someone catch her and humiliate her with the knowledge of Luke's arrest. He almost felt sorry for her.

He went to the door and peered out the small window there, past the guard outside. Kristen would be here soon, he thought, and she would smile at him, and the heaviness on his heart would be lifted.

He should never have gotten her involved in this.

He started to turn away from the window, but just before he did, he saw the outer door open, and Kristen stepped inside. She stopped at a table, conferred with one of the clerks, then glanced toward the room he was in.

She was so beautiful, he thought. Her hair hadn't changed color in all these years, and it still looked like silken threads his fingers ached to touch. Someday, he thought...then rebuked himself, certain that day would never come.

He stepped away from the door as Kristen came toward it, and when she opened it, he watched the way the fluorescent bulbs overhead sent shimmering rods of light scurrying across her chignon. She wore the nostalgic scent of memory and heartache and innocent seduction.

She smiled, her pastel eyes luminous as they beheld him. "Hi, Luke. How was your night?"

He could no more ignore that smile than he could ignore the sunshine he always watched rise over the skyline on his morning jogs. "Fantastic," he lied with a grin. "Slept like a baby."

Kristen wasn't fooled. Had she ever been? he wondered. "You look like you used to look when you were hung over after one of your wild orgies."

"Nasty rumors," Luke said, his wicked grin spreading to his eyes. "I never got hangovers."

She laughed then, shaking her head like an old friend with an always incorrigible pal. All grown-up, he thought again. Gone were the giggles, the blushes, the gullibility. She was a woman now.

"Just the same," she said, getting back to the subject, "you don't look like you got much sleep in that cell."

"Oh, it wasn't so bad," he said.

"No big deal, huh?" she asked, seeing right through the way he discounted the crisis. "Just another Thursday night, right? Good food, relaxation, quiet?"

One corner of his lip curled upward. "Hey, I didn't say I'd argue if you got me out of here."

"No, I didn't think so," Kristen said. "So, are you ready?"

He held up a hand and gestured toward the door. "Just lead the way," he said. "I'm in your hands."

Something about his suddenly serious tone, the trusting offering, made Kristen feel even closer to Luke than she had eleven years ago. It would be all right, she thought. Everything would be all right, because he was back in her life. She wouldn't let him down this time, either, no matter what it took to clear his name.

SUNLIGHT FROM THE WORLD outside entered the little hospital room like a shy visitor afraid to come inside. Hank Gentry plugged the final cord into the VCR he'd brought from home, and inserted a videocassette of *Duck Soup.* He had read a book about laughter being the best medicine, and had convinced himself that the Marx Brothers might have just the healing power Sherry needed.

"Wait till you see this," he told her. "It'll crack you up."

Sherry managed to smile. "If you wanted to crack me up," she said weakly, "you should have brought those home movies of us in Rio."

Hank sat next to her on the bed as the credits rolled. "The ones where I stumbled onto the stage and sang 'Blue Suede Shoes'? You were horrified."

Sherry laughed . . . for the first time in days. "And then . . . you convinced the drummer in the band to let you play 'Inna Gadda da Vida.' It was so awful. . . ." Her words tumbled into laughter again, and Hank laughed, too, savoring every ounce of life he heard in that sound.

"Did Luke tape all of that?" Hank asked.

"Just about," Sherry said. "Until that well-endowed barmaid started hitting on him."

"Ol' Luke," Hank said. "He's always drawn the women, hasn't he?"

"Out of the woodwork," Sherry said. "One of these days he's gonna get caught. I want to be there to dance at his wedding."

The thought made them both quietly pensive and Hank took her frail, cold hand and kissed her knuckles. In his best Groucho Marx voice, he said, "The day

Luke Wade gets married, my dear, is the day we both do the cancan on a jet-ski across the Mississippi."

Sherry surrendered to laughter again, and Hank knew that as long as he lived, no sound would be so magical. The laughter gave him a healing release from his dreads and anxieties, making him truly believe that his wife was on her way to recovering yet again.

If only the laughter worked as well on her, he thought. If only he could get her home again.

IT DIDN'T TAKE LONG for Kristen to get Luke released on a $20,000 bond. Within two hours, they stood outside the courthouse beside her car, smiling at each other like teenagers with secrets that only the other shared. He looked so good standing there, she thought, with the wind whipping through his hair, lending a pink glow to his nose and stubbled jaw. His hands were resting indolently in the pockets of a green flight jacket, but his eyes gleamed as if he secretly teetered on the edge of laughter.

"What's so funny?" Kristen asked, her nerves tingling.

"You," he said. "You look so professional in that trench coat. Do they have some kind of lawyer store where you guys go to buy your clothes?"

Kristen inclined her head and looked at his own coat. "And you look like something out of *Top Gun* Where'd you get a flight jacket, Luke?"

"Stole it." His irreverent answer was followed by a chuckle, making her laugh along with him.

"You did not."

"You never know," he said. "I might have enough skeletons in my closet to keep you busy for a long time."

"Like I said," Kristen told him, "you haven't changed. You're still as full of bull as you ever were."

"And you still look nineteen," he said.

"Nineteen." Kristen's smile wilted with the reminder of the worst year of her life, the year she had lost Luke once and for all. "I'd say the same thing, but you were never nineteen, were you, Luke?"

He glanced off into the distance. His eyes still held a trace of amusement, the way they always had when she hit a nerve. Luke didn't like giving things away... sometimes not even to her. "No, I guess I never was."

She leaned back against her car, holding her briefcase in front of her with both hands. "Do you remember the day you joined the Army, Luke? When we were all at the bus station saying goodbye?"

Luke laughed, but there was no fondness—no nostalgic magic—in the sound. "Yeah, I remember. Aunt Margaret smiled more that day than the whole time I lived with her." He brought his eyes back to Kristen. "But you didn't."

Her eyes clouded, and suddenly she felt like that nineteen-year-old standing at the station, realizing for the final time that Luke Wade was fading from her life. "I was proud of you," she said, forcing a smile. "You looked so handsome in your uniform. And you had so much purpose that day, so much pride. But...I knew how much I'd miss you." She paused, then found her voice again. "I thought I'd hear from you. That you'd write. Something."

Luke reached inside his jacket pocket and pulled out a pair of sunglasses. He put them on, instantly shielding his eyes. "We both got busy, and I've never been a letter writer. What can I say?"

Kristen swallowed the old emotion that, no matter how she fought it, still never let go of her. After a moment she found her voice again. "Well, now is what really matters, isn't it?" She cleared her throat, took a deep breath and told herself she wouldn't let the hurtful memories get in the way of the good ones. "We need to get together this afternoon, Luke, after you've had a chance to rest a little. I can't pretend this case is going to be easy. Our best approach is going to be finding whoever set you up." She squinted in the cold sweeping over the pavement and studied him gravely. "Do you know who it could be? Any enemies that you can think of?"

Luke cocked a one-sided grin, again discounting his plight. "I haven't slept with anybody's wife, haven't kicked anybody's dog, haven't insulted anybody's mother. Who would want to do something like this to me?"

"Well, I don't know," she said. "But we've got to figure it out." She checked her watch. "Can we meet at three o'clock?"

"Sure," he said. "My house or yours?"

Kristen opened her car door and tossed her briefcase on the seat. "I was thinking more along the lines of my office. That's where I usually meet with clients."

Instantly, the shutters over Luke's eyes closed, and she saw him stiffening before her eyes. She had reduced him to the status of ordinary client, and he didn't like it. But was it wise to take him to her home, let him enter so far into her life, let him see how she lived, how she mothered, how she relaxed? Was it wise to take him back into her heart, when he'd only fade out of sight again as soon as he had the chance?

The answer came as quickly as a heartbeat. Yes, it was wise, because he was Luke. That was all the reason she needed.

"But on second thought," she added, "let's just meet at my house."

Luke slid his hands into his pockets and nodded. "All right. Your place, three o'clock."

Kristen got into her car and shut the door. "See you later, Luke,' she said through the open window.

"Yeah," he said. The beginnings of amusement—as if he knew something she didn't—curled across Luke's mouth.

She cranked her engine and frowned, bewildered at the way he still stood beside her car, grinning down at her.

"Bye."

"Bye," he said.

She shifted into drive and started to pull away, but before she had gone more than a foot, Luke reached out and stopped her. He leaned into the open window and pulled off his shades, revealing the full force of those hypnotic eyes again. With a trace of laughter he asked, "You mind giving me a ride, babe? The cops kept my car for evidence, and forgot to provide me with the complimentary limousine service they usually offer."

Kristen leaned her head back on the seat, years-old laughter welling up inside her. "Why didn't you say something?"

He chuckled deeply, his face a little too close, his smile a little too compelling. How many times had he stood like this, leaning into the window of her rusty Mustang, teasing her, when she was barely old enough to drive? "I didn't have the heart. You looked so efficient. It's that trench coat. I guess it intimidates me."

Kristen's laughter floated on a moan. "You've never been intimidated in your life. Get in."

Still chuckling, Luke ambled around the car and slid in. And as they pulled away, Kristen felt less than nineteen. She felt like the fifteen-year-old who had believed that Luke Wade had invented heartbeats, who had laughed with him and endured his teasing, who would have followed him blindly anywhere he led her. "When you've finished laughing at me," she said, still grinning, "you can tell me where you live."

"That's all right," Luke said, his voice deep and lazy. "I didn't really want to go home, anyway. First I wanted to go buy a pack of cigarettes before I go into respiratory distress."

"Ah," Kristen said. "I knew something was missing. It was the perpetual cigarette. What's the second place?"

Luke's amusement faded, and a shadow passed over his expression as he looked out the window. "The hospital," he said quietly. "To see how my partner's wife is doing."

Kristen pulled into the traffic and glanced over at him, aware that the teasing note had left his voice. "I'll take you there. Do you mind if I go with you? I'd like to see if he has any ideas about who could have set you up."

"Sure," Luke said. "Don't expect him to be too social, though. He's real down about Sherry's leukemia. She's at the Atlanta Cancer Institute for her treatment, but she's having a real bad time right now."

Kristen's eyes rounded in alarmed compassion, and she looked at Luke again. "Is she dying?"

"Hell no!" Luke said quickly, as though the mere act of denial could stop what was inevitable. He set his eyes on her dashboard, stared at the lock on the glove compartment. A slow frown cut between his brows. "I hope not."

Kristen didn't press further as she pulled into a convenience store parking lot for Luke's cigarettes. She went in with him, aware of the attentive eyes of the young girl behind the counter as he bought a pack of cigarettes and a newspaper.

When they were back in the car, he rolled down the window, lit up and took a slow, relaxing drag. "Ah," he said with a long sigh. "Best smoke I've ever had."

One side of Kristen's mouth cocked up in a grin, for the cigarette completed the picture she had remembered of him.

"You know," he said, exhaling out the window so the smoke wouldn't fill the car, "I really should quit. Anything that means this much to me has got to be destructive."

"Is that why you haven't quit?" she asked lightly. "Because you're afraid of investing yourself in anything more satisfying?"

He laughed, as if he knew she was practicing some kind of amateur psychology on him. "Babe, if I ever find anything more satisfying than a good cigarette, and I know it won't kill me or land me back in jail, I'll quit so fast that my system will go into shock.''

"I guess lung cancer is a pretty flimsy reason to quit," she said. "Even though you threw it up to me every time I wanted to smoke.''

"Did I?" Luke asked, as if he didn't remember.

"Sure did," Kristen told him. "You said you had the market cornered on stupidity and if you ever caught me with a cigarette you'd be so disappointed you'd never speak to me again.''

"And you bought it?" Luke asked, laughing.

"Of course," Kristen said. "Didn't want to risk making my 'big brother' mad.''

Luke didn't laugh, as she'd expected. Instead, he put his sunglasses back on and drew on the cigarette again. "Too bad I didn't listen to my own advice," he said.

He finished his cigarette and tossed the butt out the window, then shook out the newspaper and began scanning the pages.

"It's in Section C," she said soberly. "Page three.''

Luke looked over at her, his eyes apprehensive. "Pretty bad?"

Kristen shrugged. "It could be worse. It just gives the facts.''

"The facts," Luke muttered, turning to the article entitled, "Local Man Arrested for Ammunitions Plant Theft." He read the article quickly, then crumpled the paper and set his elbow on the car door, stroking his lip with his finger. "Funny how condemning a bunch of facts can look when the newspaper reports them.''

Kristen groped for something to comfort him. "It's a small piece, Luke. Not that many people will read it."

"No," he agreed sarcastically. "Just a few hundred potential clients, every friend I have in town and my dear, sweet Aunt Margaret."

Kristen swallowed and changed lanes as the hospital came into view. "Aunt Margaret knew before the paper came out," she said quietly. "I asked my mother to talk to her last night."

Luke's expression changed, and he tapped his chin with restless fingertips. "Terrific," he said. "She's probably already called the judge and convinced him to give me twenty years."

Kristen sighed. "I guess she took it the way you'd expect," she said. "She was upset."

Luke gave a bitter laugh. "Upset? Don't you think that's an understatement?"

Kristen wished she could tell him that Aunt Margaret supported and loved him, and believed in his innocence. But they both knew that wasn't the case.

She pulled into the parking lot of the hospital, found a space and cut off her engine. "Look, I'll just wait downstairs in the lobby if you want...."

Luke looked up at the windows, as if he knew instinctively which one was Sherry's. "It's okay," he said. "You can come up to her floor."

They sat still for a moment, neither making a move to get out, and finally Luke spoke again. "Sometimes my own problems seem so small when I compare them to what Hank and Sherry are going through."

Kristen looked over at Luke, wishing that just once he'd worry for himself. "Your problems aren't small, Luke. They're big this time."

He laughed mirthlessly. "I know, babe. My head's not that thick. It's just that she's up there, going through God knows what...."

"Are you close to her?" she asked quietly.

"Yeah," he whispered. "Real close." He glanced aside at her, and for a moment she thought he would leave it at that—one of those many Luke-secrets he didn't care to share. But after a moment, he went on.

"Hank's my best friend," he said. "We met in basic training, and we got assigned together after that. When we got out of the Army, we started our security business, and we've been together ever since. And Sherry, well, she's one of my best friends, too. I was with him when he met her." He pulled out another cigarette, lit it and leaned his head back on the seat.

"She was a dancer at a nightclub in Vegas, and Hank took one look at her legs and it was lust at first sight. I said, 'You jerk, that woman has men lined up at her door. What would she want with you?'"

Luke laughed then and shook his head. "Hank told me he was gonna marry that girl, bet me a thousand bucks, no less. Damn if I didn't lose."

The amusement in his eyes faded into soul-deep sadness, and he looked up at the hospital windows again, seeing a memory, instead. "I hope she'll be all right."

Kristen didn't know the woman or the man, but oddly, she felt Luke's pain as if it were her own. She set her hand on his shoulder. "She will," she said, wishing she had the power to make it so.

Luke sat up straighter and opened the car door. "Yeah, she'll be fine," he said with waning conviction. "Come on, let's go."

Kristen hesitated. "Maybe I shouldn't go with you," she said, suddenly feeling like an intruder now that she knew just how bad Sherry's condition was.

"It's okay," he assured her. "She can't have visitors, anyway. Hank'll come out to see us."

"Still," she said. "He won't be up to answering my questions. Maybe I should wait a day or so...."

Luke's smile returned. "Kristy, I'm headed for prison. He's my best friend. He'll do what he can to help me. Besides," he added, a soft sparkle in his eyes, "he's waited all these years to finally meet you. Who am I to deny him that now?"

It was a moment after Luke had gotten out of the car before Kristen realized she was holding her breath. Maybe, she thought with the faintest stirring of hope. Maybe he had talked about her because she'd meant more to him than a mere relative or past friend. Maybe there was more. Just a little bit more.

But that hope died almost as quickly as it had been born. Luke had probably spoken of her the way an older brother would have. An older cousin. A neighbor who'd watched her grow up. Luke would never think of her in any other way.

She got out of the car and started to follow him toward the hospital, trying desperately to accept things as they were. But the acceptance she'd felt years ago wouldn't return. The truth made her angry this time, made her feel shortchanged. But she knew that the truth was altered and bent every day. Maybe there was still a chance to make Luke see her differently.

Maybe this time he wouldn't fade away.

CHAPTER FOUR

"I HATE THESE PLACES."

Luke's baleful sentiment seemed couched in bitter memory as the hospital elevator took them to the fifth floor, where leukemia patients spent much of their lives chasing that ever-fleeing reprieve called remission.

"Yeah, me too," Kristen mumbled. "Hospitals always remind me of when my dad died. It seems like we spent weeks in his room, talking, praying, hoping."

The doors opened and Luke stepped off, his eyes focused pensively on the floor. "I remember," he said. "It was rough on you."

Kristen couldn't help slipping her hand through the crook of his elbow and giving him a gentle, affectionate squeeze. "You made it easier," she said.

He smiled down at her, feeling awkward because of the open gesture. "Did I?"

"Yeah, you did," she said with a sigh as she remembered the quiet night they'd shared in his car, driving aimlessly, not exchanging a word. "You took me away from the relatives and condolence calls, and didn't expect me to be strong."

"You were anyway, though," he said.

Kristen smiled and let go of his arm. "Well, it wasn't as if I was the only one who'd ever lost a parent."

She saw the shadow of melancholy pass over his face, and years-old tension stiffen his shoulders as he looked up the long corridor. "No, but sometimes I think it was probably a little better to have them snatched away, like mine were, instead of them lingering on in a place like this. I've always hated long goodbyes."

Kristen met his eyes and saw that they weren't just talking about death anymore. "I don't know," she said. "Sometimes long goodbyes are better than unfinished business."

"Well, you get unfinished business no matter how you say goodbye," Luke said. "It's just a question of making the cleanest break."

He looked back up the hall, saw a nurse coming with a tray of medications and walked toward her.

"Excuse me," he said quietly. "Could you please take a message to Hank Gentry in 513?"

"Of course," the nurse said, her voice low.

"Tell him Luke's here. I'll wait for him in the waiting room."

Kristen followed Luke to the small room where a game show blared on a television set, and a weary-looking woman sat with two squirming young children. They giggled as they moved all over the couch, oblivious to the sadness and disease that surrounded them.

"Hey, Nance," Luke said, smiling at the woman and lifting one of the twin boys as if he knew the child intimately. "How's it goin'?"

The woman, bleached blond and in her fifties, had obviously been beautiful in her prime before the lines of fatigue and distress did their job on her complexion. She smiled wanly up at Luke. "Okay, Luke. How are you? Hank said something about your being arrested yesterday."

Luke sat down, setting the wiggling boy on his feet and letting him run back to the couch to join his brother in a wrestling match. "Yeah, but we'll get it worked out. I have a good lawyer." He smiled at Kristen, standing tentatively in the doorway. "Kristy, this is Sherry's mom, Nancy. And these rowdy little guys are Hank and Sherry's two-year-old twins, Jake and Josh. Nance, this is my oldest and best friend, Kristen Jordan."

A surge of warmth shot through Kristen at Luke's words, and smiling, she shook Nancy's hand. "How's your daughter?" she asked.

"Not very well, I'm afraid," she said. "I'm about to go in and see her when Hank comes out. He's taking the boys for a few hours." She glanced at her watch, then out the door. "That is, *if* he ever comes out. He forgets sometimes that I want to be with her as much as he does."

She leaned her head back on the wall and closed her eyes, and one of the boys, the one with the Dennis the Menace cowlick in his hair, crawled into her lap and pressed a surprise kiss on her chin. Nancy opened her eyes and smiled, as if the kiss had provided her with the strength she needed to get her through the morning.

"You love Nanna?" she asked the boy.

"Nope," he said with a teasing grin.

Her hands moved quickly to his ribs, attacking him with a punishing tickle. "Yes, you do, you little monster!"

The other twin got into the act, until both were giggling boisterously and collapsing onto the floor. Kristen couldn't help laughing with them, but when she glanced at Luke, she saw the pensive sadness in his eyes, as if at that very moment he were considering the possibility that the boys were soon to lose their mother, and that Nancy was about to lose her only child.

"Can you guys hold it down?" a man said from the doorway. "There are sick people up here."

Kristen looked up to see a sandy-haired man of about Luke's size filling the doorway, smiling down at the twins, who simultaneously abandoned their grandmother and launched themselves into his arms. Laughing, he stooped and hugged them, then acknowledged Luke's presence.

"Luke..." He swallowed and stood up, and the boys resumed rolling on the couch. "Hey, man, I'm sorry. I should have come for you last night, but Sherry wasn't doing very well, and I just couldn't leave her."

"No problem," Luke said. "Kristy got me out."

Hank regarded Kristen, who sat a little closer to Luke than a mere acquaintance would, and he smiled. "So he called you, huh? I honestly didn't know if he would."

Kristen's smile faltered, and she glanced at Luke, confused. "Why not? He knew I'd come."

"Yeah, well, Luke doesn't always think of Luke, does he?"

Luke shifted in his seat, and Kristen noticed his obvious discomfort. Characteristically, he changed the subject. "I know you're busy man," he told Hank. "But I really need to go over some things with you. Someone has set me up, and I could be in a lot of trouble. You think while Nancy's with Sherry we could take the kids someplace where we can talk?"

Hank looked at the kids, rubbed his bloodshot, fatigued eyes, scratched his two-days' growth of stubble and nodded reluctantly. "I guess. But obviously it'll have to be somewhere they can run wild, or we won't get a word in."

"How about the park across the street?" Kristen asked.

Hank shook his head. "No way. When we go to the park, I spend the whole time trying to keep them from killing themselves on the slides and monkey bars. How about the lake? You know, Luke? Where we used to go fishing?"

Luke got to his feet. "All right, if I can still remember how to get there."

"No problem," Hank said, separating the boys as one started to cry. "I go there sometimes by myself, just to think. I know it by heart."

"Okay," Luke said. "We'll follow you guys in Kristen's car." He looked over his shoulder to Nancy, who was hurriedly straightening the clutter the boys had left.

"Hey, give Sherry a hug for me, will you?"

Nancy looked distracted as she glanced up at him. "I will," she said, then left the room and disappeared down the hall.

THE PRIVATE SPOT Hank led them to on Lake Heritage would have been impossible to stumble on, and Luke explained that they'd found it once by boat, then negotiated a path out and figured out how to get there by car. "The fishing's great," Luke said, dragging on a cigarette and flicking it out the open window of Kristen's car as they pulled to a stop. "But the quiet's even better."

"Not today," Kristen said with a grin as the twins tumbled out of the car up ahead of them and took off toward the water, carrying the miniature fishing poles they had stopped by Hank's house to get.

Luke and Kristen got out of the car and met Hank beside his. Kristen noted the pale cast to Hank's skin, as if he hadn't been outside the hospital in days, and the dead-tired weariness in the dry lines of his face.

He slid up onto the hood of his car, his eyes following his sons, who were comically sticking their poles into the water, as if they expected to harpoon a fish.

"You okay, man?" Luke asked him quietly.

"I'll live." He brought his bloodshot eyes back to Luke. "How 'bout you?"

"I'm good," Luke said.

It was against Kristen's nature to sit out by a lake on a workday, with the wind blowing through her hair, and make idle conversation. "He'll be better when we find out who could have set him up," she said.

"Set you up?" Hank asked. "How do you know someone set you up?"

"How do I know?" Luke laughed cynically. "Man, there were enough explosives in the trunk of my car to start a small war. And I sure as hell didn't put them there."

"Oh, yeah," Hank muttered. He narrowed his eyes, as if thinking through the problem, then shook his head. "I'm sorry, Luke. I don't have a clue who it could be, either. Maybe somebody at the ammunitions plant?"

"Who?" Kristen asked impatiently. "Hank, we need names. Luke's in serious trouble."

Hank looked down at the ground. "Well, there was that guy, what was his name—Mahoney? Didn't he have a copy of the blueprint of our security system?"

"He was one of the first people the police checked," Kristen said, jotting down the name anyway, "but that doesn't rule him out. Do you remember seeing anyone near Luke's car any time in the past few days?"

Hank shook his head, and offered a palms-up shrug and an apologetic look to Luke. "I'm sorry, man. I don't think I've even seen your car in a couple of weeks. I've been so wrapped up with Sherry." He rubbed his face and gazed back at his kids as a soft glaze misted over his eyes, as if the mention of his wife's name had dragged his attention away from Luke's troubles and back to his own. "I better get back to the hospital pretty soon. She might need me."

"Her mother's there," Luke said. "Let her have some time with Sherry. You need a break."

"A break?" Hank said, as if the words came close to angering him. "She's lying in that hospital room about to just hand over her life, and you think I need a break?"

"I guess not." Luke watched as Hank slid off the car and turned his back to them, and Kristen set a hand on Luke's arm. He looked down at her, and she saw despair in his eyes. Setting his hand over hers, he looked at Hank.

"Hank?"

Hank turned around, looked into Luke's face. "The truth," Luke said. "How bad is she?"

"The truth?" Tears filled Hank's eyes, and he spun around, putting his back to them again. "She's freakin' dyin', man. That's the truth!"

Luke looked as if the breath had been knocked out of him, and he took a helpless step backward. Instinctively, Kristen tightened her hold on his arm.

"The thing is," Hank said, checking his anger and turning to face them again, "as long as I'm there with her, reminding her that she has things to live for, like me and those kids, and people who love her, and memories that make her laugh... I almost feel like I can get her through this, that she'll hang on a little tighter. And then, one day, she'll wake up and be herself again. And I can take her home."

Kristen's eyes stung with incipient tears, and she slipped her hand out from under Luke's and shrank back against the car, respecting the intimate, emotional moment between the two friends.

"Is there anything I can do, pal?" Luke asked in a barely audible voice.

Hank laughed mirthlessly and threw up his hands. "Oh, I wish." He took a deep breath, steadied himself and focused his eyes on a cloud overhead. "Typical Luke. We came out here to talk about how to keep you out of prison, and you wind up asking *me* if there's anything *you* can do." He kicked at a tree stump breaking the ground, and shook his head. "I'm a miserable human being."

"Why?" Luke asked, setting his hands on his hips. "Because you don't have all the answers?"

"Because I should be there for you," Hank said. "I should have bailed you out last night when you called. I shouldn't have taken for granted that you'd call her, when you swore you never would!"

Pain and surprise flashed through Kristen's eyes. Luke cast a guilty look at her over his shoulder, then tore his gaze away and looked out toward the kids.

"You were busy, man," Luke said. "You aren't some kind of superhuman. You can't do everything at once."

"I've lost control," Hank said, his shoulders slumping in defeat. "I can't do a godforsaken thing about Sherry, and now you—"

"Look, don't worry about me," Luke cut in. "Just take care of yourself and Sherry. I'll be fine. It takes more than a night in jail to get me down."

Hank turned around and looked Kristen fully in the eyes, concern sharpening his steady gaze. "Are you going to get him off?" he asked.

Kristen inhaled a deep, unsteady breath, and realized that she really couldn't consider any other possibility. "Yes," she said without a doubt.

Hank breathed a heavy sigh, and nodded grimly. "I've got to get back to Sherry then," he said. "It's getting close to the kids' nap time, and Nancy will want to get them home."

"Yeah." Luke issued a ragged sigh. "Let me know when Sherry can have visitors, okay?"

"Sure," Hank said vacantly. He turned around and called for the boys, who came running, brandishing their wet poles. "Call me if there's anything I can do," Hank said before he left.

"Same here," Luke said, and watched his troubled friend get into his car.

THE RIDE BACK TO TOWN was quiet, but finally Kristen posed the question that had been plaguing her since they'd left Hank. "Luke?"

"Yeah, babe," he said, dragging on his cigarette, then holding it out the window to keep the car from filling up with smoke.

"What Hank said, about you swearing you'd never call me—"

Luke shifted uncomfortably in his seat, and tossed the cigarette out the window with a flick of his wrist. "He was just talking," he said, adjusting his sunglasses. "It didn't mean anything."

Kristen stared straight ahead as she drove, unconvinced. "Why, Luke? Why didn't you want to call me?"

Luke laid his head back on the headrest, and stared up at the ceiling, not answering. After a moment, Kristen thought he'd discarded the question completely. "Luke?"

"Because I didn't figure you needed Luke Wade back in your life after all this time, okay?"

Kristen glanced over at him, and swallowed. "Even if you needed me?" she asked.

"Yeah," he said. "Even then." He looked out the window to the buildings they passed, his expression hidden by his sunglasses, but he couldn't hide the tight line of his lips. "But I guess I'm not as strong as I used to be," he said. "Because I did call you, after all, didn't I?"

Kristen didn't answer, for there didn't seem to be anything left to say. He saw it as a sign of weakness to have called her, and that, while strangely confusing, left her feeling annoyed and a little sad. It meant that he would be leaving again, as soon as he was strong; it meant that after he was done counting on her, she couldn't count on him. *It's just a question of making the cleanest break.*

"Hey, you okay?" Luke asked softly, after a stretch of tense silence.

"Yeah," she whispered. "I'm okay. Just tell me where you live."

He rubbed his chin, as if wondering whether to let the subject drop. Finally, he muttered, "The corner of Magnet and Sycamore. In the north end of town."

She nodded. "I know where that is. It's a nice area."

"Surprised?"

Kristen looked over at him. "About what?"

"That I live in a decent neighborhood, instead of some roach-infested slum somewhere?"

Kristen came to a red light and slammed her foot on the brake, jerking the car to a halt. Genuine offense colored her cheeks. "What is it you think about me, Luke? That I'm some snob with a file full of opinions on how you turned out?"

"No," he said. "It's just that you know me so well. Probably better than anybody else. And most of the people who really know me, like Aunt Margaret, consider me no-account trash who's got prison coming to him."

"Aunt Margaret has never really known you," Kristen shot back. "And if you think that I've spent the past eleven years thinking you were some kind of junkie sifting through the garbage in the low-income section of town, then you don't know *me* very well."

"Hey, don't get so hot," Luke said, his face registering genuine surprise. "I didn't mean anything about you."

"Right," Kristen said. "You meant it about yourself. *You're* the one who sees yourself at the bottom of the ladder looking up at the decent, respectable people on top. And as long as you see yourself that way, then you can't blame Aunt Margaret for seeing you that way, too. But I don't, Luke. And you know it. *Don't you?*"

"Yeah," he said quickly. "Sure I do. That's why I called you."

She grew quiet then, and riveted her eyes on the road as she drove.

Luke propped his elbow on the window and stroked his lip with his thumb. Damn, he hadn't meant to shake her up like that, he thought. He glanced back at her, and realized, deep in some region of his heart, that she had, indeed, grown up. Gone was the little worshipful girl who thought he'd hung the moon. Now she was a woman with a temper to match her convictions. He had forgotten how good it felt to be around her.

His callused thumb scraped across the shadowy stubble over his lip. He needed a shave, he thought, and a shower. And a little time to think. Still, he hated to see her leave him just yet. "So... you still coming back around three?"

Kristen glanced at Luke, and the innocence and poignance in her eyes jolted him. Michelle Pfieffer couldn't hold a candle to Kristen's pale beauty, he thought. No one ever had.

"Well, I guess we could do it now, since we're already together. I just need to check in at the office, to see if I have to return any important messages."

"You can do that while I take a shower and change," Luke said, assessing her face for any sign of retreat.

There was none. "Okay, fine. We really do need to get right to work on your case. We don't have any more time to waste."

Wasted time... Luke's mind drifted back to all the years since he'd seen Kristen, all the times he'd thought of her and picked up the phone to call, only to hang up and tell himself that he owed her more than that. Maybe those were *his* wasted years, he thought, but not hers. She'd come so far without him....

He only hoped he hadn't made a mistake, letting himself back into her life.

KRISTEN STEPPED into Luke's house with the same awkward admiration that she had felt years ago. His house was bigger than her own home, and decorated in masculine earth tones with expensive accessories that bespoke success and pride. "Luke, it's beautiful," she said with a frown, as if his modesty and humility were incongruous, juxtaposed with such confident decor. "Did you do all this yourself?"

"Not really," Luke said with a self-conscious grin. "Sherry decorated most of it for me. When I bought the house, I only had a threadbare couch and a beanbag for furniture. She literally took me by the hand to the furniture store and made me pick out some things. The next thing I knew, I'd spent a ton of money and she was hiring people to slap up wallpaper all over the place."

"So she's a decorator?" Kristen asked, wishing she'd had the chance to get to know Sherry before her health had failed her. Maybe she still would, Kristen thought. Maybe Hank's faithful vigil would pay off.

"No, she's not a decorator," Luke said with a smile. "She just likes to spend other people's money. 'Course, I approved everything as we went along. I really like how it turned out."

He led her into the kitchen, which was clean, except for a few breakfast dishes from the day before. He pulled out a chair for her. "You can spread out here," he said. "And the phone's on the wall there. I'll be out of the shower in ten minutes, and then we can work."

"Okay." Kristen set her briefcase on the table and started to open it, but Luke leaned over, hooked a gentle finger under her chin and made her look up at him. "I'm sorry, Kristy," he said softly.

"For what?"

"For making you mad, back in the car."

Kristen sighed and pulled his hand away from her chin, closing it in her own. "It only makes me angry when you play the part of the bad boy who couldn't be good if his life depended on it. The truth is that you run a successful business, you have close friends, and you have a good life. It's almost like you're trying to pull some kind of joke on those of us who knew you before. But even then, I looked up to you, Luke. I never saw you the way you saw yourself. Don't forget that, okay?''

Luke's eyes softened as he gazed into hers, contemplating her faith in him. He'd never consciously cultivated it. It had been a gift.

He cupped his hand around the nape of her neck and pulled her toward him. Dropping a soft kiss on her forehead, he whispered, "I couldn't forget if I tried."

And then he left her sitting there alone, and disappeared into the back of the house.

Fifteen minutes later, while she waited for John to come to the phone, Kristen held the receiver between her shoulder and ear and looked over the messages her secretary had given her. Down the hall, she could hear the shower running, and the subtle changes in its sound as Luke moved beneath it. Her heart still thudded from the chaste kiss on her forehead, and she cursed herself for being so affected by him.

The music on the hold line cut off, and John picked up midsentence, mumbling orders to his secretary as he brought the receiver to his mouth. "Kristen," he said. "Where are you?"

"I'm with a client," she said. "Luke Wade."

"Look, I need to know if you're going to be available to help me on the Genpack case. I've got to get going on it, and—"

"I guess not," she cut in, trying to take the offensive. "This is a pretty serious case, John. I have my work cut out for me."

John sighed heavily, and she could tell that he was annoyed. "Kristen, come on. You aren't really going to take this, are you?"

"Yes!" she said. "We agreed that it was time I started handling my own cases, didn't we? Were the promotion and the office and the pep talks all just pacifiers?"

"No, of course not," John said. "And I'm not trying to stand in your way. It's just . . . are you sure you're up to this?"

Kristen wilted and propped her chin on the heel of her hand. "No, actually," she admitted. "I'm scared to death of losing this case." She sighed and shifted her papers around. "I was hoping I could count on you for some advice when I need it. Not just criticism."

John was quiet for a moment, but finally he mumbled, "Okay, Jordan. If you have to take it, take it. And I'll help if I can. But you have to realize that the partners aren't going to be thrilled about this when they hear. Lost causes don't play very well at the meetings, you know."

"I know that," she said. "But I didn't go into law for a free ride. If I can't help someone I care about, how can I ever help someone I don't even know?"

"It isn't always that simple," John said. But then, as if he had no more time to allot to the phone call, he ended with, "we'll talk later."

Kristen got up and hung the phone back on the wall. She heard the shower cut off, and turned in the direction of the bedroom. In her mind, she imagined Luke stepping out, beads of water dripping over his tanned skin, mingling in the hair on his chest, trickling down his hard stomach. . . .

Trying to halt her train of thought, she sat down to study the paperwork before her. There were so many questions to be answered about the years she had lost with him. There were things the prosecutors might use against him, things that needed explanation.

Like how he could have forgotten me so easily . . .

She swallowed and thought of the way he had looked at her just moments ago, and had whispered, "I couldn't forget if I tried." *Had* he tried? she wondered.

Deep in the house, she heard more water running, and wondered if he was shaving. She wondered if he'd use fresh after-shave, the kind that always made her heart race and her mouth go dry, and her senses heighten. She wondered if he could read her feelings in her eyes.

The air was growing hot, so she slipped off her blazer and hung it over a chair, and tried to relax so she could think. But it was hard to think when her emotions raged out of control—not to mention her hormones. She'd never been able to think clearly when she was with Luke.

She went back to the table, and gave concentration her mightiest effort. There was so much she didn't know, and what she did know, she couldn't tell the jury. Gut feelings were inadmissible as evidence. She pictured herself in the courtroom, addressing the jury, with Luke sitting at the defense table.

Somehow, she didn't think telling them that he'd always been there for her and that he only got into trouble because it was expected of him, would sway the jury at all. She didn't think they'd believe that beneath his rough and ready-to-pounce persona there was nothing but a soft heart and a nurturing soul.

She looked up and saw him coming into the kitchen, wearing a pair of faded jeans and no shirt. The clean scent of soap and after-shave followed him into the room, and she breathed it in, swallowed and diverted her eyes as he went to the coffee pot and filled it with water.

"Feel better?" she asked, but the words came out a little too hoarsely.

"Yeah," he said. He sat down at the table, at a right angle to her, and braced himself on his elbows. Her eyes strayed to the bulge of his biceps, then across to the strong chest that boasted of his workout regimen. When, at last, her eyes made their way back to his face, she could see that he'd thought over his plight while he showered, and his manner was a little quieter. "Did you call the office?"

"Uh-huh. I told them I'd be here most of the day."

He nodded and cocked a half grin. "Did they tell you that the prosecutor called and said it was just a bad joke, and I don't have to go to trial for something I didn't do?"

Kristen couldn't seem to return that grin. "No, Luke. It's no joke. It's real."

He sighed and rubbed his face wearily. It was only then that she saw how tired he was. "Damn," he said. "I can't believe this is happening."

Kristen leaned toward him and stopped just short of taking his hand. "Luke, you're not going to prison. I won't let you. But we have a lot of hard work ahead of us. I need to know every detail of what's happened to you since I last saw you. Anything on your record that the prosecutors might have dug up. Anything anyone might be able to say about you. I need to know where you've been, who your friends were, who your enemies were, where you worked, what you did there . . . everything.''

Luke brought his sad eyes back to her. ''I don't even know where to start,'' he said.

''That's easy,'' Kristen said. ''Start with the day you left me.''

CHAPTER FIVE

"START WITH THE DAY YOU LEFT ME."

For the next few hours as they talked, Kristen's words haunted Luke. So much time had been wasted in his life, he realized. So many years of bided time while he let her grow up and make her way in the world without him.

By the time Kristen had complete information about the years since they'd last seen each other, she was on Luke's sofa with her clipboard on her lap, her shoes kicked off and her bare feet curled beneath her.

Talking about himself wasn't easy for Luke, and like a psychologist searching for answers, she had prodded him and questioned him, pausing to probe details that surprised her, yet truly had no pertinence to her case. It reminded him of the nights they'd sat in the yard outside her house, talking and talking and talking, solving all the mysteries of the world and creating new ones of their own. She had been his best friend, and he had missed her.

Now, as he spoke about the security business he and Hank had built from scratch, he watched her face become animated with interest, her eyes brighten and even though she jotted something on her clipboard now and then, he could see that he had her full attention. She'd never stopped caring. Just as he had never stopped caring for her.

"So," he said with a sigh when he'd come to the end of his history. "What do you think?"

Kristen lowered her eyes to the notes in her lap, and a tiny frown formed a crease between her feathery brows. Luke propped his arm across the back of the couch and touched that wrinkle in her forehead with his finger. She looked up at him.

"What's wrong?" he asked. "Tell me what you're thinking."

Kristen swallowed. "Luke, I have to suggest a possibility that I know hasn't even crossed your mind," she said. "And you aren't going to like it. But as your lawyer, I have to consider it."

"What?" he asked, bracing himself.

She took a deep breath, and he could see that she considered her words very carefully. "Hank," she said finally. "He knew how to break through the security system, he had the blueprint of the building—"

"No." Luke's denial was so sudden and so vehement that Kristen jumped. "Hank did not set me up."

"I'm not saying he did," Kristen responded, leaning toward him and setting a calming hand on his arm. "I'm just saying that we can't rule anything out."

Luke sprang off the couch, paced across the room and turned back to her, obviously torn. "I've known Hank for years. You *know* when someone is capable of something like that. Besides, you met the man. He's a basket case over his wife. You think he took the time to sneak out of her hospital room and break into the ammunitions plant, then plant the explosives in my car, then call the cops and tell them where to look? Why would he do that? It doesn't make sense.''

"I don't know why,'' Kristen said, getting to her feet and facing him squarely, her expression telling him that she doubted the possibility, as well, even though as his lawyer she had to consider it. "But Luke, all of the stolen explosives weren't found in your car. A lot more of them were stolen. Whoever stole them had some purpose for them, and just used you as a scapegoat. Someone to take the heat while they did the dirty work.''

"What dirty work?'' Luke asked.

"Making bombs, selling them. I don't know. If Hank—''

"Hank did not steal those explosives!'' Luke's voice shook the house and startled Kristen again. "He's as much a victim of circumstance as I am!''

"I know,'' Kristen said, trying to calm him with an outstretched hand. "You're right. You are.'' She swallowed and pushed her fingers through her hair, realized that her hands were shaking. "I shouldn't have even brought it up.''

"He's the best friend I've had since...'' Luke's voice faded out, and he looked at her again, the anger draining from his expression as his confession found its way to his lips. "Since you,'' he whispered.

Her blue eyes—so blue that they created an ocean of peacefulness in his soul—met his in silent enchantment. "Sometimes friends can let you down,'' she whispered.

Luke went back to the couch, set his elbows on his knees, clasped his hands in front of his face and closed his eyes. "I'm not claiming Hank's a saint," he said more quietly. "But he's no more a thief than I am."

He met Kristen's open gaze. "You know the way you believe in me, Kristy? The way you just knew without asking that I was innocent? Well, that's how I feel about Hank."

Kristen sank back on the couch. "Okay, Luke," she said.

He turned to face her, his troubled gaze embracing her again. "I mean, where would I be without your faith in me? Where would Hank be without mine in him?"

"But it isn't blind faith," Kristen said. "I can see the clear picture of Luke Wade. I have years of facts to substantiate my faith."

"Spoken like a true lawyer," he said, grinning. "But you know better. Since I was thirteen years old, you've always been there for me."

"Until you lost interest," she said with a wan smile.

"*I* lost interest? You were the one with the line of boyfriends forming at your door. Hell, there was a different guy at your house every night from the time you turned fifteen. I was just trying to stay out of the way."

Kristen smiled and looked at the floor, and the sadness in her eyes confused him. "I never wanted you out of the way, Luke," she said. "I needed you."

Luke smiled and lifted her hand, fondled her fingers, soft and delicate and innocent. "You never needed me," he said. "Look how you did without me. You're happy, and successful...."

"That's a matter of opinion," she said, closing her fingers around his. "I'm a divorced mother trying the

best I can to be a superwoman. And sometimes I..."
She closed her eyes and swallowed, and thought of
telling him that sometimes she thought of him, and
wished for ten minutes just to ask his advice, or seek
his comfort, or just see his funny smile. "Sometimes
I just feel so overwhelmed by it all."

"Hey." The word was a gentle whisper, and she felt
his knuckle stroking her cheek. She opened her eyes
and met his, as his fingers laced through hers and
pulled her closer to him. "Tell me what happened.
With Eric, I mean. I've always wondered, ever since I
heard about the divorce."

Kristen laughed softly. "What's there to say? It just
didn't work out."

His eyes probed hers, as if he could see all the dis-
appointments and disillusionments of her brief marriage. "Did he hurt you?" he asked.

Kristen melted, for the question spoke volumes.
"No, he didn't hurt me," she said. "It just wasn't
right. There was too much missing."

The silence that passed between them as they looked
into each other's eyes was electric, as a lifetime of
words never spoken passed through both their minds.

He wasn't you.

That bastard should have made you happy.

I never stopped comparing....

I never stopped wishing....

She saw him wet his lips as he looked at her, felt him
pull her hand to his chest, and her heart pounded in
tandem with his. Neither of them breathed.

Kristen tilted her head back and let her tongue move
across her lips. Luke's tortured gaze followed it, and
he swallowed.

Slowly, his face descended to hers, and she closed her eyes as a tidal flood of heat washed over her. But just as she expected his lips to meet hers, his mouth settled on her cheek.

Her breath escaped in a deflated sigh, and his forehead pressed against hers. His hands came up to frame her chin, and she felt his breath on her hungry lips, lips that were aching and sensitized for a taste of him.

She dropped her face into his shoulder, knowing that tears were stinging her eyes, and pleading with her soul not to betray her now. She inhaled a deep, fortifying breath, and scooted back, slipping her hand out of his.

"It's late. I have to go pick up Courtney," she whispered.

He nodded. "Yeah."

"I'll . . . I'll call you in the morning."

He swallowed hard. "Okay."

Kristen gathered her things and started toward the door, knowing that she didn't have long to get out of his house before those renegade tears threatening her eyes teemed down her face and gave her away. "Try and get some sleep," she whispered.

"I will," he said. "You too."

IT WAS LATE THAT NIGHT as she lay in bed that Kristen found herself unable to fight the disappointment and disenchantment she'd felt that afternoon, when Luke had failed to kiss her the way she'd hoped he would. *A kiss on the cheek,* she thought miserably, as a stray tear rolled down her face. A brotherly kiss. A cousinly kiss. When would she ever realize that that was how Luke perceived her? And yet she could have sworn he'd wanted their lips to meet as well.

Kristen turned over in her bed, and tried not to remember how Luke's bare chest, sprinkled with dark hair, had felt thudding beneath her hand when he had moved it to his chest and held it there in his.

"He's the best friend I've had since you."

A best friend. That was what she was, she thought, even though for years, since she was a little girl, she had entertained fantasies of being more. But tonight he was probably sitting by his fireplace with one of the women in his life. They were probably making love on that bear rug near the hearth, and his lover was shivering from the feeling of Luke's hands moving across her....

That old feeling of resentment and jealousy washed over Kristen, taking her back to the night when she and Luke, by some coincidence, had wound up at the same swimming party. She had watched the girl he'd brought fawn over him, flaunting the bikini she wore, and moving her body against his in ways that told everyone there that she could be Luke's for the asking. His interest in the girl had seemed subdued, almost grudging, as if he didn't want Kristen to know he had sexual impulses. But Kristen had noticed when he disappeared early in the evening, and didn't come back....

There was always another woman for Luke. A prettier woman. A more experienced one. And knowing that had always haunted her at night, and taken the focus off the dates she chose, and the sparks that might have been, and the interest that could have burgeoned if she hadn't compared everyone she met to Luke.

And now she was a mother, and a lawyer, and she had no business still feeling this way about someone who'd demonstrated time and time again that she was not someone he wanted to think of in that way.

Other women might incite passion, wildness and reckless behavior in Luke. But she inspired a kiss on the cheek.

Nothing more.

Her tears soaked into her pillow, making sleep a struggle. And when she finally surrendered and dreamed, it was Luke's face she saw, and this time she was the one he left the party with. This time she was the one he wanted.

I ALMOST KISSED HER. The knowledge of how close he'd come raged through his head, inspiring a dull ache that centered in his groin. Damn! How could he have been so stupid?

Luke pulled his foot up onto the windowsill where he sat, hugged his knee and leaned his head back on the casing. She'd been willing, he thought with a subtle twist of his heart. She had expected him to kiss her. But if he had . . . oh, if he had . . .

His breathing quickened and he closed his eyes and told himself that, no matter what it took, he wouldn't let himself be that weak again.

But the disappointment in her face came back to him, and he realized that if he had a choice between seeing that pain again and surrendering to what he'd wanted since she was thirteen years old, he'd take the coward's way out. He only hoped it didn't come to that. Because if it did, he didn't know if he could live with himself.

BY MORNING, Kristen was angry with herself for wasting precious energy fantasizing about Luke. She had to defend him in court in a few weeks, and she had no business mooning over him like some starry-eyed girl. Deciding that she would adopt her best professional persona today and keep things strictly business, she called Luke, and asked to meet him in her office at ten. She also asked him to get Hank to join them, as well.

Kristen noted the hesitation in his voice, as if he recognized the change in her tone and was put off by it, but she told herself that it was better for him to notice it now, so that, once and for all, they could get back on the right track.

HANK GENTRY LOOKED at his watch and counted the hours that Sherry had been asleep. Too long, he thought. She wasn't fighting anymore. She was losing the battle, but by God, he wouldn't let her stop fighting.

He noted a difference in her breathing and moved to her bed to sit beside her. "Sherry?" he asked gently. "You awake, love?"

Her eyes fluttered open, the green of them providing a startling contrast to the death-gray color of her skin. Still, a suggestion of a smile curled her lips infinitesimally upward. "I am now," she said.

He took her hand, so cold and limp, and laced his fingers through hers. "I have to leave for a while this morning," he said, stroking her forehead. His hand followed the line of her scalp, only barely sprinkled with remaining wisps of hair. "I have to meet with Luke's lawyer, to try to get him out of this mess. Your mom is coming to stay with you."

Sherry's weak smile faded, and concern haunted her eyes. "What about the boys? I don't want them left with a stranger."

"No stranger," he said. "Your mom's friend Ethel is keeping them."

Sherry managed a laugh that ended in a breathless cough. "They'll run all over her. Poor Ethel isn't up to those rascals."

"She'll be fine," he said. "But right now, I don't want you left alone. Okay?"

"Okay." She sank back against the pillow and closed her eyes. For a moment, Hank thought he'd lost her to sleep again.

"Hey, Gentry," she whispered after a moment, not opening her eyes.

"Yeah, love?"

"Before you go, send the hospital hairdresser up."

The subtle dimple in Hank's left cheek showed as he grinned. "The hairdresser?" He combed his fingers through the sparse wisps. "You want a permanent or something?" he asked, chuckling.

Sherry's eyes came open, alive with a hint of laughter. "I've decided to get it all shaved off," she said, her words uttered with great effort. "That way... it'll look deliberate. I'm not the wig type... but I have a great head... don't you think?"

Hank couldn't help laughing. Only she could transform baldness into a fashion statement. "I think you'll look great," he said. "Talk about a low-maintenance hairstyle ."

"Yeah," Sherry said, smiling. "I might keep wearing it like that when it grows back in. Do you think it'll frighten the kids?"

"Hell, no," Hank said. "They'll want theirs shaved, too. We'll all do it,"

Sherry laughed at a mental family portrait, but her laughter died on a faint intake of breath, and a sudden sadness settled in her eyes. "I wish I could see them. Can't you sneak them in or something?"

Hank kissed her cheek. "No way, love. Your resistance is too low. If you were to get a virus or something..." His voice trailed off, but he didn't have to finish. They both knew what that would mean.

But he couldn't brook the sadness in her eyes, any more than he could put her life in danger. "I'll tell you what," he said softly. "I'll borrow Luke's camcorder, and we'll take some videos of them. They can talk to you that way. Then, when they start wearing you out, you can just turn them off."

Sherry smiled. "All right. I guess if that's all I can get..."

There was a knock on the door and Nancy stuck her head inside. Sherry tried to sit up. "Come in, Mom," she said.

Her mother stepped inside, her concerned eyes first assessing her daughter's waning condition before she spoke. Forcing a smile that almost looked genuine, she said, "Hank, Luke's waiting for you."

"I'm going." He bent over his wife and pressed a kiss on her cheek. Then, addressing her mother, he said, "I left a number by the phone where I'll be. Call me if . . . if you need me, okay?"

Her mother nodded grimly, then rallied and pulled two crisp papers out of the bag she'd brought. She brandished them for Sherry. "Jake and Josh made these for you," she said.

Sherry managed to sit up slightly, and slapped a delighted hand over her mouth. "Finger paintings?" The word was spoken with more energy than Hank had heard in her voice all morning. "You let them *finger paint*?"

"They're naturals," Nancy said. "The paint is made of pudding, by the way."

"Which explains the mouth print on Josh's," Sherry said.

"That's a kiss," Nancy informed her matter-of-factly. "Especially for you." She laughed then, forgetting her worries about her daughter for a moment. "You should have *seen* the mess!"

Knowing Sherry was in good hands, Hank slipped out of the room to find Luke.

KRISTEN SAT RIGID in the staff meeting that morning, occasionally jotting down notes pertaining to one case or another. Distracted, she watched out the glass wall for Luke and Hank, and checked her watch for the fiftieth time in an hour, as one of the partners droned on about a takeover case he was working on.

"Kristen, are we keeping you from something?" the senior partner asked when the speaker finished.

Kristen recognized the reprimand and countered it with her own. "Yes, actually. I have a meeting at ten. I didn't expect this meeting to run over."

"We have a lot on the agenda today," Robert said. "But if you need to leave, we could skip a few items and get to the case you're working on." He shuffled the files on his desk, pulled hers out. "U.S. v. Wade, isn't it?"

"Yes." Kristen shifted in her chair as the attention of all the lawyers in the firm focused on her. "A crate of explosives was found in my client's trunk a couple of days ago, and they were part of what was stolen from the ammunitions plant a month ago. He maintains that someone planted them there—"

"The guy's got a record," John said matter-of-factly. "Drugs. And tell them about his expertise in the Army."

Kristen's eyes met and held those of her mentor. "I was going to," she said, not disguising the vexation in her voice. She turned back to the other attorneys, who listened with censure in their expressions. But she was determined not to wilt. "He was in the ordnance corps of the Army. He knows how to assemble and disassemble bombs—"

"And he just happens to have installed the security system at the plant in question," John cut in.

Kristen compressed her lips and turned to face the man who had taught her more than anyone else in the firm. One of the lessons she had learned well was not to be anyone's doormat. Not even his. "Excuse me, John," she bit out, "but this is *my* case."

John propped an elbow on the back of his chair and gestured for her to go on.

"Those things are all circumstantial evidence," she said. "And I know better than anyone that I have my work cut out for me."

Laura Ashton, the partner who had also become her friend over the past two years, leaned forward and frowned. "Kristen, why would you take a case like this?"

"Because he didn't do it," she said adamantly, drilling out her point. "I've known him most of my life, and I *know* he didn't do it."

Robert closed his file and steepled his hands in front of his face. "He doesn't sound like the type of client we generally like to represent, Kristen."

"You mean because he isn't the head of a major corporation or the son of a Fortune 500 mogul?"

Her colleagues began to moan and roll their eyes, and Kristen's face flushed with angry heat. "This is not a *pro bono* case," she said, enunciating the words distinctly. "His fee will be covered. And as for his 'type,' his caliber is miles above the inside traders and embezzlers that we'd prefer to represent."

"Kristen, we're just thinking of you," Robert said. "You have to have a strategy when you build a career. You can't take on losing cases and expect to get anywhere with them."

"You just got a promotion, for heaven's sake," Laura added.

Kristen looked from one face to another. "Then you're telling me that I can't take this case?" she asked stiffly.

A hush fell over the room, and finally Robert dropped his hands. "No, Kristen. I won't tell you that. The decision, at this point, is still yours."

"Good," Kristen said, closing her file on Luke and scraping her chair back from the table. "Then if you'll excuse me, my client is waiting."

But as she left her colleagues in the conference room, something told Kristen that the subject wasn't closed. It was clear that they felt she'd made a bad decision.

Somehow, she vowed, she'd just have to prove that they were wrong.

KRISTEN'S OFFICE SMELLED of fresh air, and Luke let his eyes wander over her things as Hank told him about Sherry's plan to shave her head. It sounded like something Hank's wife might have done even before she'd suffered the side effects of her treatment.

He saw a framed picture of a child on the credenza behind Kristen's desk, and idly, he got up and walked around the desk, picked it up and smiled. "Courtney," he mumbled. "She looks just like her mother. Beautiful."

Hank inclined his head and assessed his friend with squinted eyes. "You know, I've always thought you had a thing for her. Is there a chance—"

"No." Luke set down the picture and turned back to Hank. "No chance."

"Uh-huh," Hank said, gazing at Luke with a decided lack of belief. "What is it with you? You act like she's some kind of forbidden fruit."

"She is forbidden fruit," Luke said. "She always has been."

Hank grinned and shook his head wearily. "So you're just going to sit around torturing yourself and pretending you don't care about her?"

"She knows I care about her," he said. "And I'd rather torture myself than her."

"How do you know you're not torturing her already?" Hank asked with a grin.

"I know, okay?" Luke plopped back into his chair. "Now can we drop this, please?"

"Fine," Hank said. "We don't have to talk about it. But take it from me, it won't go away."

"Take it from you?" Luke repeated, a tugging at his lips. "What do you know about it?"

"A lot, Buddy," Hank said, sobering a little. "A lot."

The door opened, and Luke looked up to see Kristen rushing in, her face pale as porcelain and framed by her loose hair, which hung just below her shoulders in a froth of spiral curls. "Sorry to keep you waiting, guys," she said, dropping her file on the desk and flitting to the file cabinet, where she found the papers she needed.

Luke noted the way she avoided his eyes, and he drew his brows together, redefining the permanent lines between them. "Everything okay?" he asked.

She gave him a cursory glance, then sat down and reviewed Luke's file. "Yeah. Fine. Just a meeting that ran over." She moved her attention to Hank, and leaned forward. "I know you're in a hurry to get back to Sherry, Hank. How is she?"

"I don't know," he said. "Last night I thought she'd gotten worse, but this morning she seemed in good spirits. I really think she's better today."

"Good," she said. "I promise I won't keep you long. I needed you here this morning so we could go over what happened every day that you and Luke were working on the security system at the plant. I need to know who you talked to, who you saw, when you had access to the explosives, everything.''

And before Luke had time to mention how much he liked her office or the picture of Courtney or the way she was wearing her hair, Kristen had launched into a rapid-fire inquisition that left no room for conversation.

They'd been at it for over an hour when Kristen's telephone rang. "Kristen Jordan," she answered briskly.

A woman's hoarse, shaky voice greeted her. "Uh, Miss Jordan? This is Nancy, Sherry's mother?"

"Yes, Nancy," Kristen said, moving her eyes to Hank, who had snapped to complete attention.

"Could I please speak to Hank for a moment?"

Kristen handed the phone to Hank and met Luke's eyes in silent sympathy. He looked over at Hank, who'd gone pale.

"What is it, Nancy?" he asked.

They waited for some sign of relief on Hank's face, a sign that all was not as bad as they feared, but that sign didn't come.

"Oh, God," Hank moaned, lowering his head and covering his eyes with his hands. "Okay. I'm coming. I'll be right there."

He hung up the phone and got to his feet, and when he looked back at Luke, his eyes were misting. "I have to go. Sherry's..." He stopped, swallowed, tried again. "She's got a nosebleed." His lips trembled, and he turned to the door. "God, her platelet count is so low that they can't get it to stop."

Luke was on his feet and behind Hank before he could reach the door. "I'll drive you," he said.

"No." Hank shook his head emphatically. "No, I'm fine. I want you to stay here and finish this with Kristen. You've got to stop thinking about me and work out your own problems."

"But, Hank—"

"I mean it," Hank said, as if Luke's gesture of sympathy angered him. "I'll call you later."

Luke set a hand on Hank's shoulder and squeezed hard. "If there's anything I can do. Anything at all—"

"I know," Hank said, setting his hand over Luke's.

Luke watched his friend disappear out of sight, and finally he turned back to Kristen and closed the door behind him.

"A nosebleed. I guess that could be pretty serious, but not fatal or anything. Don't you think?"

Kristen lowered herself back into her chair. "She's in good hands, Luke."

He nodded and sat back down. "Yeah, I guess."

A moment of silence stretched between them as they looked at each other—really looked at each other—for the first time that morning. Now that her guard was down, he realized that it had been up for the past hour.

The worry on his face changed into a softer, more pensive look, and he leaned back in his chair, propped his elbow on the armrest and gazed at her. "I like your hair that way," he said.

He noted a subtle blushing of her cheeks, and she looked back down at the file, turned a few pages, then picked up her pen. "Where were we?"

"I said I like your hair that way," Luke pressed, demanding a response.

"Thank you," she said pointedly. "Now where were we?"

Luke made a grand gesture of shrugging. "I don't know. Somewhere in the middle of pretending we hardly know each other."

Kristen saw that her strategy was futile, so she sighed deeply and leaned back in her chair. "I'm just trying to get some work done," she said. "There are a lot of things we have to cover."

"Fine," Luke said. "We'll cover them. But do you have to keep shooting questions like some prosecutor trying to trip me up? We're on the same side, remember?"

Kristen's lips stretched taut, and she folded her hands in front of her. As she did, he noticed they were shaking. "Luke, what do you want?"

Luke slapped his legs and stood up, leaned over her desk until his face was too close to hers. "How about a little cordiality? We were getting along just fine yesterday."

"Well, maybe that's the problem," Kristen fired back. "Maybe we were getting along too well." She came to her feet and went to her window, keeping her back to him.

"Too well? What are you talking about?" Luke asked. "Nothing happened. Did it?" The question was genuine, as if Luke feared he had missed something.

Kristen shook her head, and he saw her swallow. "No," she said. "But it occurred to me last night that if I'm going to be an effective lawyer for you, you have to stop treating me like that little girl who had a crush on her self-proclaimed big brother."

She felt Luke coming up behind her, felt the warmth of his body reaching out to her. He smelled of that tantalizing after-shave, and for a moment she thought of asking him to stop wearing it for the duration of this case. But that would be silly, she thought. Luke's charisma wasn't limited to the after-shave he wore.

"I never knew you had a crush on me." His voice was a gentle whisper against her neck that made her shiver. "And I may have tried to be a lot of things to you, but a big brother was never one of them."

"All right, then," Kristen said, her voice still crisp and cool as she kept her eyes on the street below her window. "A cousin. A neighbor. Whatever."

"Yeah," he whispered, and she could hear the confusion in his voice. "Whatever." He stepped up beside her, forced her eyes to meet his. "You really had a crush on me?"

The slight grin in his eyes, as if the revelation was a pleasant one, made her smile as well. "Come on Luke. You knew I did. I was your biggest fan."

It was Luke's turn to look out the window. "I guess I was too busy worshiping you to notice."

"Worshiping me?" She laughed out loud, relief from the exchanged confessions lightening her mood a little. "You can't be serious. The older I got, the more you ignored me."

When he looked at her again, his expression was clearly earnest. "Oh, I never ignored you, babe. That couldn't be done."

Kristen felt a painful lump in her throat. A lump that said it might have all been a mistake, that all the wasted years might have been a sad, miserable joke. "But you never *ever* touched me, or made any move at all toward me. It was so platonic that my mother would have trusted you in my bed!''

"Your mother would have been a fool.''

Kristen's heart stumbled into triple time, and she wet her lips and swallowed again. His eyes held no trace of amusement, and for the first time in her life, she realized that he wasn't toying with her. He was deadly serious. "Luke, if I wasn't some helpless little cousin to you, then what was I? Really, it's important. I need to know.''

He thrust his fists deeply into his pockets and gazed at her for a long moment. She noted a subtle change in the depth of his breath, and realized that the moment was as taxing to him as it was to her. "Someone too good for me," he said at last. "Someone who needed her wings so she could fly as high as she could.''

"My wings?" Kristen asked on a breath of surprise. "But didn't you know that wings are no good without a breeze to launch them?''

Luke's smile told her that he had no regrets at all. "You did just fine without me, kiddo.''

Kristen looked at him, assessing him for whatever emotion he might still harbor for her. The *kiddo* rang in her head like a reminder of the years he'd let pass without a word or a note or a phone call. And something told her that his confession today was nothing more than a clever letdown. He could see her feelings in her eyes as clearly as he'd read her when she was a child. And he didn't want to humiliate her.

She went back to her desk and sat down, and opened the file again. "Yes, well . . . we'd better get back to work, Luke. We'll be at this all day as it is.''

Luke noted the change in her mood. She was back to being the cool professional. Some inner voice told him to let it go at that. The crush she'd admitted to was history, and even if he'd realized it then, he wouldn't have acted on it, because it wouldn't have changed a damned thing.

Kristen's life was too stable for her to get involved with someone who kept winding up on the wrong side of the law. And he owed it to her to keep it that way.

IT WAS LATE AFTERNOON when Luke finally left Kristen's office and headed toward the hospital to check on Sherry. Several times during the day, he'd called to try to get information on her condition. "Critical" was the latest report.

He felt guilty that he hadn't given Sherry *more* thought today. He'd been too caught up in his case, and in his closeness to Kristen, and in the confession she'd made that morning.

I was your biggest fan.

Funny, he hadn't felt that when she was sixteen and they wound up at the same swimming party and he had to sit there and pretend that his pulse wasn't thundering in reaction to the bikini she wore, and that he wasn't bothered by the guys swarming around her.... He'd tried his best to feign interest in the girl he'd brought as his date. What was her name? Cindy? Karen? Hell, he couldn't even remember what she looked like now. Just that he'd used her that night in a way that made him berate himself for weeks afterward. And no matter how hard he'd tried to pretend, she just hadn't smelled like Kristen, and her kisses had done little to alter the beat of his heart.

The hospital came into sight, and he saw a space beside Hank's car and pulled his Harley into it. Hank could see what Kristen did to him. Even distracted by Sherry's illness, he'd noticed it today. Luke decided he'd have to make sure to watch that. The romantic feelings he had for Kristen would serve absolutely no purpose. Neither would talk about what might have been. He wouldn't let himself think of it anymore.

But telling himself that was as effective as telling himself not to breathe. Kristen was as fixed in his mind as she was in his heart. And no matter how many years had passed between them, he'd never stop thinking of her.

Still, he thought as he went toward the hospital, he'd give it a hell of a try.

He got on the elevator, glanced around and saw a father with a little girl of no more than four, holding a wreath in her hand that read, "It's a boy." Luke smiled.

"I have a baby brother," she announced, her eyes wide and excited.

"You do?" he said. He laughed and looked at the father, extended his hand to shake his. "Congratulations. Was he born today?"

"A few hours ago," the child's father said, flicking a cigar out of his pocket and handing it to Luke. "Seven pounds, eight ounces."

The numbers meant little to Luke, but from the pride in the man's voice, he figured it was a healthy weight. The elevator stopped on the maternity floor, and he watched them get out.

As the doors closed, a desolate sense of loss swept over him. *Seven pounds, eight ounces.* He supposed he'd never hand out cigars of his own.

A fleeting thought of Courtney, smiling in a gold frame on Kristen's credenza, skittered through his mind. She was so pretty. So much like her mother. He wished he'd been there to see her when she was born. He wondered if Eric had bragged about her weight and passed out cigars, or if he'd stayed at home that night to watch football.

He chuckled slightly, and realized that he was being ridiculous. Of course Eric had been with Kristen. She was no fool, and Luke knew that, as she got older, she had chosen her dates carefully. He knew she'd chosen her husband that way, as well.

It had just always been so hard for him to find anyone good enough for Kristen. There was something wrong with every one of them. One was a smart aleck. Another was a snob. Another leered at her too much. And some were simply not her intellectual equals. But he'd learned early on to keep his mouth shut and let her find out on her own.

But when he'd heard she was getting serious with Eric, he hadn't been able to sit idly by. He'd dug into Eric's history, found out all about him and even confronted him about his intentions. Eric hadn't appreciated the subtle interrogation, and had told him to kindly step out of her life, that he could take over from there.

And Luke had done just that.

Maybe if he hadn't bowed out so easily, Kristen could have avoided making a mistake.

He got off the elevator on Sherry's floor, went to her room in hopes of finding Hank and saw that the door was open and the bed was empty. An alarm rang out in his heart, and he turned around, searching the halls for someone—anyone—who looked as if they might know what was going on.

A nurse came out of a room across the hall, and he grabbed her arm. "Sherry Gentry. Where is she?"

"She's been moved to a laminar air flow room," the nurse said.

Luke took a few seconds to catch his breath. That was better, he told himself, than what he had initially feared. A laminar airflow room, where no germs could penetrate the sterile, bubblelike walls, a room where only the sickest patients were treated. "Oh. I guess her husband's with her, huh?"

"Yes," the nurse said. "And her mother."

"Okay." Luke raked his hand through his hair, and stood motionless for a moment. "Is she going to be all right?"

The nurse didn't hedge, and he realized that she had to deal with death every day, and that she'd learned to confront it with honesty. "I don't know. She's critical right now. We just have to wait and see."

Luke closed his eyes, and the nurse added, "But she has the very best doctors. Really, they're doing everything they can for her."

He nodded and looked in the direction of the special rooms, knowing that he couldn't go in. He wasn't family, no matter how much he felt as if he was. "Look, could you tell her husband that Luke is here?"

"Of course," the nurse said. "I'll give him the message right now, but the doctor's with them. He might be a while."

"Oh." Luke let out a deep sigh, then glanced toward the elevator. "Look, never mind. He's got a lot on his mind. I'll just call later or something. I wanted to go down and give some blood, anyway."

"That's good," she said. "She needs it."

When the nurse went on, Luke pressed the elevator button and waited for the doors to open. He should have come earlier, he thought. This latest complication in Sherry's illness might be the one that did her in, but he'd been too busy worrying about saving his rear end to care.

Upbraiding himself, he got off the elevator and cut across the lobby to the room he frequented at least three times a week to give blood. The thought of Hank hanging on to Sherry's life made him shudder. Years ago, when their greatest worry had been getting through basic training, he'd never dreamed that they'd have to face such disasters when they got older. Wasn't life supposed to go smoothly if you toed the line and did things by the book?

That was what he'd done for the past few years, but somehow it didn't change who he was...who he'd always been.

When he was finished donating blood, he went out to his bike, sat for a moment, then decided that he could at least leave Hank a note, asking him to call him if he got a chance, to update him on Sherry's condition. He checked his pockets for paper, and found only a pen.

Luke got off his motorcycle and went to Hank's car, aware that Hank kept a clipboard with paper under his seat, for jotting down directions and figuring estimates when he was on the job. He slid into Hank's driver's seat, reached under the passenger seat and slid out the clipboard. Along with it came a brown paper sack.

He lifted the clipboard, and the sack fell to the floor, spilling its contents. Muttering a curse, he reached down to retrieve it.

His hand froze.

On the floor was a roll of cord, the kind that easily passed for telephone cording. Luke recognized it as the kind used to detonate bombs. Behind it fell three packs of lithium wafer batteries, the kind used in watches, calculators and sometimes even in the bombs he and Hank had been trained to assemble.

Take it easy, Luke told himself. *It's not what it seems.*

His hand shook as he jammed the cord and batteries into the sack and pushed it back under the seat. There was an explanation. There had to be.

Forgetting the note and swallowing the growing knot of fear rising to his throat, Luke got back on his Harley, cranked it and pulled out of the parking lot in a daze.

Victim of circumstance. Coincidence. Hank did not set me up.... He pulled out onto the highway in front of the hospital, and drove for nearly a mile with no destination, no direction in mind.

"It was just a roll of cord," he told himself aloud, as if to put his questions to rest once and for all. "And some batteries. It means nothing. Nothing."

The sound of a siren coming up behind him restored his concentration on the road, and he glanced in his rearview mirror and started to pull over to let the squad cars—two of them—pass.

It wasn't until he'd come to a complete stop that it occurred to Luke that they weren't passing him. Instead, they had pulled to a halt behind and in front of him, blocking him in.

Before he'd had time to evaluate what was going on, one of the officers was at his bike, pulling him off and slamming him against the hood of the police car.

"What the hell is going on!" Luke shouted, his face pressed to the car as the cop cuffed his hands behind his back. "I didn't do anything, man!"

"Shut up," the officer said. "You're under arrest."

"For what!"

"For planting the bomb that blew up the federal building today. It's called terrorism, pal. And you're gonna be locked up for a long time."

Horror washed over Luke as the words sank in, and too stunned to defend himself, he allowed them to drag him to their car.

CHAPTER SIX

THE LIGHTS IN THE ROOM felt like stifling beams of heat beating down on him, and Luke leaned forward on the table, rubbed his eyes roughly and looked up at the team of cops whose attention was centered on him. Not just ordinary cops for his case, he thought with a dry twist of his stomach. These were FBI agents, from the terrorism task force.

How much worse could it get?

The men were circling around him with hatred in their eyes, as if he'd been responsible for everything from the TWA explosion to the hijacking of the *Achille Lauro*. A federal building blown up... damn!

Luke cleared his throat, wet his dry lips and addressed Barron, the cop who'd been conducting the bulk of the interrogation. "You didn't tell me... was anyone killed?"

"You answer our questions and we'll answer yours."

"I told you," Luke said. "Not until you let me speak to my lawyer. I just want to know—"

"Two people were injured, Wade," one of the others said bitterly. "If they die, we're gonna nail you to the wall."

Luke closed his eyes and dropped his forehead in his shaking hands.

The cop who'd shared the news with him leaned over the table, his face too close to Luke's. Luke looked up at him without backing away. "But there could have been hundreds of casualties. Before the bomb threat, that building was full."

"There was a bomb threat?" Luke asked, his eyebrows shooting up. "Did they get it on tape? They could analyze the voice, and they'd see—"

"We're not stupid, Wade," Barron said. "We know you wouldn't have made the call yourself."

"I told you I didn't do it!" Luke said through his teeth. "I don't know anything about this!"

A large man who'd hardly said two words since he came into the room but who seemed to wield a lot of authority over the others, shifted slightly in his chair. "Let him call his lawyer," he said quietly. "This is wasting our time."

Leaning forward, Luke sought the man's eyes. "Look, I have nothing to hide. I'll tell you whatever you want to know. But not until she gets here."

He sat back as the officers ambled out of the room, and in the hall he could hear a crowd of reporters yelling questions. Already, he could picture Aunt Margaret's reaction when word got out. Luke Wade, thief, was bad enough. But Luke Wade, terrorist?

The memory of those batteries and the cord in Hank's car came back to him, but the whole situation was too big, he thought, too amazing to be Hank's doing. Why would Hank be designing bombs to blow up buildings, and why on earth would he set up Luke to take the fall? It didn't make sense. He was on the wrong track, even thinking of Hank, so he vowed to put the thought out of his mind. There had to be an explanation, he thought, and he would get it as soon as he had the chance. Until then, he'd keep his mouth shut. No one would believe him, anyway.

He wondered what Kristen's reaction would be when they told her, and just how long it would be before she, too, stopped believing in him. The way it looked to him now, time was running out on faith all around. And that clock just wouldn't stop ticking.

"IT'S GETTING LATE," Eric Jordan said, his hurried voice shooting across the telephone line. "I have a date to get ready for. Just tell Courtney that I got her the picture of the elephant she needed for her social studies project, and I'll drop it by tomorrow."

"Why can't you tell her?" Kristen asked, trying to keep her voice low so that Courtney wouldn't know that her father didn't have time to speak to her.

"I told you, I'm late. I'm still at the office, and I have to get home and shower—"

"Fine, Eric. I'll tell her." Her tone was clipped, and she heard Eric sigh in irritation.

"One other thing," he said. "When I talked to her on the phone this afternoon, she said you were seeing Luke Wade again."

Kristen glanced at her daughter and wished she'd learn when *not* to tell her father something. "I was never *seeing* him to begin with."

"Right," he said with a decided lack of conviction. "Whatever, I don't want Courtney around him. I don't trust that guy."

Kristen bit her lip and cupped her hand over the phone to keep Courtney from hearing. "Eric, when I start choosing your friends, you can start choosing mine. And that includes choosing who I bring around our daughter.''

The doorbell rang, and from the living room, she heard her daughter shout, ''I'll get it!''

''Someone's at the door,'' Kristen said. ''I'll tell her about the elephant.''

She hung up the phone and dashed into the living room before her daughter had the chance to invite anyone into their home.

''It's Mr. Norsworthy!'' Courtney called as she ushered John into the house.

''John, hi.'' Kristen frowned at the unexpected visit. ''If you needed to talk to me, I could have stayed late at the office.''

''That's all right,'' John said, slipping his hands under his coat and into his pants pockets. ''We had a partnership meeting this afternoon, and they asked me to stop by and talk to you.''

Kristen inhaled deeply and braced herself. She glanced at her daughter, who hovered there, waiting for whatever news he'd brought her mother, as if it had something to do with her. ''Uh, Courtney, why don't you go work on your social studies poster? Your dad said he was bringing the elephant picture by tomorrow, so you need to have the poster ready.''

Looking from one adult to the other, Courtney nodded her head and made a quick exit.

''What is it, John?'' Kristen asked, not wanting to waste time with coffee and won't-you-sit-down.

''It's the Luke Wade case,'' John said. ''They want you to drop it.''

''What? They said it was my decision. Just this morning—''

"They thought some more about it, talked it over and decided that it was a mistake. You're dragging this albatross into our firm, and it's going to make you look very bad. We're grooming you, Kristen. Not so that you can waste your time on some loser you knew when you were a kid."

"Luke Wade is not a loser!" she shouted, then brought her hand to her face and tried to calm down. She swallowed, turned back to him and straightened her posture. "What if I refuse to drop the case?"

"Don't, Kristen," John said. "It wouldn't be wise."

They stood staring at each other for a short eternity, each evaluating the lengths to which the other would go to get his way. She had just opened her mouth to speak, when the telephone rang, startling her out of her thoughts.

In the kitchen, she heard Courtney answer.

"Mommy! It's for you. Luke."

Kristen gave John a guilty look, then started to the phone, knowing that he was on her heels. Clutching the telephone to her ear, she said, "Hello?"

Luke's voice was shaky when he answered. "They got me again, kiddo. And this one's a biggie."

A cold thread of fear unwound inside Kristen, and she clutched the phone tighter. "What do you mean, they got you?"

"I've been arrested again," he said.

Kristen caught her breath. "On what charge?"

She heard a deep, rugged sigh make its way out of Luke's lungs. When he spoke, the words were racked and unsteady. "Kristen, they think I blew up the federal building today."

"Oh my God," Kristen whispered. "Luke, I'll be right there. Don't say anything until I get there. Do you understand? Not one word!"

"You got it," he said.

Kristen continued clutching the phone as she heard the click in her ear, and finally she recovered from the shock and realized that both Courtney and John were staring at her, waiting.

"What's the matter, Mommy?"

Kristen touched the counter, tried to catch her breath. "Nothing, honey."

"He's back in custody, isn't he?" John asked as if the news didn't surprise him at all.

Kristen nodded, then rallying her thoughts, leaned over to Courtney and grabbed her shoulders. "Honey, I have to go meet a client. Go pack an overnight bag. I'm taking you to your father's."

"All right!" Courtney shouted and scurried off to her room.

"Kristen..." John's voice startled her, and she turned back to him, dread and misery glittering in her eyes. "You're not going, after the partners insisted—"

"You bet I am," she said, her eyes flashing defiance. "If the partners want me off this case, they're going to have to fire me. Now, if you'll excuse me, I have a client waiting."

KRISTEN HAD COURTNEY at Eric's house before he'd even pulled into his driveway from work. But the moment his Porsche came to a halt, Courtney was out of the car and barreling toward her father.

"Daddy! Mommy has to work so I get to stay with you tonight!"

Eric gave his daughter a tentative hug and looked at Kristen over the child's head. "What's this all about?" he demanded. "I told you I had plans—"

"Eric, it's an emergency. I have a client who needs me—"

"Luke's in jail, Daddy!" Courtney blurted out, then rushed back to the car to drag out her duffel bag.

"Courtney!" Kristen tried to censor her daughter, but it was too late.

Eric's face took on that hard-as-nails look that made him so successful in business. "You can't be serious," he told Kristen. "You actually expect me to cancel my plans so you can run to Luke Wade?"

"I'm his lawyer," Kristen said. "And I'm being paid to represent him. I'd love to stand around and chat, but—"

"Kristen!" Eric said. "I told you I have a date. What do you expect me to do with her?"

"You're a real resourceful kind of guy, Eric. Figure something out. You are her father."

He loosened the tie around his neck and sighed. "What about your mother? Why can't you take her there?"

"Mom has had Courtney since she got out of school today, and she has bingo tonight. It's your turn, Eric."

Eric bit his tongue as Courtney came bouncing back to them, ecstatic that she'd have a night alone with her father. "Daddy, I brought my poster. You can help me with it!"

Kristen was already getting back in the car when Eric managed to answer. "Uh, yeah, sweetheart. Just bring it in the house and we'll...we'll see what we can do.''

"I'll be back as soon as I can," Kristen called. "Go ahead and put her to bed if I'm late. We can carry her to the car when I get here.''

She reached through the window for Courtney and gave her daughter a kiss. But before she could give her the usual lecture about minding her father and going to bed when he said, Courtney had scurried away and was chattering to her dad about her plans for their evening.

THE WAITING AREA near Sherry's new room was getting dark as dusk intruded through the narrow window at the top of the wall, but Hank was too encumbered with his sleeping sons to reach the switch to turn on the light. It didn't matter, anyway, he thought. The darkness had helped to lull the boys to sleep. Jake was already out cold on the couch next to him, and Josh he held cradled in his arms, his gentle back-and-forth motion almost making the boy surrender to sleep.

Looking away from the newscast that dominated the television screen across the room, Hank smiled down at Josh. The little boy pulled his wet thumb out of his mouth.

"Mommy?" he asked quietly.

"Nanna's with Mommy," Hank explained. "She'll be back in a little while."

The explanation didn't appease the small boy, and once again, he asked, "Mommy?"

Hank swallowed and looked away, trying not to let his son see the turmoil on his face. When he was sure his emotions were in check, he looked back down at the little face waiting for an answer. "Mommy's not feeling well right now," he whispered. "But she misses you, and she told me to give you a big hug for her."

Josh opened his arms and received his hug, and offered his father a wet kiss. *The best kind,* Hank thought. He wished he could bottle that kiss and give it to Sherry when she woke up.

Josh stuck his thumb back in his mouth and pulled the satin ribbon on his blanket close to his face, rubbing gently as his eyes began to close. Hank leaned his head back on the couch and focused on the television. He was tired. So tired. He couldn't remember the last time he'd really slept. But he couldn't afford to waste the time. He might not have much time left with Sherry.

"...police sources say that a bomb threat preceded the explosion, and that the building was subsequently evacuated except for two workers who didn't take the threat seriously...."

Hank's attention perked to life as the screen revealed the building, burned and gutted, and firefighters milling around the smoldering ruins.

"The bomb was a high-tech type often used in military operations, rather than the homemade kind usually used in terrorist attacks," a media representative for the police department told the reporter on camera. "According to our sources, it was assembled by someone who knew exactly what he was doing. The building was completely destroyed, and the two people who were injured are listed in critical condition at a local hospital.''

The color drained from Hank's face, and he felt his lungs constricting, trapping his breath. "Oh, no!" he groaned. Quickly, he laid Jake on the couch and stood up, as if doing so could add perspective to the news story.

"Channel eight has also learned that the terrorists involved issued a demand at the time of the bomb threat," the news anchor continued. "However, police sources have not yet confirmed that.''

A wave of dizziness washed over Hank, and stunned, he grabbed the back of a chair and leaned over it, trying to steady his breath. "Oh, my God!" he whispered.

"But police have confirmed that a suspect is in custody. Lucas A. Wade, of Atlanta, was booked this afternoon on several charges. Wade was released on bond just two days ago for allegedly stealing explosives from the ammunitions plant, after he was found with a trunk load of plastic explosives. We'll have more on Luke Wade, as well as interviews with the survivors of the explosion, tonight at eleven.''

Hank covered his face and sat down, as if the breath had been knocked out of him. "Aw, no," he moaned. "Aw, no.''

"Hank?''

Hank snapped upright and spun around to face his mother-in-law, who was standing in the doorway, gaping at him. "Are you all right?''

Hank swallowed and tried to catch his breath. He pointed to the television screen, where the anchor had already moved on to another story, and shook his head. "The news..."

"What?" she asked, taking his shoulders and shaking him. "What happened?"

"Luke's been arrested," he said. "For...for planting a bomb—" his voice broke off, and his face distorted in pain "—a bomb that injured two people."

"Oh, no," Nancy said. "It must be a mistake. Luke would never—"

"He *didn't*," Hank blurted, then rallied and said more cautiously, "he wouldn't. I know he wouldn't."

Nancy sat down and looked up at her weary son-in-law. "If you have to go to the police station, I'll stay here. Sherry's sleeping, anyway."

Hank swallowed and shook his head, but the sad ache of tears welled in his eyes. "No, no. I can't leave. I'm sure Kristen's with him by now." He clutched his forehead again, shook his head. "I just can't believe this happened...."

His heart pounded in triple rhythm, threatening to overcome him completely. But he didn't have time to be overwhelmed. He looked at Nancy and spoke in a steady voice. "I—I've got to get back in there to her. I don't want her left alone."

Nancy nodded and gestured to the boys. "Could you help me get them to the car? I don't want to wake them," she said.

Hank nodded. "Sure. Yeah, I can do that." He leaned over and scooped up Jake, laying the boy's head on his shoulder. As he started out of the room, he gave one last glance back at the television screen, as if he could see Luke's face there again, and determine if things were really as bad as they sounded.

It got out of hand, Luke. I didn't know....

The mental apology left him hollow and empty. For he could never say it aloud. At least, not now. Not yet.

CHAPTER SEVEN

THE BRUISE TRACING a blackening line down from Luke's brow to the crest of his cheekbone was the first thing Kristen saw when she came into the interrogation room. Luke was sitting on a cracked-vinyl sofa, his elbows braced on his knees. His clasped hands held his chin, and when he looked up at her, his expression was more serious than she could remember ever having seen.

She felt her mouth trembling, and she brought up a hand to cover it. But Kristen wasn't able to cover the tears misting in her eyes. "Luke, are you all right?"

"Yeah," he said. "I'm fine."

Her professional training told her to rein in her feelings, to sit down at the table and start asking questions. But there were instincts inside her that were stronger than training—instincts seated in her heart. Following those, she went to sit beside him on the couch, on the side where she could see the bruise more clearly, feel the tension in his muscles and comfort him in a way that she knew innately that only she could.

He didn't change his position as her weight shifted the cushion beneath him, but he turned his head to look at her. "I'm in deep shit, huh?"

The tension of her emotions drove all rational thought from her mind, and Kristen forgot not to let

her shoulder touch his, or her knee graze his knee.
And she forgot to put more distance between them.
"Yeah, you are."

She reached up with a trembling hand and touched
the bruise on his face. Sucking in a deep breath as he
inclined his head and winced, she asked, "What did
they do to you?"

"Nothing," Luke said, shaking his head and pulling her hand down to his. "They were just in a real big
hurry to snap those handcuffs on."

He laced his fingers through hers, squeezed, then
brought his troubled eyes back to her. "What are we
gonna do, Kristy?"

Kristen closed her eyes, forced herself to check her
emotions before they got away from her and took a
deep breath. When she opened her eyes, the tears had
gone. "We're going to get to the bottom of this," she
said. She stood up, set her things on the table and
turned back to him. "But first we have to address a
few pressing things. Starting with where you were last
night, who you saw, who you talked to—anything to
hold up your alibi. And I want to know the same for
this morning before you came to my office, and after
you left."

"That's easy," Luke said. "I was at home last
night. After you left my house, I didn't see anybody.
I talked to Hank on the phone once and told him you
wanted to meet with us today, but other than that—"

"That's it?" Kristen asked as if his answer wasn't a
good one. "Nobody else?"

"Well, a nurse at the hospital who got my message
to Hank to call me back. I didn't even get her name."

"A nurse. Okay, she should be easy enough to find."

"Why?" Luke asked. "What has she got to do with anything?"

"She can confirm that you called and what time," Kristen said, jotting down that information. She looked back at him, apprehension in her eyes. "So there wasn't anyone else at all?"

Luke's eyes narrowed into an almost-smile. "Were you expecting me to be with someone?"

Kristen shrugged self-consciously. "I just...it's hard to picture Luke Wade all alone. Especially after such a stressful few days. In the old days you would have had your harem over."

"My harem?" Luke laughed then and stood up, leaned on the table facing her. "Well, let's just say I've changed my ways."

"Have you?" she asked, no humor in her dull voice. Then, shaking her head, she went back to her notes. "What about this morning?"

"Nothing to tell," Luke said. "I met Hank at the hospital, and he followed me straight to your office."

"Okay, what about after you left my office?"

"I went to the hospital to see about Sherry," Luke said. "Only she was in a new room and Hank was talking to her doctor. So I went down and gave blood, and then I went out to Hank's car—"

The sudden way he let his sentence die snagged Kristen's attention, and she looked up at him. "What?"

Luke rallied and shook his head. "Nothing," he said a little too emphatically. "I left a note for him to call me. In his car."

Something about the look on Luke's face and the fragmented way he offered that particular explanation alerted Kristen that something wasn't right. "He has a phone in his car?" she asked, confused.

"No," Luke said. "Why?"

"Well, you said you asked him to call you in his car."

"No," Luke said, shaking his head. "I *said* I left a note in his car for him to call me. That's all, okay? I left the note and drove away."

"Okay," Kristen said, perplexed by his sudden defensiveness. "And then what did you do?"

"I got in my car and started to drive home, but that's when the cops pulled me over." He moved a chair out with a scraping sound and slumped into it. "Oh, hell. Why would anybody do this to me?"

The sheer helplessness of his question left Kristen unable to speak for a moment, then she went to sit beside him. "I don't know, Luke."

He looked up at her, saw the tears in her eyes and, as if her opinion meant everything to him, he met her eyes directly. "Kristen, I swear. I've never hurt anybody intentionally, and as much trouble as I've been in in my life, I can't remember ever making a real enemy. Hell, I'm no saint, everybody knows that. But I've never made anybody mad enough to want me put away."

"Maybe it's not that," Kristen said. "Maybe it's come down to you or whoever did this, and given your background, they figured you were easy to set up. Desperate people do desperate things."

"Kristen, I don't know *anybody* who would blow up a building with people in it. Desperate or not." He paused, his breathing labored, as if the thought of the people in that building was like a fist pounding into his spleen. "They think I did it. The ones lying in the hospital with burns...their families...everybody thinks I did it."

The words were uttered with such despair that Kristen couldn't contain her tears any longer, and she leaned over and rested her forehead on his shoulder. As if she were the one who needed reassurances, Luke took her shoulders and made her look at him. "Hey, don't cry," he whispered. "I'll get out of this."

Kristen tried to buck up and nod, but more tears rolled down her cheeks. Gently, he pulled her into his arms and held her. She tried to swallow and muffle her sobs, but they kept coming. Kristen closed her eyes and allowed herself to melt in his strength, in his fortitude. His scent was like a relaxant, filtering through her lungs, and his warmth was a blanket of security that none other had ever matched.

Finally, after a short eternity, she forced herself to pull back enough to look at him. "We don't have long," she said in a hoarse voice, wiping her eyes with shaking hands. "They're going to start questioning you in half an hour. We really have to talk some more." Her voice broke when he didn't let her go, and breathing in another hiccuping sob, she reached up with her tear-damp hand and framed his face, carefully covering the bruise. "I want so much to get you out of this," she said. "But it's so big. You need someone more experienced. Someone who's handled cases like this before."

"I want you," Luke whispered. "I couldn't go through this with anyone else."

Kristen closed her eyes. "But what if I blow it, and you wind up going to prison?"

Luke tipped her chin up and forced her to look at him. Her lips were so close to his, she could smell the clean, warm scent of his breath. "Kristy, I believe in you."

The words gave her a subtle strength. "I believe in you, too."

Luke's arms closed tighter around her, and he pulled her into a crushing hug, one that she didn't want to break. They held each other for a fragment of time, and she wrestled the urge to steal more from the moment, and kiss him. But she didn't, and finally he released her.

"Did they tell you anything?" he asked.

Kristen wiped her face again and stepped back, nodding. Trying to refocus her thoughts, she sifted through the papers in her briefcase. "They told me some. One of my friends in the press told me a lot more. Apparently whoever set that bomb had a demand to go with it."

"What kind of demand?" Luke asked.

Kristen referred to the notes she'd jotted before she'd come into the room. "That a man named Samuel Bates be released from prison. They said they had more bombs and would blow up more buildings until he was released." She looked at Luke, her eyes assessing him with intense hope. "Do you know Samuel Bates, Luke?"

Luke racked his brain for the name, but came up empty. "No. It doesn't even sound familiar."

"Are you sure? Someone from your past? The Army?"

"No. Who is he? Why is he in prison?"

Kristen shuffled her papers. "Apparently he's in for attempted murder, after he shot a city councilman. I'm hiring a private detective, Luke. I'm going to have his background checked. I think if we can start with him and work backward, we might be able to link him to whoever is setting you up."

"A private detective," Luke said, beginning to look a little less distraught. "Good."

"I'm also going to have a lot of other things checked out, too. I have to tell you that the U.S. Attorney is going to do everything he has to do to link Bates to you. I have to be one step ahead of him."

"Right. But meanwhile, they're going to be questioning me. Kristen, I don't have anything to hide. I can tell them anything they want to know."

"All right," Kristen said, "but I'm going to be right beside you the whole time. If I tell you to stop talking, then do it. It may be that they're getting some kind of interpretation from what you're saying that you aren't aware of. We have to be very careful. Sometimes even the truth, as innocent as it may seem, can be indicting."

Luke nodded and got up, and Kristen could see the worry in his eyes. "I guess I'll be here for a while? I mean, they don't let people charged with terrorism just wander the streets at will."

Kristen shook her head. "It could be weeks before the grand jury hearing, unless the U.S. Attorney pressures them to expedite things. You can't stay in jail all that time."

"Will they let me out on bond?" he asked.

Kristen sighed and tried to imagine what the magistrate would do. "I was thinking...if I could get the magistrate to agree to release you into my custody, maybe I could get him to set bond. I've known him socially for a couple of years, and he knows I can be trusted. The bond would be high, but..."

Luke paced across the room, staring at the cracks in the yellowing tiles. "Kristy, when I posted bond for the first charge it cost me everything I had in savings, and then I still had to borrow some. It's still tied up. I don't think I'll be able to come up with any more. My business isn't worth anything with all this publicity, so I can't use it for collateral. And I used the equity in my house for the surety for the last charge."

"We'll come up with something, Luke," she said, frowning as if sheer determination could get the job done. "I won't let you stay in jail."

"Come here," he whispered. Again, he pulled her into his arms, but this time his embrace seemed so tentative that Kristen could feel him slipping away already. Through her tears she looked up at him, and pressed a kiss on his chin. "I love you, Luke," she whispered.

The sharp catch in his breath was enough answer as he tightened his hold on her, for she didn't want a response. It was enough for Luke to know that he wasn't alone.

IT WAS AFTER TEN when Kristen got back to Eric's condominium, and the first thing she noticed was that his car, usually parked in the drive, wasn't there. Biting her lip, she turned off her engine and went to the door.

As she expected, his note was stuck to the glass with a piece of tape. "I took Courtney to your mother's," it read. "I caught her before she left for bingo and she agreed to keep her."

Anger made her face redden, and Kristen clutched the note tighter and read on.

"About Luke Wade," Eric had written. "If you get him out of jail, I don't want that hood around my daughter. I mean it."

Kristen wadded the note in her hand, slammed it against the front door and watched the paper bounce to the ground and roll back from the cement step. *Damn him,* she thought. He couldn't take one night to exercise some rare parental responsibility, but he had the audacity to malign Luke!

She bit her lip and stormed back to her car, shifted into reverse and screeched out of the driveway.

Eric had never liked Luke, Kristen reflected, even when they had first started dating and she was only eighteen. Eric had been jealous of the relationship she'd had with Luke, even to the point of warning her to stay away from him, that he was "bad news." She would never forget the day she'd come home from the mall with her mother, only to find the two men engaged in quiet yet obviously hostile conversation that halted abruptly when she drove up. Luke hadn't said a word, but had given Eric a scathing look that sent a shiver down her spine, and had turned around, ambled across the street and disappeared into his house.

"What was that about?" she'd asked suspiciously, turning on Eric. "What did you say to him?"

"What did *I* say to *him*?" he'd repeated incredulously. "That guy comes over here and asks me my intentions toward you, like it's any of his damn business, and you automatically assume that I started it?"

"He's my friend," she had said. "He watches out for me."

"Yeah, well, you need to watch out for him." He had pulled her into his arms, and she remembered having felt strangely divided. Half of her was content to bask in Eric's affection—but that other half, the part of herself she'd never been able to control, wanted nothing more than to lose herself in Luke. "I don't want you around him anymore," Eric had continued. "You're my girl, and from now on I'll watch out for you."

Broken promises, she thought with a dull headache as she negotiated the streets to her mother's. Eric was full of broken promises. He had no more watched out for her than he did for Courtney now. Just an occasional note explaining his "concern." Eric was a delegator... he didn't like doing the dirty work, like loving and caring and cultivating a relationship, himself. She almost felt sorry for the date he had abandoned Courtney for tonight.

She parked the car in her mother's driveway and got out, and turned around in the darkness, staring across the street to the house where Luke used to live. It hadn't changed much, she thought, even though so much time had passed. Through the curtains, she could see the one lamp shining that Aunt Margaret always kept on when she slept, and she wondered if the woman had heard of Luke's plight yet. Of course she had, Kristen told herself. If Aunt Margaret hadn't heard it on the news or read about it firsthand, there were any number of busybodies who would love breaking the news to her. She only wished the woman could put aside those feelings she'd always had toward Luke, and this once, be there for him. But that was a lot to ask.

Quietly, she slipped into her mother's house, and saw her mother dozing on the couch with David Letterman on the television screen engaged in a segment involving stupid pet tricks. A dog was pulling the trousers off of a man lying on the floor, and the audience was howling in laughter.

Kristen tiptoed through the house and found her daughter, sleeping soundly in the same bed Kristen had slept in as a child. She looked so peaceful, so quiet, lying under the covers, and suddenly sadness washed over Kristen. Courtney had been so excited about staying with her dad tonight. Kristen wondered how Eric had explained away his lack of time to spend with her, or if he'd given one second's thought to the girl's fragile feelings.

She sat down on the bed, her weight shifting the mattress, and reached out to sweep the hair back from Courtney's little face. Courtney opened her eyes. "Hi, Mommy," she whispered.

"Hi, pumpkin. You wanna go home?"

"Um-hmm," she said with a sigh, then closed her eyes again. "Daddy brought me here because he had a date."

"I know," Kristen said.

"She was real pretty," Courtney said, opening her eyes again. "I don't blame him at all."

"I know, pumpkin. I know." The acceptance in the little girl's voice, pardoning her father, twisted Kristen's heart. "Go back to sleep," she said. "We'll just spend the night here."

"Will you sleep with me?" Courtney asked.

"I sure will," Kristen said. "But first I need to wake Grandma and tell her I'm home. She thinks she's waiting up for me."

"Okay, Mommy," Courtney said, snuggling down into her sheets. "I'll keep it warm for you."

Kristen leaned over and dropped a kiss on Courtney's warm little cheek, then went back to the living room. Quietly, she sat down next to her mother. "Mom?"

Her mother's eyes popped open, and she looked around, trying to orient herself. "Oh! I must have dozed off...."

"I'm sorry I'm so late," Kristen said. "But the questioning went on forever. We're just going to stay over here. I don't want to take Courtney back out tonight. I'm sorry Eric finked out on me."

Her mother rubbed her eyes, patted her hair and looked at her daughter. "She was trying to be a real trooper when he brought her, but I could tell she was hurt that he didn't want her tonight. She kept talking about how it was fine with her because his date was real pretty."

"Yeah," Kristen said. "She said that to me, too. I imagine Eric spelled that out to her. 'You wouldn't want me to miss a date with such a pretty lady, now would you?' He makes me sick. Do you know that he called Luke a hood and said he didn't want him around Courtney?"

Edith's forehead wrinkled in a tired frown. "How is Luke?"

Kristen slumped back on the couch and shook her head. "He's in jail, Mom, and for the life of me, I don't know how I'm going to get him out. The U.S. Attorney is going to ask for preventative detention. That means Luke would be denied bond, and would have to stay in jail until his indictment hearing, and unless I come up with something substantial to prove his innocence, there's no doubt in my mind he'll be indicted." She swallowed and took a deep shaky breath, and felt those tears returning to her eyes.

"Oh, Mom, I just can't stand the thought of him sitting in jail all that time. If he's out, he can help me find who set him up. They have to make a mistake sooner or later."

Edith took Kristen's hand, squeezed it. "If you need a character witness," she said, "I'll be glad to testify. Luke would never do the things they're accusing him of. I can't tell you how many times I thanked God that he was around when you were growing up." She sat up, straightened her clothes and rubbed her eyes. "Without your father, there were times when I was just lost. But Luke always seemed to pop up and take care of things. If your car broke down, Luke fixed it. If you were lonely, Luke talked to you. If you had boy troubles, Luke advised you. I really depended on him back then, and he never let me down."

Kristen's heart ached at the memories that were so vivid, yet so far in the past. "Yeah, I did, too."

A quiet moment passed as both mother and daughter stared idly at the television screen, recalling the past. "And I'll tell you a little secret," her mother added. "Deep in my heart, I think I always hoped that someday the two of you would . . . well, get married."

Kristen looked at her mother, surprise brightening her eyes. "Did you really, Mom? Even when he kept getting into so much trouble?"

Edith smiled. "I knew that if anybody could keep Luke Wade out of trouble, you could. I figured you were just what he needed."

Kristen stared down at the lines on her palms and shook her head dolefully. "Well, he saw things differently, I guess, because he just sort of drifted away. He never even wrote once after he went into the Army. I never understood it."

"Luke has funny ways," Edith said thoughtfully. "And very noble ideas for someone who's been accused, by his own aunt, of being no good. He probably thought he was doing what was best for you."

Kristen laughed mirthlessly. "He told me this morning that he saw me as someone too good for him. I thought, what a clever letdown."

"Letdown?" Her mother gave her a sideways glance, and Kristen noted a perceptive grin forming on her lips. "What would he have to let you down from?"

"From any hope I might be harboring, that someday, maybe the two of us—"

"Kristen," her mother cut in, looking at her more closely. "Are you in love with him?"

The question was so sudden that Kristen felt her defenses rising, but somehow she needed to be honest. "Mom, I've loved Luke Wade since I was nine years old. And as much as I've tried to forget him, I can't. He has some kind of hold on my heart, and no matter how far away he is, or how *he* feels about me, he won't let go."

The age lines around Edith's eyes altered as she arched her brows and smiled. "I hope he never does."

Kristen sighed at the intensity of her mother's wish. "He doesn't even know it," she whispered. "To him, I'm just an accidental relative who cares about him. And I can't even figure out how to get the money to keep him out of jail. Even if the magistrate sets bond, I don't know how we'll raise it." She looked at her mother, her eyes helpless and distant. "I'd give every cent I had to get him out, Mom, but it wouldn't be enough."

Her mother sucked in a quick breath as an idea took form. "Why don't you ask Margaret? She inherited a nice nest egg when Ed died. Maybe she could help."

Kristen regarded her mother with skepticism. "According to Luke, she wouldn't give him the time of day, much less the money to bail him out of jail."

"Well, maybe Luke's wrong. Margaret's a good person. I admit that she short changed Luke when he was growing up, but I honestly don't think she realized what she was doing to him. In her own way, I think she loves him. And I think she would help him in his time of need."

Kristen let her eyes drift to the television, where David Letterman was interviewing some up-and-coming star she couldn't name. The comical banter had no effect, for the thought of Luke sleeping in a jail cell tonight wouldn't leave her mind. "Maybe you're right, Mom," she said. "It's worth a try. I'll go talk to her in the morning."

CHAPTER EIGHT

NOT MUCH HAD CHANGED about the old neighbor-hood, or Aunt Margaret's house, or the woman her-self. Kristen found her in the back yard early the next morning, on her knees scrubbing out the planters that held the potted flowers she had tended for years with much more love than she'd ever offered Luke. She hadn't heard Kristen walking up the brick pathway that led through the gate and to the back patio, and for a moment, Kristen stood back and watched her.

"Hi, Aunt Margaret," she said finally.

Margaret jumped and swung around, as if she'd been caught doing something shameful, and when she saw Kristen she slapped on a smile and scampered to her feet. The woman had lost weight, Kristen noted, since she'd seen her a couple of months ago, and she had to wonder if it had anything to do with the news of Luke.

"Kristen! I wasn't expecting you!"

They exchanged quick, spontaneous hugs, and Margaret grabbed a towel and dried her hands. "Come in, dear. We'll have some coffee. My, you're up awfully early."

"I have to be in court in a little while," Kristen said, following her from the patio into the kitchen that had been freshly painted and retiled in white. Perfection,

Kristen thought as she looked around her. That was what Aunt Margaret had always strived for. "I wanted to talk to you before I left."

"Oh? About what?"

"About Luke."

Margaret's hand froze over the freshly ground bag of coffee, and she hardened her eyes on the wall behind her counter top. "I really have nothing to say on that subject, dear."

Kristen sighed and pulled out a chair at Margaret's big breakfast table, the same table Luke had eaten at a thousand times when he was a boy. She recalled the few times she had eaten here with them, when between each bite, Luke had suffered Aunt Margaret's scathing critical orders: "Sit up straight, Luke," or "Don't gulp your food," or "Put your napkin in your lap," or "Get your elbows off the table." Kristen had always been self-conscious eating in front of the woman herself, even though Aunt Margaret's tongue-lashings only seemed directed at Luke.

"Aunt Margaret, he's back in jail again. The charges are very serious."

"Yes, I heard it on the news. Believe me," she said with a sarcastic laugh that revealed more bitterness than she realized. "I'm quite aware of how serious they must be. Terrorists don't fare well in this country."

"But Luke is not a terrorist," Kristen said, schooling her voice to hide her rising anger. "He's being set up. Someone planted those explosives in his car, and later planted the bomb in that building. Luke is innocent."

"Uh-huh," Margaret said skeptically, turning back to face Kristen with stiff lips and hard, stubborn eyes. "Luke always could convince you of anything."

"And you were always quick to believe the worst about him."

They stared at each other for a long moment, and finally Margaret turned back to the sink, wet a dishrag and began to scrub the counter in jerky motions. "I gave him a roof over his head, I fed him, I bought him clothes to wear. I shouldn't be faulted for not being able to control him. My sister was wild, too, and she raised him that way. There wasn't one thing I was ever able to do about it." She turned back to the coffeepot, poured two cups and set one down in front of Kristen. "You know, I never had one minute of trouble from my own children. That ought to tell you something."

Again, Kristen tried to control her anger, but it wouldn't be tamed any more than Luke had been as a child. "It does tell me something. It tells me that your own children knew they were loved and appreciated—and even respected. Luke didn't have those luxuries."

"Respect!" Margaret remained standing, clutching the hot cup in her hand as she gaped at Kristen with a sarcastically amused smile. "You've got to be kidding. That boy was in trouble every time I turned around. He never came home on time, he sneaked out of the house after everyone had gone to bed, he skipped school every chance he got." She sat down, braced her hands on the table and drilled her gray eyes into Kristen's. "What about the respect he had for Ed and me? Huh? What about that?"

Mottled patches of red colored Kristen's cheeks, and she felt her lips trembling. "Aunt Margaret, he was just a kid when he came to live with you. He'd lost his parents, the only people in the world he knew loved him. Why couldn't you have shown just a little patience, a little understanding?"

"I never asked to raise him!" Margaret blurted. "I had done a good job with my own children. They're decent, respectable people. My Johnny is the president of a bank! But then Luke came along and shattered my reputation. Everything I'd worked for all my life was ruined the first time he got himself into trouble."

Tears stung Kristen's eyes, and she realized that she'd made a mistake in coming here. Margaret would never in a million years help with Luke's bond. And Kristen herself would rather die than ask for the woman's help. Kristen stood and pushed back her chair. "I feel sorry for you," she said in a cracked voice.

"Me?" Margaret asked, her eyes still flashing livid fire.

"Yes, you. Because you'll never have the chance to know what a good and loving person Luke is. You cheated yourself out of finding that out. And someday you're going to regret it."

Margaret compressed her lips and looked up at Kristen, and she saw a hint of tears glistening in the woman's dull eyes. "I did the best I could," she said.

"Yeah," Kristen said without conviction. "What you did was to make him an outcast in your home. Did it ever occur to you that Luke got into so much trouble because of that? That maybe if he was disliked because he was a troublemaker, that was just a little bit easier to bear than being disliked because he wasn't worthy of your love?"

"Yes, well, you tell that to the judge when you get to court," Margaret said. "See how your psychoanalysis of him stands up against an exploding bomb and two people in the burn unit." She banged her fist on the table, shaking her whole body. "I won't take responsibility for the kind of person he is! I won't do it!"

"Well, I will!" Kristen said, and before she had to hear another word, she turned and left Margaret's house, slamming the door.

Her mother wasn't home when Kristen made her way back across the street, for Edith had agreed to drive Courtney to school while Kristen spoke to Margaret. Kristen stumbled into the house, determined to get this crying spell over with before her mother came back.

She sat down at the kitchen table, dropped her face in her cupped hands and sobbed with every ounce of energy in her body. What was she going to do?

She wiped her tears, as if by doing so she could wipe away the pain and misery and grab back a little of the control she saw slipping away. Last night, she had spoken to all the bail bondsmen she'd been accustomed to dealing with in the past. All had refused to post bond for Luke in the event that the magistrate set it at all, because due to the seriousness of his crime, they feared he would jump bond and leave the country. It was too much of a risk for such a serious crime, they'd said.

Now she grabbed her briefcase and, with shaking hands, pulled out her book with the phone numbers of some bail bondsmen she knew personally. Deciding to give it one more try, she called the one she had dealt with most often, a man she'd even dated once or twice. When he answered, she cleared her throat. "Um, Jack? This is Kristen Jordan again. How are you?"

"Same as last night, Kristen," he said. "Have you seen the magistrate yet?"

Kristen rested her chin in her hand. "Not yet, Jack. But I'm going to see him in two hours. I'm going to ask him to deny the prosecutor's request for preventative detention and release Luke into my custody."

"*Your* custody?" the bondsman asked. "Are you serious?"

"Yes," Kristen said. "That's how sure I am of him. I'll take full responsibility for him. The magistrate knows me and you know me. My word has to count for something."

Jack laughed. "Kristen, you can't do that. He could sneak off in the night—"

"I'm talking about moving him into my house with me," she said, her voice wobbling. "Jack, Luke is my cousin. I won't let him out of my sight for a moment."

She heard the hesitation in Jack's voice, and finally he made a concession. "I'll tell you what. If you can talk the magistrate into that, I'll put up fifty thousand dollars. But that's all."

"But I can't get him down that low! The best I can hope for is a million dollars surety with one hundred thousand cash. Where will I get the rest?"

"It's all I'm willing to do, Kristen, and only because it's you. If I know you, you can convince him to let him out for fifty thousand in cash and, if it's more, you'll just have to scrape it together somehow. Take it or leave it."

She thought for a moment, flipped through the pages of her address book and finally realized this was the best offer she was likely to get. "All right, all right," she said. "I'll take it. I'll get the funds somehow."

She thanked him and hung up the phone, then slumped over the table, massaging her temples.

Her mother touched her trembling hand, and Kristen looked up at her. "I take it Margaret didn't come through?" Edith asked.

Tears returned to Kristen's eyes, and she shook her head. "I didn't even ask her. Luke's right. She hates him. She'd pay *them* to lock him up."

"I don't believe that," Edith said.

"Believe it," Kristen told her. "Now I've got to find someone to put up the rest of his bond, assuming the magistrate agrees to set it. But I don't know these other bondsmen very well, and my word doesn't mean that much to them." She sat back, trying not to look as overwhelmed as she felt.

Her mother set down her purse and went to the stove. "I'll get you some coffee."

In the next half hour, Kristen called ten bondsmen, all of whom refused to grant Luke the rest of the money. Finally, she pushed the telephone away and sat back, limp with emotion. "I can't believe this," she whispered. "No one will loan us the money."

"What about the partners at the firm?" her mother asked. "Why don't you ask them for some help? Maybe they have a little more pull."

"I can't," Kristen said, fresh despair coursing over her as last night's orders from John came back to her. She took a fortifying sip of her coffee, and met her mother's eyes. "Last night the partners ordered me to drop Luke's case. I refused." She breathed a humorless laugh at her audacity. "I actually told them that the only way they could get me off this case would be to fire me."

"Good for you," her mother said quietly, though she couldn't hide the worry in her eyes.

Kristen nodded dolefully. "Yeah, good for me. I may not have a job this morning, but you know something? I was wrong last night when I said that. Even if they fire me, I'm *still* not dropping Luke's case."

She went to the sink, splashed some cold water on her face and dried it with a paper towel. Then, turning back to her mother, she took a deep breath and said, "Well, it's time for me to sit down and figure out where I'm going to come up with the money."

"Why do you have to do it now?" her mother asked. "Why can't you wait for the magistrate's ruling?"

"I could," Kristen said, "but I need to know what I have to work with. After this hearing, I won't have another chance. If he rules in my favor, I need to be able to act on it."

She pulled out her bankbook and flipped through the pages until she came to the place where she kept her savings account balance. "I have thirteen thousand dollars in here," she said. "And I have some IRAs I could cash in. That would bring me up to twenty." She did some figuring on one of the blank pages in her bankbook. "We have a credit union at work. I might be able to borrow a little from that, assuming I still have a job."

Her mother reached across the table and touched her hand, made her look up at her. "Honey, aren't you forgetting something?"

Kristen set her chin on her hand, and fixed her eyes on her mother. "Daddy's money?"

"*Your* money," her mother clarified. "He set up the trust fund for you, and you've never touched a cent."

"Mom, I can't." She looked down at her figures, as if miraculously something in the numbers might have changed.

"Honey, you've got twenty-five thousand dollars plus interest just sitting there."

"But I was saving it for you, Mom. You might need it someday."

Edith wouldn't be swayed. "Kristen, it was for your college. You were just too stubborn to touch it."

"I managed without it, Mom. I never really felt like that was my money. Daddy worked all his life for it, and I've just been saving it for—"

"For someone you love," Edith cut in. "It doesn't have to be me, honey. Who better than Luke?"

Kristen breathed out a broken sob, and closed her hand over her mouth. "Are you sure, Mom? What if you need it someday?"

"We'll get it back when this is all over," her mother said. "For now, Luke needs it more than I do. That's what counts."

Kristen got up and embraced her mother in a bone-crushing hug. "I love you, Mom. Thank you."

"Don't thank me," her mother said, laughing. "It's your money, not mine."

"Thank you for your blessings," Kristen began, piling her things back into her briefcase. "Now if I can just convince the magistrate."

She started toward the door, but her mother stopped her. "Honey?"

"Uh-huh?"

"Are you really going to move Luke into your house?"

Kristen shrugged. "I have to, Mom. I have no choice."

A tiny smile played on her mother's lips, and Kristen tried to ignore it. "Nothing's going to happen, Mom. Luke doesn't see me that way."

"I have a feeling Luke's vision is about to clear," her mother said. "If it hasn't already."

Kristen took a deep breath and left the house, wondering if she was setting herself up for the biggest heartbreak of her life.

A BURST OF ICY AIR from the vent over his head sent a shiver down Hank Gentry's spine as he stared in disbelief at the article on the front page—the article that implied that Luke was a terrorist.

"Those friggin' jackasses!" he said in a harsh whisper, turning back to his mother-in-law, who sat in the waiting room with him. "Just because the man had some explosives in his car doesn't mean he's a terrorist, for Pete's sake! Did you read this crap?"

"I read it," Nancy said, clutching her arms tighter around her to battle the cold.

"Did they ever once think that he might not know a damned thing about that bomb? That it had nothing to do with him?"

Nancy looked up at him, a frown creasing her brow. "Calm down, Hank. You can't do anything about it."

Hank flung the newspaper against the wall and raked both hands through his hair. "Damn it, don't you think I know that? They'll set his bond sky-high, if they allow it at all. Where's he gonna get that kind of money?"

"He'll get it," Nancy said.

"How?" He turned back to her, his face red with rage. "He sure as hell won't get it from our company account. I emptied that out already, trying to come up with the money to pay for this treatment that's just making Sherry sicker and sicker—"

Nancy got up slowly and went to her son-in-law, put her arms around him and pressed her forehead against his. In her eyes, he saw deep fatigue and worry, but she also saw a lot of love—love that he'd come to take for granted. "If it weren't for you, Sherry would have died a long time ago," Nancy said. "You know that. Whatever you had to do to get the money, it bought her some time. It was worth it."

His eyes brimmed with stinging tears, tears that made him angry. Brushing them away with the back of his wrist, he said, "Nancy, buying her time is like buying her more agony. She fights and fights, and the drugs make her so sick."

He caught his breath and walked out of the waiting room, and Nancy followed. Together, they went to the glass window at Sherry's room, where they could see her lying in a sterile plastic tent that covered most of

her tiny form. Her nose was packed from the nosebleed that the doctors still hadn't managed to control, and it had swollen to four times its size. Her eyes,
black as if she'd been in a fight, were swollen shut.

"She's made it through this point before," her
mother said in a stiff voice, making Hank nod in
agreement. "We've got to keep her fighting until we
can get her into remission again."

Hank stepped away from the window and leaned
against the wall, and tears pushed over his lashes
again. "Damn it, it's just that I don't know what I'm
making her fight for. For *her* life, or for mine? The
things she has to go through just for one more day in
the sunshine..."

"Or one more hug from her children," Nancy
whispered. "Hank, Sherry's fighting for us, but
mostly she's fighting for herself. We can't give up before she does."

Hank breathed in a broken sob and looked through
the window again. A nurse in a sterile gown, cap and
mask had gone in, and was checking Sherry's vital
signs. Sherry didn't move.

"Oh, God, I'm not ready to let her go," Hank said
in a high-pitched whisper. "And I don't know if that
makes me a selfish bastard or not."

"If it does," Nancy said, "then I'm just as guilty.
Come on, Hank. Let's go back and wait for the
doctor."

She hooked her arm through Hank's, and leaning
on her, Hank went back to the waiting room.

SOMETHING'S NOT RIGHT, Luke thought as he looked
down at the papers the bail bondsman had brought

him. The amount was only fifty thousand dollars, and he was sure the judge had posted bond at one hundred thousand—and then only after Kristen had spent nearly an hour laying out all the reasons why he shouldn't follow the U.S. Attorney's recommendation to lock him up until his trial. She had planted herself in front of the magistrate, practically refusing to take no for an answer. Finally, she had won. "Where's the rest?" he asked, looking up at the man across the table from him.

"Not my problem, pal," Jack said, taking the signed paper back and handing him another haphazardly typed legal document, and scribbling an upside-down X on the signature line there. "Now sign this."

Luke skimmed it quickly, and read that he was being released into Kristen's custody, and that she was taking complete responsibility for his whereabouts. "What the hell—"

"Sign it," Kristen said from behind him, and he turned in his chair and looked up at her.

"It was the only way he'd give us the money," she said. "Just sign it."

"But it says here I'll be living with you in your home. When you told the judge you'd be responsible, I didn't know you meant that you were moving me into your house!"

"That's right," Kristen said, carefully controlling her voice. "You're coming home with me. I gave my word to the judge and to Jack that you'd be with me. So you're stuck."

Luke's eyebrows knitted together as he stared at her, and finally, he turned back to the paper in front of him. "Sounds to me like you're the one who got stuck," he muttered. "Besides, this isn't enough money, anyway."

"I know," Kristen said, the strain on her face beginning to show in the pale pink color of her cheeks as she pulled out the chair next to him and sat down. "Don't worry. I've come up with the rest. Just sign the paper, Luke."

"Where? Where did you get it? I want to know."

Hesitating one last time, Luke sighed loudly, then finally scrawled his name. "I'll tell you later, okay? Just sign it."

Luke sighed loudly, telling Kristen that signing that paper was against his better judgment. He thrust the paper back to Jack and shrugged. "What now?"

"We go home," Kristen said wearily. "And we get to work."

Luke nodded and stood up then shook Jack's hand. The man seemed reluctant to shake it, as if he wasn't accustomed to getting buddy-buddy with the criminals he bailed out. Luke pretended not to notice. "I appreciate it, man. Really."

"I did it as a favor to Kristen," Jack said. "If you skip out, it'll be on her head."

Luke held the man's steady gaze, not wavering, but he didn't reply. At this point, he figured, no one would believe anything he had to say, anyway. No one but Kristen.

He waited for the man to leave, then turned back to her, watching her sort through the papers in the file in her briefcase. "Hey, Kristy?"

Kristen glanced up, and he could see in her eyes that she was hiding something—something he needed to know.

"Where'd you get the other half?"

"I . . . it's mine. I had some money saved up—"

"Fifty thousand dollars?" he asked, astounded. "Kristy, you can't do that. I'd rather stay in jail than take money from you."

Kristen dropped her head, wishing she hadn't told him. "Luke, I'll get it back. It was just sitting in the bank, anyway."

"No, I don't buy it," Luke said. "Nobody has fifty grand just lying around in the bank."

"Well, some of it was in savings," she said, "and I liquidated a few investments—not very good ones, so don't worry. But the bulk of it was from the trust fund my father left me for school. I never did use it, because I was able to get loans—"

"Kristen, you can't do this!" His tone was weighted with finality, and he shook his head. "This is too much. I feel like I'm losing control here. I can't stand this."

"Luke, it's no big deal," Kristen said, stepping toward him, her eyes full of conviction. "Please, I want to do this. My mom even wants me to do it."

He turned away from her, every muscle in his body rejecting her sacrifice. When he turned back around, his face was the color of a raging fire. "Your father left that money to *you*," he said. "If he saved that kind of money working for the telephone company, then it meant something to him. I guaran-damn-tee you he didn't mean it to bail some loser out of jail!"

"Don't you dare call yourself a loser!" Kristen shouted. "And you have no right to determine what my father wanted me to do with that money. If I knew my dad, he would have gladly given it to you himself, for all the times you were there for me after he died. You were *always* there when I needed you, Luke. You let me depend on you. Why can't you depend on me a little?"

"Because I've never had to depend on anyone before," he said, the corners of his mouth twitching. He turned away from her, his back stiff and rigid. "Not since Aunt Margaret. And when I left her, I swore I'd never do it again."

Kristen stepped up behind him, laid a trembling hand on his back, pressed her face against his shirt. It bore the sweet, unique scent of Luke, and she closed her eyes. "Please help me help you, Luke," she whispered. "I'd die if you went to prison for something you didn't do. And I need you out of jail to help me find who's setting you up."

She heard him swallow, felt his heartbeat hammering through his back, felt his muscles relax in reluctant acceptance of the sacrificial gift she offered him.

"Oh, Kristy," he whispered. "Why the hell do you care that much about me?"

"Because of who you are," she whispered vaguely, knowing that was the best explanation she could give him at the moment.

He turned around and pulled her against him then, crushing her to him, and she could feel his breath against her neck. "I've never, in all these years, found anyone like you," he said. "And God help me, I've tried."

"Don't try anymore," she said, knowing she was treading on dangerously thin ice. "Because I'm here. And I'm not going anywhere."

CHAPTER NINE

LUKE FELT THE UNIQUE SENSE of family as he sat at the dinner table with Kristen and Courtney, but he told himself to throw his barriers up and not get too comfortable. Family was a dangerous feeling—a singing sensation that only left him on a false high. But beneath that false high, he felt destined to have the rug pulled out from under him. He couldn't afford to get his emotions tied up with Kristen again, and he sure couldn't afford to get involved with Courtney.

But those were the ramblings of his mind, and his heart had other things to say. It told him he deserved this moment of sunshine after so long in the cold. It told him that what he gained in seeing both of them smile at him was worth any pain he would have to endure later on.

"Luke, was my mommy pretty when she was a little girl?" Courtney asked as she helped her mother clear the table.

Luke stacked the plates that hadn't been moved yet and carried them to the sink himself. "She was a knockout." He glanced at Kristen, who wore a pensive, gentle smile, then brought his eyes back to the flaxen-haired urchin standing next to him, looking up at him with wide blue eyes. "She looked a lot like you."

"Not much," Courtney countered. "I saw her picture. Yours, too. You were smoking a cigarette."

The slash in Luke's cheek deepened in amusement, and he set the plates next to the sink and turned back to the child. "Was I?"

"Yeah," Courtney said. "And you were real young."

Luke met Kristen's amused eyes, and he felt the kind of reprimand only a child could offer. "Too young," he said. "I had a lot of bad habits back then."

"Do you still smoke?" Courtney asked, awed.

"Uh..." Luke looked up at Kristen again, saw her shoulders shaking with silent laughter. "Well...yeah. Sometimes."

"Are you going to smoke tonight?" the child asked.

Luke looked as if he'd been backed into a corner. "Not in the house," he said. "I never smoke in other people's houses."

Courtney didn't take her big, admiring eyes from him. "One time my daddy bought me some candy cigarettes, and my friend Janie and I stood out in the yard and pretended we were smoking. We looked so cool."

Luke stopped smiling and he bent over and slipped his hands under Courtney's armpits. He lifted her onto the counter, then braced his hands beside her and bent down until he was level with her face. "You listen to me, kiddo. Smoking is about the worst thing you can do to yourself. It smells bad, it makes you cough, and it looks awful. But by the time you realize that, it's so hard to quit that you just go on letting it control you."

"But you're tough, aren't you?" Courtney asked. "Mommy says you're about the strongest person she knows. Why don't you quit?"

Luke cast a sidelong glance at Kristen and noted the way she tried to suppress her grin. Quietly, she dried her hands, crossed her arms and waited for Luke's answer.

Luke brought his eyes back to the little girl waiting patiently, seriously, for an answer. "You know you're right?" he said. "I am tough. And the reason I've never quit before, is that the right person never asked me to. But if you think I should..."

"I do," Courtney said, nodding with all the seriousness of a doctor pointing out the hazards of chemical dependence.

"Then I'll quit," Luke said.

"Wait a minute." Kristen was skeptical as she turned back to Luke. "Don't make promises you can't keep, Luke. Especially to a little girl who believes every word."

Luke met her eyes, the challenge they'd given him adding new life to his eyes. "Have I ever made a promise I didn't keep?"

Her amusement faded and she gazed at him for a long moment. "I don't remember you making all that many promises, period," she said softly, a smile still hovering on the edge of her lips. "But the ones you made, you kept."

"That's right," he said. "And I'll keep this one." He dug into his pocket and pulled out the pack of cigarettes that seemed to be a fixed part of his anatomy. He handed it to her. "Would you like the honors?"

Kristen bit her lip, took the cigarettes and, with exaggerated delight, tossed them into the trash can. "I can't believe you let me do that," she said. "I knew Courtney could be persuasive, but I didn't think anyone could make Luke Wade stop smoking."

"It's those big Thompson eyes," he said with a grin. "I never could resist them." Kristen glanced back at him, her face flushing with subtle heat, but he was looking at Courtney.

"What kind of eyes?" Courtney asked.

"Thompson," he said. "It was your mother's maiden name."

"But I'm a Jordan," she said.

"That's all right, kiddo. You've got enough of your mom in you to keep ol' Luke in line."

Smiling pensively, Kristen piled the plates in the sink and began scraping them. "Are you finished with your beer?"

Luke picked up the glass, brought it to his lips and stopped cold when he saw Courtney's face take on that serious expression again. "Did you know drinking drugs is as bad as smoking cigarettes?" she asked.

Kristen couldn't help laughing, in spite of her daughter's serious expression. "Honey, let Luke enjoy his beer. He's had a bad day."

"No, that's okay," Luke said, pushing the glass away. "She's absolutely right. I'll stop now before I catch myself making any more promises." He grabbed Courtney by the waist and pulled her off the counter, set her gently on her feet. "Now, how about a mean game of Go Fish?"

"All right!" Courtney shouted, and scurried off to her room in search of her deck of cards.

Luke leaned back on the counter next to Kristen, and assessed her smug smile once again. "You're enjoying this, aren't you?"

Kristen tried without success to suppress her grin. "I have to admit, it's fun watching someone whip you into shape."

"Hell, I'll be a candidate for the priesthood before I bust out of this joint," Luke said.

"I don't think there's any danger of that," Kristen said, slapping his chest playfully. He caught her hand and pulled her against him as they laughed. Suddenly, as her face came so close to his, their laughter faded at the same moment, and both sobered as sudden awareness sparked between them. Finally, Luke looked down at her dishwater-damp hand he held so naturally, and wiped it on his shirt. She felt his heart beating against his hard thoracic muscles, and her own, slamming out an equally urgent message. Her gaze fell to his lips, where his tongue was slowly skimming across it, and his breath whispered slowly against her mouth.

"Are you ready?" Courtney's innocent summons came from the living room, but Luke didn't release Kristen's hand.

"Yeah," Luke whispered, knowing that the little girl couldn't hear. "I think I am."

Slowly, he brought Kristen's hand to his mouth, and without moving his eyes from hers, he kissed one soft knuckle. Then, releasing her hand, he called, "I'm coming, Courtney."

Kristen watched, mesmerized, as he left the kitchen. Her heart fluttered and shivered, and she tucked her hand into her pocket to stop the trembling. Then drawing in a deep, cleansing breath, she turned back to the dishwasher and began filling it, forcing herself not to dwell on that magic moment that had ended so quickly, or the words he'd whispered in response to Courtney's call—the words that had seemed more directed at her. Had he meant that he was ready to step over that sacred threshold of friendship? With all her heart, she wished he had.

For Kristen knew that she was ready, too.

IT WAS ALMOST Courtney's bedtime when the child talked Luke into reading her a Dr. Seuss book. Cuddled up next to him on the couch, Courtney listened with amusement as he changed his voices to suit Horton the Elephant, who claimed to be "faithful one hundred percent," as he sat on the egg for the lazy bird who had flitted off across the world.

It was nice to have a man in the house again, Courtney thought, even if he wasn't her daddy. For a split second, she entertained the traitorous thought that Daddy had never read a book to her without a lot of groaning, but Luke seemed to actually enjoy it.

She looked up at him as he read the ending, which detailed how Horton's egg hatched just as the lazy bird came back, and how it turned out to be an elephant-bird that looked just like the elephant who had cared for it all those months.

"Horton should never have sat there all that time," Courtney said when he closed the book. "He should have found Mayzie and told her to get back there and do it herself."

"Yeah," he said. "But Horton wasn't that kind of person. He thought the best of Mayzie, and he never gave up hoping that she'd be back."

"But he was an *elephant*!" Courtney said. "That was an awful thing to do to a poor elephant."

"She took advantage of him, all right," Luke said, staring at the book, though Courtney wondered if he was thinking about something else. "But that's the way it goes sometimes. Just because somebody takes advantage of you, doesn't mean you should turn on them. Maybe they had a good reason."

Courtney regarded the illustration of Horton again, then brought her eyes back to her mother, who seemed to be watching Luke as if something he'd just said struck a question in her mind. She was frowning—her thinking frown—and Courtney wondered what it meant.

Luke seemed to have noticed, but instead of meeting Kristen's eyes, he hopped up suddenly. Grabbing Courtney's hands, he pulled her to her feet. "How about I tuck you in tonight?" he asked.

"All right!" Courtney exclaimed. "Can he, Mommy?"

Kristen took a moment to answer, but finally she smiled. "Sure, honey. I'll be in to kiss you in a minute."

Kristen watched the two disappear, laughing and giggling and scheming, but she couldn't make herself join in. Something about what Luke had said, and the quiet, thoughtful way he'd said it, almost with a note of hurt in his voice, had rung a bell in Kristen's mind.

"An elephant's faithful one hundred percent."

"Maybe they had a good reason."

She shook her head and told herself she was just grasping at straws. It was a children's story, and had nothing to do with Luke's predicament. His comment hadn't meant that he knew something he wasn't telling her....

Still, the intuition nagged at her like a fading memory she couldn't quite grasp. And as if it might prove to be her final straw at some point not too far down the road, she tucked the idea away in her heart and guarded it like a fragile seed that needed planting.

COURTNEY WAS HOVERING on the outer edges of sleep when Kristen tiptoed into her room to kiss her goodnight. She looked up at Luke, who lingered in the doorway, watching the little girl with the most poignant expression she had ever seen on his face.

Quietly, she went out into the hall and stood behind Luke.

"How can you ever bear to let her out of your sight?" he asked.

Kristen smiled. "You get used to it," she said. "You just learn to let go a little as they grow."

Luke shook his head, negating the simplicity of her answer. "I was never any good at letting go."

She took his hand and pulled him away from the doorway, and with a reluctant smile, he followed her back into the living room.

"She's really special, Kristy," he said, dropping back onto the couch.

"I know," Kristen said. "She's my lifeline. I don't know what I'd do without her." She cocked her head and offered him an amused smile. "So, do you want another shot at that beer I bought for you, now that she's asleep?''

"Nope," he said, flashing her a devilish grin. "I think maybe it's time I cleaned up my act. Besides, I need a clear head tonight."

The remark was ambiguous, for Kristen didn't know if he referred to having control over his hormones, or wanting to go over the facts of his case again. She lowered herself to the couch, leaned back in the plush corner and pulled her feet beneath her. "Courtney really likes you," she said. "I appreciate the time you spent with her tonight."

"Hey, don't thank me," Luke said quietly. "I'm the one who came out on the winning end." He tilted his head, propped it on his hand, carefully avoiding the bruise that colored his cheekbone. "Tell me about ol' Eric. Does he spend a lot of time with her?"

"Only when it's convenient," Kristen said. "His social calendar is a little too demanding for a five-year-old girl. That's why it meant so much to her to have you choose to spend time with her tonight. She usually just gets leftovers, you know?"

Luke smiled. "She reminds me so much of you. How old were you when I moved in with Ed and Margaret?"

"About nine," Kristen said. She looked down at her ankle, traced the bone with her finger. "If I could have one wish for Courtney, it would be that she'd have a Luke in her life. Someone to watch over her the way you always watched over me."

Luke kept his serious eyes on her, and Kristen felt a warm blush coloring her cheeks as she looked up at him. "I guess I could have done a lot worse than to have you think of me as a cousin, huh?"

Luke shrugged. "And I could have done a lot worse than to have you to watch over," he said.

A quiet moment passed between them, and Kristen turned sideways on the couch and propped her chin in her hand. "Luke, I'm going to ask you something, and I want you to be perfectly honest with me, okay?"

Those lines between Luke's brows deepened. "That depends," he said.

"I was wondering whether you're watching over somebody else right now," she ventured cautiously. "Somebody you're trying to protect. It's just…every now and then I get this nagging feeling that you're not telling me everything."

Luke looked away, as if the question was ludicrous, but suddenly she could see the tension in every line of his body. "Kristen, I've told you everything I know, okay? If I knew anything else, don't you think I'd use it to get myself off the hook?"

Kristen gazed at him without answering for an eloquent moment, wondering why he couldn't look at her when he said it. "I don't know, Luke," she said.

Luke shook his head with vivid frustration, and as he leaned forward, setting his elbows on his knees, she knew that she'd pushed him too far. "Kristen, you're the only one I've got who trusts me. If I lose that—"

"I trust you," she said adamantly. "It's not that. It's just that I know that sense of honor you have, and Luke, *somebody's* responsible for what's been happening to you."

Luke laughed then, throwing her off guard, and finally met her eyes again. "Only you, Kristy. Only you could ever look past the blurs and smears in my past and see honor.''

"You see it, too, Luke," she said. "And you know it. You hide it away, like it's a little secret. That's what makes you so special."

Luke leaned back, trying not to let his expression reveal his true feelings as he looked at her. "No, Kristy," he whispered. "*You're* what makes me so special." He touched her temple with his finger, tapped twice. "Right in here."

She swallowed, knowing that her closeness to him was leading her too far, but she was powerless to fight it. "No," she whispered back, taking his hand and moving it to her heart. "Right in here."

The look on Luke's face as he sat with his hand over her heart was so blatantly vulnerable, so startlingly alarmed, that she took pity on him and let his hand go. Slowly, he moved it to his thigh, but his eyes remained softly on her.

"Good night, Luke," she whispered, rising slightly on her knees and pressing a soft, chaste kiss just below his lip. She felt his late-day stubble graze across her mouth, breathed the intoxicating scent of cigarettes and wind, savored the way his eyes closed in response.

"Sleep well," she whispered, then started to her room.

LUKE WASN'T SURE how long he had sat in the dark after she'd gone to bed. Maybe two hours...maybe three. Fleetingly, he thought of going to the guest room she had made up for him, and calling it a night. But he couldn't shake the feeling of having Kristen move his hand to her heart, or the sweet, seductive kiss, or the adoration that was unmistakable in her eyes.

He closed his eyes and thought of the heavy-lidded, I-know-what-I'm-doing way she had leaned over to kiss him. Maybe her fantasies weren't so far removed from his. Maybe...

He stopped and lassoed his thoughts back in, and told himself that he was buying trouble, on the installment plan, and that he didn't have what it took to make those kinds of payments.

Don't do it, Wade, he told himself urgently. *Don't make a mistake you'll regret for the rest of your life.*

Kristen didn't need someone with terrorism, murder and burglary on his record. She needed someone who could help her get where he knew she was going. Someone who realized how special she was, and could help her to reach her potential.

The problem was, he'd never yet met a soul who measured up to her.

His gaze drifted up the dark hall to Kristen's bedroom, and his groin tightened at the mental image of her lying in bed in her gown, her bare feet peeking out from under the covers, and her hair spread around her face.

His mouth went dry, and his heartbeat accelerated.

Damn. He wanted a cigarette. That was the cause of all this nervous energy. Withdrawal.

But it wasn't the need for a cigarette that bothered him as he stared at Kristen's bedroom door, left slightly ajar. And a promise was a promise. He wasn't going to break it. At least, not the one he'd made to Courtney.

He just wasn't certain he was strong enough to keep the one he'd made to himself.

Taking a deep, miserable breath, he got up and went to his room, turned on the light and sat down on the bed. She had turned back the covers, and without pulling up the spread, he lay down. Instantly, he smelled her scent in the sheets, even though they were freshly laundered. The feel of the bed, the wallpaper, the carpet... they all spelled Kristen.

He closed his eyes and told himself that he wasn't getting anywhere tonight. He should be thinking of staying out of prison, trying to figure out this mess he was in....

But he'd never spent the night this close to her before, and for the life of him, he didn't know how he'd make it until morning, for he felt himself growing weaker with every second that passed.

Kristen lay awake in her bed, and wondered if Luke had gone to sleep yet. Her heart had pounded ever since she'd left him alone, as if she anticipated the impossible...that he would come to her, and she'd suddenly be more than his cousin, or the "girl next door," and be transformed into some sexy vixen who'd bring him to his knees.

It was hot, she thought, reaching up to unbutton a few more buttons of the old-fashioned, sleeveless white linen gown she wore. She turned over, tried to get comfortable and failed.

She closed her eyes and lay still, letting the warmth of just knowing that he loved her, in his own way, wash over her like the comfort of her down bed-spread. Chaste love was almost as sweet as romantic love, she told herself, and she'd take it from Luke any way she could get it. If only she could stop wanting . . . wishing . . .

If only she had one clue that the chemistry she'd felt smoldering between them tonight hadn't been one-sided. It had felt mutual, she thought. The way he had looked at her, and whispered that he thought he was ready. And the way he had said that she was the one who made him special. Hadn't those words meant something?

She felt a quick draft in the room, then heard a slight click that she was sure had come from his door down the hall. He'd probably just gone to bed, she thought. He had probably watched television without giving her another thought, and now he was settling down for the night.

A subtle change in the air, a sudden charge in the atmosphere, a slight shift in the scents of the room, sent her heart into triple time, and slowly, she opened her eyes.

The darkness greeted her like a fog, and she looked around her room. Suddenly, she saw the reason for the trip-hammer in her heart.

Luke sat in the chair across from her bed, elbows braced on his knees, his chin propped on his folded hands, quietly watching her.

She met his eyes in the semidarkness and saw him swallow. But he didn't move another muscle.

Slowly, Kristen sat up in bed, unaware that one shoulder of her gown dropped a few inches down her arm, or that her hair fell around her shoulders in sensual disarray.

"Luke?" she whispered.

"Shhh." Luke lowered his face, until his forehead pressed against his knuckles, until his eyes no longer gave him away. "Don't talk," he whispered. "Just listen. There are a few things I've got to say...."

CHAPTER TEN

SHE WAS A SILHOUETTE against the moonlight beaming from the window at her back—a silhouette with angel eyes and wet lips, a silhouette with a dark, sweet expression that could crack the strongest heart into a million pieces. Luke drew in a deep, shuddering breath, and tightened his fingers into a fist.

"When you were fifteen," he whispered, so quietly that she almost couldn't hear, "I started to lose my sanity—one date at a time. *Your* dates..."

He stopped and swallowed, brought his eyes back to hers, and he saw her head tilt in wonder, and her eyes sparkle with a glimmer of tears. "I used to sit in the window of my bedroom across the street from you, and watch when those guys brought you home. I'd watch them kiss you...."

He shook his head helplessly. "And you were so beautiful...."

"Luke." Kristen moved to the edge of the bed, her bare feet touching the carpet, and he held out a hand to stop her.

"No. Let me finish. I have to say this."

He saw the lone tear fall over her lashes, and catch the moonlight as it made its way down her cheek.

"I couldn't let you know how I felt, because it would ruin everything. I knew that you could love me, maybe even in that way, but I didn't want you to. I wanted something better for you." He lifted a hand, desperately trying to illustrate his point, but still found it difficult. "I wanted...for you to be more than I was, more than you could be with me. I wanted you to have a shot at everything you deserved, without me to drag you down. And the only way to do that was to stand back and let you grow away from me."

He heard the soft catch in her breathing, saw the tears flowing faster down her cheeks and prayed he hadn't made a mistake in telling her. His heart froze in his chest when she got off the bed and knelt in front of him, taking his hands.

"Don't you know," she asked in a hoarse whisper, "that *everything* I am, I am because of you?" He lowered his head, but she raised herself up on her knees, and forced his tormented eyes to meet hers. "Still, eleven years later, I weigh everything I do against what you would think of it. I think of you every single day of my life."

He squeezed her hands, and she saw the tension, the misery, on his face, and knew that he wasn't offering himself to her. He was telling her why he couldn't. But she couldn't accept that. She was done with accepting.

"You're part of who I am, Luke," she whispered, stroking his hair with a warm hand. "And as hurt as I was when you faded out of my life, I've never been able to escape that."

"I never meant to hurt you," he said. His eyes misted over, and he focused on the ceiling, drawing in a deep, painful breath. "And God help me, I never meant to love you."

A surge of heartache and heart-hope swelled inside her, and Kristen let go of his hands and slowly leaned forward, pressing her lips against the indentation at the base of his neck. She felt a low moan deep in his chest, a moan that spoke of the battle being waged inside his heart.

His hands moved to her arms, as if to pull her away, but somehow, the pressure wasn't there. Slowly, quietly, she reached up and released the top button on his shirt, then another, and another, as her lips followed the trail over the hair sprinkled across his chest. When she reached the waistband of his jeans, she pulled the shirt out, finished opening it and, with soft, sensuous strokes, slipped it down his arms.

"Kristen," he whispered on a broken plea, though his breath struggled with his protest. "I can't . . ."

"Shhh," she whispered against his chest, moving her hands over his rib cage. Her lips journeyed to one dark nipple nestled beneath the dark curls of hair, and she sucked lightly, drawing a deeper moan from far inside him. Knowing that she was evoking exactly the response she wanted—was so desperate for—she moved her tongue down his chest, to the flat, hard abdomen below.

"Kristen, you're playing with fire," he said sharply.

Without answering, Kristen lifted her face to his, saw the torture in his eyes, the determination not to meet her halfway. Her lips touched his in a desperate union, and in his kiss she could feel the raw desire pulsing through him. His tongue mated with hers with urgency and valor, even while his hands rested immobile on her arms.

The kiss broke, and she felt his shallow breath as her lips trailed down his chin, tasting his skin and the texture of his stubble. She moved over his throat, felt his pulse racing at breakneck speed.

Suddenly his hands moved from her arms and buried themselves in her hair, arching her head back until he and she were face-to-face, and finally, he took her mouth in another searing kiss.

But just as quickly as he gave himself to her, he withdrew. His mouth broke free, and he focused on the ceiling, as if privately beseeching some divine force to intervene before he lost himself completely.

Kristen moved her hands from him. Keeping her soft, silent eyes from his face, she began unbuttoning her gown. His eyes came back to her and his breath stilled, trapped in his lungs, as he watched the buttons open one by one, each revealing more of the flesh he had fantasized about. She heard him swallow as she came to the last button, and without opening her gown completely, she sat back on her heels and waited.

She heard the agonizing release of his breath, and slowly, his hands came up to her shoulders. She felt him tremble as he swept the gown down, pulling it open as he did.

The gown fell to her waist, leaving her breasts bare and her nipples turgid, and she beheld the deep lines around his eyes as he gazed at her. His hands froze on her shoulders, and finally, after an eternal moment, she rose, letting the garment fall as she did. Slowly, she came to her feet, and stepped out of the gown, revealing only the lacy scrap of bikini panties beneath it. Without taking her eyes from Luke's, she moved his hands up her bare stomach to her breasts, aching for his touch.

Slowly, he began to explore her body, a deep frown cutting into his forehead. His fingertips slowly traced the fullness of her breasts, circling, teasing, until at last his palms closed over her tight nipples.

He stood up and kissed her again, prolonging it as he rubbed his bare chest against hers, letting her breasts move across his ribs. His hands went around to her back, drawing her closer, and finally lowering to the small of her back. Urgently, he pressed her against him, making her suddenly aware of the hard shaft of need trapped against her belly.

As their kiss intensified, she moved her hands between them, released the snap of his jeans and slowly lowered the zipper. He grew stiff as she touched him, then shuddered with silent surrender.

"Love me, Luke," she whispered, rising on her tiptoes to fit more exactly against him.

"I do love you," he whispered. "I always have."

He lifted her from the floor, making her feel weightless in the dark moonlight, and laid her across the bed. In seconds, he had slipped out of his clothes, and he was above her, anchoring her with his weight, kissing her with driving force that hinted at the needs of the rest of his body.

He abandoned her mouth, leaving her gasping for breath, and moved down to her breasts, taking one rosebud nipple in his mouth, biting gently, then suckling it until she clutched at the bedspread beneath her to keep from crying out. His mouth released it, and his tongue traced the halfcircle beneath it, then down the center of her chest to her tight, small navel. He circled it with his tongue, while his hands moved to the lace panties still impeding them.

Slowly, he began to peel them down her legs, his lips following in a fiery trail that left her limp and helpless. He slipped the garment over her feet, kissed the arch of her foot, then trailed more wet kisses up the inside of her calf, over her delicate kneecap, and up her thigh.

Urgently, she reached for him, pulling him back to her mouth, fitting his body over hers.

In perfect orchestration they united, and slowly, he began moving inside her until they achieved the perfect union. They held still for a moment, clinging to each other, until finally their mutual needs overshadowed the satisfaction of that initial moment.

Instant delirium washed over Kristen, making her gasp for breath and cling to him for support as he moved with the passion of a man who has been without for much too long. She buried her face in his neck and tried not to cry out, but the need for expression grew until she allowed a high-pitched, whispered moan to escape from her throat.

He rolled her over until they both sat up, hugging each other in a desperate embrace as their lower bodies moved in a primitive rhythm. She felt him shudder and go rigid, then felt the vibration of his deep moan as contentment and satisfaction washed over him.

He rolled her over and stretched out above her again, not untangling himself from her, but continuing to move inside her with slow, sweet love. He looked at her, and she noted the fine sheen of perspiration on his beautiful skin, and the flush to his cheeks in the darkness. "You're going to regret this so much in the morning," he whispered.

"No," she said with absolute certainty. "Not in a million years. How can I regret something I've wanted for fifteen years?"

His mouth claimed hers again in a searing kiss that told her there was yet more hunger, more desire. She felt him hardening within her again, his startling tumescence as strong and as deep as it had been the first time around.

"I've never felt like this before, Kristy," he whispered, his breathing growing labored again. "Never. Not ever."

"Neither have I," she whispered, "except in the fantasies I had of you."

"A lot can be said for fantasies," he breathed against her lips as he began moving inside her again, "but they don't hold a candle to the real thing."

And as he kissed her, Kristen felt herself getting lost in him again, and she knew that Luke was right. A fantasy would never come close to what she was experiencing tonight.

MORNING LIGHT BEADED through the curtains in Kristen's room when she heard her familiar Saturday morning alarm.

"Mommy, hurry! We'll miss cartoons."

Kristen jerked her bedspread up to her throat and sat upright in her bed, startled at her daughter's appearance beside her bed. Quickly, she looked next to her, where Luke had been when she'd fallen asleep. To her relief, he was gone.

"Okay, honey," she said. "Go ahead and turn the television on."

"Can I go wake up Luke?" Courtney asked. "He told me to last night. He said he'd watch them with us."

"Uh . . . no, honey, let Luke sleep."

"But Mommy . . ."

Kristen looked up and saw Luke, fully dressed in a pair of jeans and a pullover shirt, leaning in the doorway with a grin on his face. "Let *me* sleep?" he asked. "I've already made breakfast."

"Breakfast?" Kristen repeated, smiling self-consciously as his eyes swept over her. Her fists clutching the bedspread tightened at her throat.

"Blueberry muffins," he said, addressing Courtney. "Do you like them?"

"Yeah!" Courtney said, and scurried out past him.

Luke took two steps into her room and gave her a wink. "Sleep well?" he asked.

She nodded. "When . . . when did you . . ."

"Go back to my room?" he asked quietly. "Around three. I didn't want Courtney to have any surprises."

"Thank you, Luke," she whispered.

He shrugged. "Why don't you take your time? Get a shower, whatever. I'll take care of Courtney."

Kristen nodded, smiling at him with poignant adoration that reached in and grabbed his heart. While he still could manage it, he started to walk away.

"Luke?"

He looked over his shoulder. "Yeah?"

"Courtney won't be here tonight," she said. "Eric has her tonight, unless he finks out."

Luke smiled and inclined his head. "It's a date," he said, then started up the hall.

"THIS IS A RERUN," Courtney said in supreme disappointment when one of her favorite cartoons came on.

"Yeah, I know," Luke commiserated, sitting at the table beside her and sipping his coffee. "I've seen it, too."

"You have? Really?" Courtney asked, her eyes widening.

"Sure. It's the one where they pretend they're circus clowns, and that cow comes along who—"

"Who thinks he's a trick horse!" Courtney started to laugh.

"Do you want me to change it?"

"No," Courtney said, her interest in the cartoon renewed. "Let's watch it together this time."

Luke laughed and messed up her blond hair, and wondered at how happy he was this morning. Not a common feeling for someone facing federal charges of theft and terrorism. Still, feeling the way he did today, he couldn't entertain the idea of anything not working out. Kristen loved him, and his love for her was no longer a secret.

The doorbell rang, and Courtney sprang up. "I'll get it!"

"No way, kiddo," Luke said, grabbing her arm and heading for the door himself. "You don't know who's there. I'll answer it."

Courtney allowed him to answer it, but she didn't fail to make her appearance there. She peered out as soon as the door cracked open. "Mr. Norsworthy!" Courtney shouted, as if he were a long-lost friend of the family. Taking his hand, she drew him into the house. "This is my mommy's friend Luke," she said. "He spent the night here last night. I helped make up his bed."

Luke extended his hand, not certain whose hand he was shaking. What was apparent, however, was the blatant disgust on the man's face. "Luke Wade," he said.

"I know who you are," Norsworthy said. He turned back to Courtney. "Where's your mother?"

"In the shower," Courtney said without ceremony. "Do you like cartoons?"

John Norsworthy ignored the question and focused his hard eyes on Luke. Recognizing the censure, and sensing that the man must hold some sort of authority over Kristen, he looked down at Courtney. "Why don't you go finish watching for us?" he said. "I'll be there in a minute."

Courtney began to retreat to the couch, but her attention wasn't on the cartoons. Suddenly, she seemed as aware as Luke that John wasn't happy.

"I'll send Courtney to tell her you're here," Luke offered.

"No, that's all right," John said, tapping the knot in his tie, as though to make sure it was still there. "I'd almost rather speak to you, anyway. Kristen and I work together at the law firm. She had a good career going until she lost all her professional sense and started representing you. Did you know she had just gotten a promotion, a new office, a shot at a partnership?"

The color drained from Luke's face. "If you have something to say to me, say it."

"All right," John said. "The bottom line is that I came in here two days ago and told her that the partners had decided to order her to drop your case. She refused. That's not good. She's very valuable to our firm, but not so valuable that she can't be replaced."

Luke felt as if he'd been struck, and he stepped back against the foyer wall. "Just tell me one thing," he said. "Why don't they want her to represent me? I can cover the expenses. I'm good for it."

"It's not the money," John said, waving his hand as if to dismiss the idea. "It's the reputation. This case won't do anything but ruin hers." He looked around him, at the evidence that Luke had made himself at home. "From the way things look, her judgment is long gone. Cousin or not, it's unprofessional to move your client into your home with you. Unprofessional, and unacceptable."

"We didn't have a choice, man," Luke said, regaining his fight and stepping toward John again. "It was the only way the magistrate would agree to set bond."

"So she's responsible for you, is she?" John asked. "You don't give a damn about what it's doing to her."

"You don't *know* what it's doing to her!" Luke bit out. "Who do you think you are?"

"I'm someone who cares about the career she's spent years building for herself," John snapped back. "Do her a favor and find somebody else to represent you. Leave her alone, or you'll be hurting her more than you know."

"Luke would never hurt my mommy."

Courtney's voice drew their full attention to the little girl standing in her gown, clutching her teddy bear to her chest. "You wouldn't hurt Mommy, would you, Luke?"

A lump of emotion rose in Luke's throat at the innocent faith and certainty in Courtney's voice, and suddenly, he wasn't sure at all. He dropped his head, rubbed the back of his neck. "Not on purpose," he said.

"Then let her off the hook," John told him. "Find another lawyer. Don't drag her down with you. She's too good for that."

Luke didn't respond as John opened the door. Muttering "Tell her to call me," he closed the door behind him.

And suddenly, a cold, shattering reality assaulted Luke. Kristen could never be his. Not as long as he was in this mess. But the joy of having loved her last night was too great, too secure, and he wasn't ready to abandon it just yet. Somehow, he'd make himself worthy of her. Somehow, he'd get out of this mess. The only thing to do was find some way out. Some answer. Some clue.

He remembered the wire in Hank's car, and decided that another day couldn't go by without his confronting him. Hank had at least part of the answer. If it took everything in him, he'd get the rest. It wasn't just his life that was affected now, he thought.

It was Kristen's too, because she loved him.

COURTNEY AND LUKE were quiet—too quiet—when Kristen emerged from her bedroom. She had taken the time to wash and dry her hair, and had rolled it into soft curls that fell around her shoulders. She'd even taken the time to carefully apply her makeup. Now she wondered if she'd taken too long.

She looked at them sitting side by side on the sofa, their faces grim and sober, but she couldn't help smiling at the serious way Courtney cuddled close to Luke.

"So where are the muffins?" she asked.

"In the kitchen," Courtney said quietly.

Kristen looked curiously at Luke. When his dull eyes met hers, she was certain that something was wrong. "What is it?" she asked.

"You had a visitor," he said.

"Mr. Norsworthy," Courtney added, her bottom lip puckered with indignation. "He's not my friend anymore. He was mean to Luke."

"Oh no." The words came out on a deflated sigh, and Kristen lowered herself to a chair across from them. "I'm sorry, Luke."

Luke breathed a mirthless laugh. "*You're* sorry? You're jeopardizing your job for me, and *you're* sorry?"

Kristen came to her feet and went into the kitchen, anxious to hide her despair from Courtney. As she knew he would, Luke followed her.

She went to the sink and turned on the water, but discovered that there were no dishes to wash. Luke had already done them.

"Why didn't you tell me?" he asked softly from behind her.

She turned around and met his eyes—melted in them. "Because it didn't make any difference at all. Whether they fire me or not, I'm still representing you."

"But Kristy, you're throwing away everything you've spent your entire adult life building. I can't let you do it."

"You don't have a choice!" she said. "If they let me go because of this, then I'm better off. I don't want to be associated with people who have so little faith in my professional judgment. I'm a *good* attorney, Luke, and I can make it with or without them."

Luke leaned back against the table and rubbed his face harshly with his callused hands. "Damn it, Kristy, it makes me feel so helpless. It's like I'm just trapped in this situation, taking, taking, taking, and there's nothing I can *do* to stop you from going down with me!"

"There's something you can do," Kristen said, looking at him with a beseeching directness in her eyes. "You can help me figure out who's setting you up, *before* this even goes to trial. You can help me prove them all wrong."

Luke rubbed the back of his neck and nodded, but his silence bore an eloquence that he wasn't aware of.

"Where do we start, Luke?" she asked.

"The hospital," Luke said in a flat, metallic voice. "I have to talk to Hank."

"Why?" she asked cautiously, knowing that the question erected that barrier in Luke's eyes yet again.

"Just . . . to get some things sorted out. Maybe he's thought of something."

She didn't believe him, but she trusted him. And so, without demanding further explanation, Kristen got Courtney dressed to go to her father's.

CHAPTER ELEVEN

IF HE HADN'T BEEN ABLE to tell from Sherry's lingering nosebleed that her condition was getting worse, Hank would have known it from the worry in the doctor's usually hopeful face the moment he walked out into the hall with him that morning. "We did a bone marrow today," said Dr. Gordon, who'd struggled through this long battle of disease, remission and more disease with them. He tapped his pencil on his chin, then scratched the eraser against a forehead pleated with the burden of his profession. "Her platelet count is down to zero," he said.

"But you've been giving her so many transfusions," Hank argued, as if pure logic could turn the disease around.

The doctor turned his hands palm up and shook his head. "She isn't responding. We're going to keep transfusing her, and we're trying a new drug tomorrow. But at the moment, our main concern is controlling the hemorrhaging."

Hank slumped over in his chair, settling his chin on hands that were shaky with fatigue, stress and near panic. "She's got a fever," he said, as if the doctor didn't know. "The nurse said it was 106 degrees. What about brain damage?"

"We're doing our best to control it," Dr. Gordon replied evasively, as if brain damage were the least of his worries at the moment. "Meanwhile, we've got to keep trying to get her platelet count back up. Her body's begun manufacturing antibodies, and she's rejecting platelets as fast as we transfuse her. If we could find some other family members—sisters, brothers—who could give more compatible blood..."

"She's an only child," Hank said, as if that in itself were a death sentence. "And her father's passed away. Her mother's the only one."

Dr. Gordon shook his head. "Her mother gave yesterday. We can't take more from her until at least tomorrow."

"So what do we do?" Hank asked, his voice beginning to quiver. "Just give up?"

"No, of course not." Dr. Gordon walked to the window to Sherry's room, holding her test results in his hand as if studying them once more might shed one more ray of light on her illness. "We keep transfusing her with nonfamily donor blood, anyway. If we can bombard her bloodstream with enough platelets, sometimes we can neutralize the antibodies. Then we can get some of the good platelets in. It's a long shot, but it's all we've got."

"I gave blood this morning," Hank said with a moan of despair, looking at the bandage, still fresh on his arm. "What else can I do? There must be something. I can't just sit here and watch her slip into coma!"

The doctor turned back to him, new hope lighting up his face. "You can mobilize as many friends as you can, and ask them to donate blood. And you can keep talking to Sherry, trying to pull her back from this semicoma. Sometimes, just when you think you've lost them, they come back. And Sherry's strong."

"Yeah, Doc," Hank said, letting his eyes drift to the window through which he could see his wife, lying limply on the bed that looked like her funeral bier. "She's the strongest person I know."

"Do whatever it takes to appeal to that strength," Dr. Gordon said. "Yell at her, challenge her, but whatever it takes, pull her out." He slapped a hand on Hank's shoulder, squeezed and forced Hank to meet his clear, thoughtful eyes. "Just know that it takes a lot more than this to make me give up."

"Yeah," Hank said, blinking back the tears stinging his eyes. "Thanks, Doc."

He waited for a moment until the doctor had gone, then returned to the sterile area at the entrance to Sherry's room, slipped a gown over his clothes, stepped into the paper boots that went over his shoes and put on the cap and mask that would keep him from transporting germs into the room. Then, stepping through the door and under the plastic bubble that made up her shrinking world, he went to her bedside.

"Wake up, Sherry," he said in a wobbly voice. "Please God, wake her up."

There was no response, but he kept standing beside her, watching her breathing patterns, watching her peaceful slumber. But she wasn't at peace, yet, he told himself. She was in misery. Her lips were black, and her nose—packed with gauze that did little to stop the bleeding—was bruised and purple, the color extending to the circles beneath both eyes.

I have to pull her back, he told himself, but something deep inside him, some growing sense of compassion, questioned him ruthlessly like a voice from the other side.

What are you bringing her back for? More pain? More agony? More failure?

Hadn't she earned a chance to rest?

He thought of Josh and Jake, and realized that she hadn't said goodbye. She hadn't made her peace with leaving them. She hadn't prepared to slip away just yet.

And God knew, he wasn't ready.

He lowered himself to the bed beside her, collapsing from the weight of his emotion, and dropped his head until fat tears plopped onto her gown, leaving large wet stains. He wondered if they contained germs that could do her harm, and feverishly wiped at his eyes, trying to dry them.

"Sherry, please wake up," he cried in a louder voice. "Please! Damn you, I'm not ready to say goodbye yet! I won't do it!"

When there was still no response, he stood up, leaned over her again and felt fury like none he'd ever experienced seething inside him. "Damn it, Sherry, you're making me so *angry*! You're just letting yourself slip away. I'll never forgive you if you stop fighting now! Do you hear me, Sherry? I'll never forgive you!"

In the quiet that followed, he could have sworn he heard a heavy sigh pouring from her throat, and a distinct change in her breathing. Was she coming back? he wondered, taking her hand and holding it to his mouth, every fiber of his being pleading for her to make the effort.

"Come on, baby, you can do it," he said. "Just fight it. Just a little longer. That's all I ask. You've never been a quitter. Don't quit on me now."

He saw her lips move infinitesimally, and suddenly she squeezed his hand. "Oh, thank God," he whispered on a broken suspiration, focusing his blurring eyes on the ceiling. "Thank God, love. You haven't left me yet."

LUKE AND KRISTEN found Nancy in the lobby of the hospital with the phone book spread out on her lap, frantically dialing on the lobby phone as the boys ran races across the floor, oblivious to the pain their mother suffered upstairs.

"Nancy?" Luke called as he started toward her.

The woman looked up, and from the circles under her eyes and the red, swollen patches beside them, he wondered how long it had been since she'd slept. "Is everything all right?"

"Luke!" She sprang to her feet and darted across the floor to take his arms. Her eyes were almost wild as she confronted him. "I've been calling everybody I know. When's the last time you gave blood? We can't stop her nosebleed!"

Luke took her arms, tried to steady her. "I gave the day before yesterday. I think they'll take it again today."

"Good," she said, struggling to contain her tears. "Nobody's home. We need a lot more donors, and I've been calling everybody—"

Kristen stepped forward and took the woman's clammy hands. "Look, I can give, and I have a lot of friends in town. Let me call some people."

"Oh, thank you," Nancy whispered, and dropped back to the couch as Kristen picked up the phone and started dialing.

One of the boys tripped over a shoelace and fell, and his wail echoed over the entire first floor. Luke snatched him up and held him close, as if that tiny boy's cry were Sherry's anguish, Hank's despair and Nancy's horror.

Jake paused in his wailing to shake his finger at the floor, and angrily shouted, "Bad floor!"

"That's right," Luke whispered. "That bad floor hurt Jake." It seemed so simple, he thought, confronting the source of the pain. If only the culprit were always so apparent. Jake's crying abated somewhat at the release of his anger, and soon Josh found an aquarium against the wall, and his twin squirmed to get down and dash toward it.

Kristen hung up the phone and turned back to Nancy. "I just spoke to my mother," she said. "She's going to call all the ladies in her Sunday School class, her women's auxiliary group and her bingo club. Then she's going to come herself to give, and she's offered to watch the kids for you for the rest of the day."

"Oh, God bless her!" Nancy whispered, her eyes filling with tears again. "That would be such a help!"

"Now, where do we go to give blood?" Kristen asked, looking around.

Nancy stood up and took her hand. "I'll take you and introduce you myself," she said.

The blood donor room was abuzz with activity, and it became apparent to Kristen as she watched the staff bustle around that Sherry wasn't the only patient on the leukemia floor who was in dire need of platelets. There was only one spare chair at the moment, so Luke left Kristen there and slipped upstairs to see Hank.

As she sat in the chair waiting for a technician to come and take the vital blood from her arm, she felt a sense of accomplishment. At least she was able to do something for this woman who meant so much to Luke, even if she hadn't been able to do much for him yet.

Before much longer, she hoped she could do a lot more.

"You're a godsend," the technician said, as though Kristen weren't one of hundreds who would come in to donate blood that day. "That poor girl is upstairs bleeding and bleeding. This blood might be her only hope."

Kristen watched as her arm was prepared for the needle, then closed her eyes as it was inserted. "Tell me something," she said. "Why is a nosebleed so critical in a leukemia patient?"

"Because she can literally drown in it," the technician said. "It bleeds into her throat." She checked the bag to make sure the blood was flowing the way it should, then resumed her explanation. "It takes a team of doctors and nurses to control it. They have to go in through the mouth and pack it to stop the flow into the throat, and then try to control the front. It's very dangerous, and painful."

"But the platelets help?"

"If they can get her body to stop rejecting them," she said, "then her blood will start clotting again."

Kristen closed her eyes, and imagined how futile the whole ordeal seemed. "Don't you ever get overwhelmed with all this?"

"Sure I do, honey," the technician said. "We all do. But we can't give up. We keep doing everything in our power, and maybe one thing will work. I've seen it happen over and over. Sherry's been here before, and the doctors got her into remission. It might happen again."

Kristen looked around her, at the other chairs full of friends and neighbors and relatives of other patients, and wondered if that hope was as easy for them to hold on to. It was all they had, she realized, as she thought of Nancy sitting on the lobby couch with that phone book in her lap. Hope was all that was keeping Nancy going.

HANK'S EYES WERE ALIGHT with hope as he came out of Sherry's room to meet Luke, once the doctors had gone in to check her. "She squeezed my hand," he told Luke. "I think she's waking up."

"Good. I'm waiting to give blood. Kristen got her mother to make some phone calls. We'll have donors coming in droves before the day's out."

"Thanks, buddy," Hank said, pulling off his surgical gown and tossing it into a wastebasket. He did the same with the mask, cap and boots, then slowly led Luke toward the waiting room. "Man, I'm tired," he said. "It was a hellacious night." He looked up at Luke suddenly, and redirected his worry toward his friend. "Hey, I heard about the new arrest. What's going on?"

Luke plopped onto the couch and braced his elbows on his knees. "They think I blew up the federal building," he said, assessing his friend for any change in his expression.

An almost imperceptible twitch of Hank's mouth was the only change in his face, but Luke noticed it at once. "Yeah, I heard. But you have an alibi, right? I mean, you can prove that you didn't do it?"

"The funny thing about my alibis," Luke said, a despairingly cynical note to his voice, "is that they don't know exactly when the bomb was planted. It could have been any time. It had a timer."

"Yeah, but only for twelve hours, right? You could prove where you were for twelve hours."

"How did you know that?" Luke's question came suddenly, and he sat up slowly and centered his gaze on Hank.

Before Luke's eyes, Hank's expression went blank, and he could see his friend beginning to withdraw. "I don't know. Maybe I heard it on the news."

"It wasn't on the news," Luke said quietly, not wanting to frighten Hank away before he'd gleaned what he needed to know.

"Well, hell, Luke. Everybody knows that a bomb doesn't distinguish between a.m. and p.m. It doesn't take a genius to figure out that a bomb with a timer probably had an ordinary clock attached."

Luke sat back, telling himself Hank was right. He would have made the same assumption himself, with or without inside knowledge. "Yeah." He looked down at his hands, touched his fingertips together.

"Anyway, there was a demand that went with it. Whoever planted it said they wanted some guy named Bates released from prison."

"Bates?" Hank's curiosity came across as more genuine this time. "Who the hell is he?"

"I don't know. But I have a feeling I'm gonna find out real soon. The U.S. Attorney's office is doing everything they can to link the guy with me. Even if they can't, chances are that if I don't come up with whoever framed me fast, I'm in a lot of trouble. We're talking about terrorism."

Hank stood up then, looked out the window, turning his back completely to Luke. "I wish I could help, buddy," he said quietly.

Luke stared at his hands again. His palms began to dampen, and he told himself to ask about the cord and batteries. But some level of compassion deep inside him warned him that it wasn't the time. The problem was, there wasn't a right time. And his time was running out almost as fast as Sherry's.

Finally, because he had no choice, he forced out the words. "Hank, the other day, I came by the hospital to give blood, and I was going to leave a note in your car."

"I didn't see it," Hank said, turning back to face him.

Luke looked up at him, met his tired, bloodshot eyes. "No, I never wrote it. I reached under your seat to get paper off your clipboard, and when I pulled it out . . . I saw a bag with some batteries and detonator cord."

Hank stiffened instantly and his expression betrayed instant alarm. He held out a stemming hand, shaking his head. "Hey, wait a minute. You're not going to pin this on me, Luke."

"I'm not trying to pin anything on you," Luke said quietly. "I was just hoping you had a reason for buying that kind of cord."

A crimson wave splashed across Hank's face, and his teeth clamped together. "And you call yourself my friend? They found the RDX in *your* car, pal, not mine! Just because you were snooping around in my car—"

"I was not snooping," Luke said, coming to his feet. "It was an accident that I found it. I'm not accusing you of anything. I just want to know what you were doing with it."

"I don't have time for the third degree from you," Hank sneered through his teeth, rage rampant in every muscle of his face. "My wife's in there fighting for her life! You have your problems, and I have mine!"

"Just answer the question!" Luke said. "That's all I want. Just an answer."

"I did *not* plant that bomb," Hank said, biting off each word. "Is that good enough for you?"

They heard footsteps in the hall, and Luke turned and saw Kristen, looking pale and a little flushed. He turned away and leveled his eyes on the ground.

"I have to get back to my wife, *pal*," Hank bit out, then pushed past Kristen and headed back up the hall.

Kristen watched Hank's retreat, then settled her eyes on Luke. "What was that all about?"

"Nothing," Luke said, peering after his friend as he donned his sterile gown again and went back into the room. "Hank's nerves are just ragged right now. He's got a lot on his mind."

Kristen looked in Hank's direction, a frown furrowing her brow. "Yeah, I can imagine," she whispered.

WHEN THEY FINALLY LEFT the hospital, Sherry had completely regained consciousness, but Kristen hadn't missed the unmistakable antagonism drifting between Luke and Hank. Something told her that it had to do with Luke's case, but Luke still wasn't talking.

They spent the day digging through old newspapers, trying to find names of anyone and everyone who might be tied to Samuel Bates. Then she called a friend who worked at city hall, and even though it was Saturday, talked her into letting them in to look up some more of Bates's records. Luke searched through the things they'd found, old clips and articles, evasive bits of evidence about a man whom, days before, he'd never heard of. And through it all he remained quiet, as if his frustration level were reaching an explosive peak. For the life of her, there was nothing Kirsten could do about it.

He was lying on her bed in nothing but a pair of faded jeans, staring up at the ceiling with worried, pensive eyes, when Kristen finished her bath that night. Shyly, almost awkwardly, she climbed onto the bed beside him, sat on her feet and looked down at him.

From somewhere beneath that frown, he found a smile for her.

"What's wrong?" she asked.

"Oh, nothing," he said. "I'm going down for some terrorist act I didn't commit, one of my closest friends is dying, I'm ruining your life. . . ."

"Nobody's ruining anybody's life," Kristen whispered, tracing her fingernail down the center of his chest. "Sherry's going to pull through like she has before, and your very capable and devoted attorney is going to see you completely exonerated."

Luke bent his arm and set his hand on her shoulder, stroked the length of her bare arm, down to the mark on the vein where she'd given her blood. He rubbed his thumb across the needle mark, then brought his eyes back to her. "It was a good thing you did, getting all those people to give blood."

"I didn't do anything," Kristen said. "My mom did it all."

"Yeah, well, I intend to thank her, too."

She moved her hand to his arms, big and bulging with muscles that attested to his pride in himself, and she traced the swell of one vein at the joint. There, he had two marks, one fresh, the other healing. Two others, barely visible, graced the other arm. "How often do you give?" she asked quietly.

"Lately, every couple of days," he said. "I figure since they give it back after they take the platelets, it's no big deal."

She touched his face, stroked her gentle fingertips down the angle of his jaw, and he caught her wrist with his hand. Slowly, he moved his mouth to her fingertips, kissed one, bathing it in the warm wetness of his mouth.

"You smell like an angel," he whispered, drawing her down beside him.

She stretched out on the bed and laid her head on his chest, soaking up the feeling of perfect belonging as he stroked his fingers through her hair. "You seem so sad tonight," she said. "So distant."

"I'm here," he said.

She looked up at him, savoring the feel and touch of his face, as if she knew that the end was on its way. "We don't have to make love tonight," she whispered. "Just lie here with me. Hold me."

He lay still for a moment, holding her as she had asked, but after a while, he hooked a finger under her chin and brought her face up to his. "How can I hold you and not make love to you?" he asked on a hoarse whisper.

Her lips met his in a gentle victory, and as he pulled her above him, she felt his body coming to sweet, pulsing life. Their kiss was long, sweet, unhurried, but his body expressed a deeper urgency as she moved slowly against him.

"I love you, Kristy," he whispered against her lips as his hands moved under her clothes.

And as beautiful as those four words were to her ears, they left her with a strange sense of loss... as if she might be hearing them for the last time.

LUKE WAITED until Kristen was asleep before he slipped out of bed, pulled on his clothes and made his way through the dark house. Quietly, he opened the door to the garage and stepped outside.

His old, battered Harley sat where he'd left it; his car was still being held as evidence. He couldn't start it without waking Kristen, he thought. And if he woke her, she'd want to know where he was going—and why.

Instead of opening the garage, he released the kickstand and wheeled the bike out the garage's side door, into the night. A cool breeze was whipping up, reminding him of other times, years ago, when he'd slipped out of Aunt Margaret's house at night and gone for a ride. But this wasn't pleasure, he thought. And the defiance was much more serious. He was in Kristen's custody, but he couldn't find out what he needed to know as long as she was with him.

He walked his bike to the stop sign at the end of the street, well out of earshot of Kristen and her neighbors, then straddled it and kick-started it. The engine roared to life, and Luke pulled on the helmet strapped over the back, hooked it under his chin and took off into the wind.

He drove for fifteen minutes, threading through town, before he reached the long, sparsely inhabited street where Hank had built his house years ago, when both of them felt on top of the world. But that was before they'd been dragged down by disease and deception; that was when they'd trusted life and each other.

He cut off his bike before he reached Hank's driveway, in case Nancy had decided to stay there with the boys that night, rather than at her own house a few miles away. He coasted into the driveway, took off his helmet and sat still for a long moment, contemplating whether he was doing the right thing.

As a friend, he trusted Hank. As a human, he believed in him. But Hank hadn't always shown good judgment, and this thing with Sherry had shaken him at his roots. Luke didn't really know what Hank might do, if he was desperate enough. Would he steal? Would he kill? Would he set up his best friend?

The conversation with Hank that morning played over in his mind as the wind swept up, bringing thick clouds overhead. It smelled of rain, just as Hank's angry denial had smelled of lies. If he hadn't done anything wrong, why hadn't he just calmly explained the cord?

Luke looked up at the clouds, took a deep breath and told himself he had no business coming here. Suspecting Hank was even worse than Hank's stark denial. But he had to know.

He wouldn't go inside the house, he thought. Just in the workroom in the back, the room connected to the garage. He knew the special panel Hank had installed to hide his valuables—what few he had. If Hank had something to hide, that would be where he'd hide it. If he didn't find anything there, he'd believe Hank, and wouldn't look any further. And the doubt would never cross his mind again.

He slid off his Harley and hung the helmet over the back, and quietly went around the house to the locked door of the storage room. He looked down at his own key chain, found the long house key that Hank had once given him when he and Sherry were going away on vacation. Luke had tried to give it back afterward, but Hank maintained that, with Sherry sick so often, he might need Luke to pick up something for him now and again, so he'd asked him to keep it.

Luke had never expected to use it to break into Hank's house.

Quietly, he slipped the key into the lock and opened the door. He stepped inside the small room, pulled the door shut behind him and flicked on the light. It took a moment for his eyes to adjust, but when they finally did, he saw nothing unusual. Hank's tools hung where they always had. Small gadgets lay in a box on the dirty hardwood table he had helped his friend build. An empty trash can sat flush against the wall.

Luke's mouth went dry as his eyes sought out the place between two beams where Hank had installed a small, invisible closet, difficult to see even when one knew it was there. He found a seam a little over an inch above the tabletop, let his eyes climb the beams beside it and saw the nail marking the top of the closet. He pulled himself up on the table, bracing himself with a knee, and grabbed a hammer hanging on the wall. Gently, he tapped the nail.

Instantly, the door popped open. Luke took a deep breath and slipped his fingers in the opening, drew the door fully open...and found what he was looking for.

Enough explosives to conquer a small country...or destroy several more buildings.

He felt his teeth coming together in a silent moan of disbelief, felt his fingers biting into the splintery board that made up the closet door, felt his stomach spinning in a nauseating sweep through the floor of his soul. "Aw, Hank," he shouted, not caring if anyone heard him. "Aw, Hank!"

Not touching the explosives, which were mixed with plasticizers to stabilize them, he slammed the door shut with all his might, then turned to the trash can sitting innocently against the wall, and launched his foot through the metal, leaving a gaping dent.

"Damn you!" he shouted, running his arm along the tabletop and knocking the tools to the floor. "Friggin' bastard!"

He turned off the light and left the room, closing the door behind him, and bolted to his bike. This time when he cranked it, he didn't pull on his helmet.

The wind pulled at his hair as he sped through town, heading for the hospital where his best friend sat like a mourning husband rather than a deceitful jackal who led a second life. His eyes stung, and he didn't know or care if it was from the gritty wind or the even grittier truth scratching at his soul.

If he'd ever in his life wanted to kill somebody, it was now.

KRISTEN STIRRED IN BED and reached out for Luke, but her hand fell on cold, empty sheets. Without opening her eyes, she snuggled farther over and reached out again, but still her hand met with emptiness.

Groggily, she opened her eyes and saw that Luke had left her bed. Turning over, she saw the clock on her bed table. Three a.m. A sense of alarm swept over her, making something in her heart react with unwarranted but instinctive fear. She sat up and slid her feet to the floor. "Luke?" she called quietly.

No answer.

She got up and turned on the light, and saw that the clothes he'd hung over the chair last night were gone, and so were his wallet and the keys that he'd tossed on her dresser.

Her heart sank as she came to her feet, and grabbing her gown at the foot of the bed, she slipped it on. "Luke?" she called louder, remembering that Courtney was with her father.

Still no answer.

Tears sprang to her eyes, and she rushed out into the hall, throwing on lights as she made her way through the house, her voice rising as she called out with a strange futility. "Luke, where are you!"

She reached the kitchen and opened the door to the garage, saw that her car was still there.

But Luke's Harley was gone.

Slowly, she backed into the kitchen and sank into a chair, slumping over the table. Fear and anger united and skeined up inside her, setting off a panic-stricken siren that made her head hurt.

He's gone... released into my custody... something he isn't telling...

Her mind groped for answers, excuses, but none came without effort. Luke was gone, and he'd sneaked away when he thought she wouldn't know.

That could only mean one thing, she thought as a miserable chill sent goose bumps prickling over her skin. He had lied to her.

"Oh, Luke," she whispered as tears made their way over her lashes, and down her fingers cupped over her mouth. "Why are you doing this? Why are you ruining everything?"

She sat alone in the kitchen long into the night, in wait for the man she couldn't help loving, even though she wasn't sure she could trust him anymore.

CHAPTER TWELVE

THE HOSPITAL CORRIDOR was virtually deserted at 3:00 a.m., except for an occasional nurse passing from one room to another. In the nursing station, Luke saw a cluster of other personnel, busy with paperwork and monitors.

Luke slipped by them unnoticed, carrying his leather jacket in his hand, aware that if they saw him, he'd be thrown out of the hospital, and *if* they knew of his recent arrests, they'd probably have the police surrounding the building before he had a chance to throw his hands above his head.

He went to the room he knew Sherry was in. The shade was pulled over her window, making it impossible for him to see if Hank was in there with her. Frustrated, he leaned back against the wall, centered his eyes on the ceiling and tried to tell himself that this was no place to vent the fury driving through his soul. He should wait until he was calmer.... But damn it, it couldn't wait. If Hank could assemble a bomb, blow up a building and frame his best friend, there was no predicting what he might do next.

Trying to decide what to do, Luke started back up the dimly lit hall. As he passed the waiting room, he saw that someone lay asleep on the couch. Pausing, he looked closer, and saw that it was Hank.

"May I help you?"

Luke jumped slightly and swung around to the nurse who had come up behind him. Taking a deep breath, he gestured toward Hank. "I was looking for him," he said. "There's been an emergency at home."

"Oh." She looked inside the waiting room, saw Hank sleeping. "All right then. Do you want me to wake him for you?"

"No thanks," Luke said. "I can do it."

He waited for the nurse to leave, then looked inside the room. The mere sight of Hank, lying there in peaceful slumber, looking innocent, made Luke's blood boil.

His mouth compressed in a hard line, and his nostrils flared with disgust as he stepped into the room. Reaching down, he shoved the man he'd served in the Army with, the man whose best man he'd been, the man whom he'd trusted to be a partner in his business.

The man who was setting him up for a crime he hadn't committed.

Hank opened his eyes, squinted up at Luke.

"Get up," Luke said.

Hank rubbed his eyes. "Whasamatter? Is it Sherry?"

"I said get up," Luke repeated through his teeth. "Now."

Hank looked fully at Luke, the tone of Luke's voice drawing him from his grogginess. He brought his feet to the floor and sat up, his face taking on a vivid defensiveness that made Luke even angrier than before. "Luke, what is it?"

"We're going outside, pal," he said. "We're gonna talk."

"Outside?" Hank swallowed and looked at his watch. "It's three-thirty. Why do you want to go outside?"

Luke bent over and grabbed the collar of Hank's shirt, and shook him as a preview of what would come if he didn't move. "Because if I beat the hell out of you right here, it might disturb the patients."

Hank sprang to his feet and jerked free of Luke, suddenly fully awake. "Get your hands off me!"

"Outside," Luke said again. "Now."

"All right!" Hank raised his hands and started toward the door. "Calm down. We'll go outside."

They didn't utter a word as they rode the elevator down, and Luke could read the fear in Hank's guilty face. He didn't meet Luke's eyes as they got off the elevator and walked somberly across the lobby floor.

The night was cool and peaceful, but it did nothing to calm Luke's mood. More than anything, he wanted a cigarette, but he hadn't bought any since he'd thrown them away for Courtney.

A promise is a promise. Damn!

"What's going on, Luke?" Hank asked him, still avoiding his eyes as they reached a small courtyard at the side of the hospital.

"How could you do that to me?" Luke blurted through his teeth. "How could you set me up? Do you know what you've done, man?"

Hank didn't answer. Luke came toward him, and he started to back away. "I don't know what you're talking about." His tone was metallic, unconvincing.

"I went to your house," Luke said as a wall stopped Hank's retreat. "I saw the RDX stacked in the closet in your workroom. Some of the same stuff they found in my car!"

Solid fear transformed Hank's face, and even in the darkness Luke could see his rage. "You broke into my house? You had no right!"

"I had a friggin' key, Hank. You gave it to me, because I was your best friend, remember?"

"Not so you could break in and sneak around—"

Before Hank could finish the words, Luke grabbed the shoulder of his shirt and slung him to the ground.

"Hey, wait a minute!" Hank cried, scrambling to his feet as Luke started toward him again. "It's not what you think. I never knew things were gonna turn out the way they did!"

"You bastard!" Luke's fist met with the stubble on Hank's jaw, reeling him back as his other fist buried itself in the flesh of Hank's stomach. Doubled over, Hank fell to his knees.

"People were almost killed!" Luke cried. "There were people in that building! They're suffering!"

"I know about suffering, okay?" Hank shouted back, new fervor entering his expression as he stayed on the ground, clutching his stomach. A trickle of blood ran from his lip down his chin. "I did it all for Sherry!"

"For *Sherry*?" The words were so absurd, so out of context, that Luke stopped advancing toward Hank, and stood dumbfounded, looking down at him. "Don't put this off on her, man. She doesn't deserve that."

"Don't you think I know that?" Hank stumbled to his feet and, still clutching his stomach, wobbled to a cement picnic table to sit down. He started to cry, and the tears rolling down his face mingled with the blood on his lip. He bowed his head and cupped his hand over his forehead. "Oh, God, Luke. It got so out of hand. I never meant for it to get so out of hand."

Luke set his hands on his hips and looked at his friend, wishing to God that he didn't feel so much pity for him. "I'm listening," he said coldly.

"We don't have insurance," Hank said, looking up at Luke, as if that one revelation explained everything. "I thought I had the system beat, Luke. Since we're self-employed, it cost too much to get individual coverage, so I figured that if one of us ever got sick, we'd just borrow some money, right?" He slammed his fist on the seat next to him, gritted his teeth and brought his moist eyes back to Luke.

"Well, nobody warned me that my wife would get leukemia! And all the treatments, all the drugs, all the doctors...I couldn't afford it, man! I had to do something."

Luke closed his eyes and paced a few steps, turned away from Hank. "What has this got to do with the explosives?"

Hank took a fortifying breath and tried to steady his voice. "When we were installing the security system at the ammunitions plant," he said, "some guys approached me. I don't even know their names. They offered me more money than I had ever imagined in my life, enough money to cover all of Sherry's treatment, if I'd find a way to get some RDX out of there and make them a couple of bombs. You have to understand, Luke. I was desperate. She was dying, and I really believed that if I just had enough money, I could save her."

"Why didn't you come to me?" Luke asked, wheeling around. "Why didn't you once ask me for help? Huh? I would have given you a loan, or gone to the bank, or whatever I had to do."

"*You* don't have that kind of money! We're talking hundreds of thousands of dollars, Luke."

"I don't care," Luke said, leaning forward and forcing his words out through his teeth. "You don't finance medical treatment by selling bombs to a bunch of terrorists!"

"I know that now!" Hank cried, standing up and starting toward Luke, desperate to make his point. "I've told myself that over and over, but it's too late. I didn't know what they were going to do with the bombs, and frankly, I didn't care. All I wanted was the money, and I didn't think I'd ever be found out. I thought I had a way figured to take a crate without it ever being missed."

"But it *was* missed," Luke said, his rage building anew as he pointed at his own chest. "And some of it turned up in *my* car!"

Hank brought his hand up to cover his face, and he sucked in a sharp sob, like a little boy who'd been caught at the most shameful crime he could imagine. "I was scared, Luke," he said in a high-pitched voice. "When I read about the theft at the ammunitions plant, I knew they'd suspect us. You have to understand how sick Sherry was for me to do what I did. I couldn't go to jail right then, and let her find out what I had done. It would have killed her."

"So you directed the heat to me, instead?"

"I thought if they found them on you, they'd leave me alone for a while." Hank rubbed his hands through his hair, unable to look at his friend. "I figured you could get out of it, Luke. You always land on your feet, and you had something I didn't have. You had time. I didn't count on the federal building being bombed, and you getting blamed for that.'"

"Just what *did* you count on?" Luke asked viciously. "Did you think they were gonna hold onto those bombs for souvenirs? Bombs *kill* people, Hank. That's what they're for!"

"I know," Hank said, drawing in a sob. "And I refused to sell them any more after the first couple. But at the time when I sold them those, I didn't think about what I was doing. All I cared about was buying Sherry some time. No matter what I had to do."

Luke uttered a curse through his teeth, then walked aside and rammed his fist against the hospital wall. "Damn you," he said, turning back to his friend. "You expect me to go to prison for you?"

"No," Hank said, his eyebrows arching with absolute certainty. "I won't let it go that far. I swear to God, I just wanted a little more time."

"Time for what?" Luke asked. "To skip town? To dig my grave deeper?"

"No!" Hank cried. "I just wanted a little more time with Sherry." He tipped his head to the side, his face a pitiful distortion of pain and weary acceptance. "She's dying, Luke. Don't you see that I can't leave her right now? I can't let her go that easy." He stepped toward Luke, his lips trembling as he spoke. "Other than my wife, you're the best friend I have in this whole world. Give me just a little more time, Luke. And then I swear, I'll turn myself in."

Luke felt his own tears threatening his eyes, and his mouth twitched as he looked at the honest misery in his friend's face. "I don't know if I can be that noble, Hank," he said.

"I know," Hank whispered. "But you come as close as anyone I know. I need you, Luke. I've never asked you for anything before, and God, I know you have every right to turn me in right now."

"If I'd done this to you," Luke said on a hoarse whisper, "you'd have killed me. You wouldn't have given it a second thought."

Hank met Luke's eyes, and nodded grimly. "You're probably right, buddy. But things aren't the other way around. And right now, all I have to count on is the fact that you have a hell of a lot more honor than I do."

Luke shook his head and turned away, tormenting, torturous thoughts flailing through his mind as he faced the decision that might be the stupidest mistake he'd ever made.

"Give me just a few more days," Hank said, setting his hand cautiously on Luke's back. "I swear, I won't let you take the fall for me. I'll turn myself in as soon as Sherry..." His voice faded off, unable to go on with the last word, but after a moment, he swallowed and said, "As soon as she improves."

But she was dying, and Luke knew it. And as much contempt as he had for Hank right now, he had equal love for Sherry and those two little boys. Hank was a hero to them, a knight in shining armor, who was always there to make things better. How could he let them know now that Hank was a thief who happened to be indirectly responsible for the injury and near death of two people, and possibly more before the real culprits were found?

"All right, Hank," Luke said at last, the words draining him of any energy that he had left in his body. "I'll keep my mouth shut for a little longer. But I'm not going down for you."

"Thank God," Hank said, his voice playing out on a note of profound relief. He reached out and grabbed Luke's arm, forced him to meet his eyes.

"Can you ever forgive me for this, Luke?" he asked.

Luke rampaged through his mind and heart for an answer, but found he came up empty. "I don't know, Hank," he said. "Some damage just can't be undone."

And then, not able to stomach the conversation any longer, Luke strode across the parking lot to his bike, and took off into the night.

He rode without his helmet, that renegade nature he'd harbored in his youth wrapping itself around him again. "What the hell!" had been his philosophy then. Life was cruel and unfair, and what was the point in fighting those odds?

A helpless feeling weighed him down, making him feel tired...so tired...as the wind blustered through his hair and hammered on his body. He had sworn to himself that he'd find a way out of this mess, just to prove himself worthy of Kristen. But now, if he had to take the fall, even for a short time, keep his mouth shut and not tell her what he knew, he was destined to drag her down. There was no way to make things easier.

His heart cried out that it wasn't fair, that for once in his life he deserved a chance at love. For once, he deserved to trust. But look where trusting got you, he thought. And if he allowed Kristen to trust him, he was setting her up for a fall just as surely as Hank had set him up. If he told her about Hank, she'd never let him keep the secret. She'd insist on turning Hank in immediately.

But he couldn't betray Hank now, even though Hank had betrayed him. For betraying him meant betraying Sherry and their innocent children. It meant snatching the father away while the mother was on her way out. That in itself was even crueler than what Hank had done to him.

He cut off his bike a block from the house, and coasted to Kristen's driveway. Then, getting off, he walked the bike back into the garage.

Quietly, he opened the door, careful not to make a noise that would wake Kristen. But instantly he saw the light glowing in the kitchen.

And Kristen was waiting for him.

Luke closed the door behind him, and stood quietly for a moment, holding his breath as he held her sad face in his gaze.

"I woke up and you were gone," she whispered, and he could hear from her voice and see from the gloss of her nose that she'd been crying. His heart throbbed.

"I had to get some air," he said. "I didn't want to wake you."

"I have a patio," she said, her lips growing stiffer though her voice remained soft.

He went into the kitchen, dropped his keys on the table and shrugged out of his jacket. "I took the bike out. I just had to think for a while. I didn't think you'd—"

"Catch you?" she asked. Her eyes filled with tears again, and he leaned toward her, but Kristen covered her face with her hand to hide her tears and stopped him with the other hand. "I want to trust you, Luke," she whispered. "I need to trust you. But when I wake up in the middle of the night and find that you've sneaked away, it gets difficult."

"I wasn't sneaking," Luke said, wanting with all his heart to take her into his arms and make her believe everything was all right. But she knew it wasn't. "I just didn't want to wake you."

"What is it, Luke?" She sniffed and looked up at him in spite of her tears. "What are you hiding from me?"

Luke drew in a deep, steadying breath. "Nothing, Kristen. I told you—"

"I can see it in your eyes," she said, her lips trembling. "I don't think you've ever lied to me before, Luke. I can't help seeing it when you are."

Luke squatted in front of her, took her face in his hands and dried her tears with the pads of his thumbs. "Babe, you're way off," he whispered. "Please, just drop it, okay? I needed some air, so I went for a ride. Just leave it at that."

Kristen sucked in a deep breath and leaned forward, laying her forehead against his shoulder. "Please don't lie to me, Luke. I don't think I can take it."

"You have to trust me," Luke whispered, a deep, miserable frown cutting into his forehead. "Please, babe, just trust me."

"I'm trying to, Luke," she whispered. "But you're going to have to help me."

"I'm doing the best I can, Kristy," he whispered, sliding his arms around her. For now, that was the best he could offer her.

And somehow, Kristen didn't expect more.

CHAPTER THIRTEEN

"COME ON, KRISTEN. It's the best he's going to get. A guilty plea will save us both a lot of time." The U.S. Attorney's telephone voice was condescending, patronizing, but it didn't intimidate Kristen in the least.

Gravely she moved the telephone from one ear to the other, and peered up the hall, where Luke had gone back to sleep in the guest room hours ago. Nothing had been resolved concerning his disappearance last night, but still, Kristen knew that no matter what he was hiding, Luke wasn't guilty. "My client is innocent, Bill," Kristen said wearily. "I intend to prove that."

"Fine," the prosecutor said. "I'll take this before a grand jury and they're bound to indict him. We're talking breaking and entering, theft, attempted murder and terrorism. Any of those indictments will land him in jail without bond until the trial—and I promise you, Kristen, no amount of tap dancing will keep him out this time—but if we make a deal I might be able to get the sentence down to ten years..."

"No deal," Kristen said again, no patience left in her tone. "If I could be at that hearing, those people would see that your evidence is so thin you can see through it. It's all circumstantial."

"A trunkload of explosives is not circumstantial," the man said, and chucked smugly. "And don't worry about it. You'll get your chance in court."

The front door opened before she could respond, and Courtney burst in, her father on her heels. "Mommy! Is Luke still here?"

Kristen leaned over for a hug, then turned her attention back to the U.S. Attorney still on the line. "Look, Bill, I have to go now. I'll speak to you tomorrow."

Chagrined at the phone call, Kristen took her daughter's duffel bag and set it on the table, and regarded Eric, still standing in the doorway, wearing a pair of khaki trousers and a designer golf shirt. "Hello, Eric."

"You didn't answer her question," her ex-husband said. "Is Luke here?"

"You know he is," Kristen said. "I told you yesterday—"

"And I told you," Eric cut in, closing the door behind him and strolling toward her with his hands in his baggy pockets, "I don't want that thug around my daughter. Either he goes, or Courtney comes back home with me."

"For what, Eric?" Kristen asked, sarcasm lacing her weary voice. "So you can take her to my mother's?"

"I'm warning you, Kristen," Eric said, pointing an authoritative finger—one that, she was sure, usually made those eighteen-year-old girls he liked to hire tremble in fear—in her face. "I'm not bluffing. I have certain parental rights, and I don't have to sit by and watch while you move that convict in here with our daughter.''

Kristen slapped Eric's finger out of her face. "He is *not* a convict! He's been accused of something he didn't do!"

"Right," Eric said without conviction. "Just get him out. Now. If you won't do it, I will."

Kristen met his eyes, defiance flecking the blue of her own. "No, Eric. He's sleeping right now."

Eric's eyes took on a dull, cold edge that almost frightened her. "Then wake him the hell up," he said.

"No need. I'm awake." Luke's voice came deep and alert from the hallway, and Kristen swung around to see him standing in the doorway of the living room, his chest bare down to his faded jeans. Unintimidated, he leaned against the casing, tipped his head indolently and regarded Eric. Seeing them together in the same room for the first time in years, Kristen had to wonder what she'd ever seen in her husband. He was handsome, yes, but not in the way that Luke wore his rugged, masculine beauty. And no matter how much he'd spent on his yuppie style, Eric would never come close to measuring up to the style Luke had always worn like those washed-out old jeans, faded in places that made her face warm.

For a moment, she felt almost sad for Eric, for it was only then that she realized her marriage to him had never really had a chance.

Luke's eyes hardened as he stared at her ex-husband. "You have something to say to me, you say it to my face."

Eric's face reddened, and Kristen knew that he hadn't expected to face Luke himself. As little as he thought of Luke, she knew that he feared him as one would fear a gang member motorcycling through the neighborhood. Luke was from a different world than Eric. Luke was from *her* world.

"I was just telling Kristen that it's either you or Courtney," Eric said. "I won't let her stay here with you in the house."

Courtney seemed even more horrified than Kristen at her father's rudeness. "Daddy, Luke's nice. Don't make him go."

The two men didn't unlock their gazes, and Kristen stepped forward and pulled her daughter back against her. How did she resolve something like this? she asked herself as tears forged their way into her eyes. Did she encourage them to slug it out like little boys? Did she risk hurting Luke by succumbing to Eric's demand? Did she risk hurting Courtney by refusing?

"You're a criminal," Eric said, his courage waxing as the silence lingered. "You've been charged with a felony, and who the hell knows what else. If I have to take Kristen to court over this, no judge in his right mind is going to think I'm being unreasonable."

Luke moved his tired gaze from Eric to Kristen, who looked at the floor with tears in her eyes. Then he saw Courtney's sad, mortified expression as she gaped up at him. "Luke is *not* a criminal," the little girl said, her bottom lip beginning to quiver. "He's my friend, Daddy. He is. Aren't you, Luke?"

Luke took in a steadying breath, and Kristen could see him summoning all the strength he owned to steady his expression. Slowly, he stepped toward Courtney, and stooped in front of her. "Sure I am, pumpkin," he said softly, finally meeting her eyes directly. "Your daddy's just looking out for you. I'd probably feel the same way if I were him.''

"Luke . . ." Kristen's voice broke in anticipation of what he was about to say.

"It's okay," he said, casting her a half glance up. "I really think it's time I was going, anyway."

"Luke, he's blackmailing us!" Kristen said, clutching her daughter's shoulders tighter, as if she would be snatched from her if she let go. "I promised the court—"

"That you'd be responsible for me," Luke said. "And you know I won't let you down. I'm not going anywhere, except home. That's where I belong, anyway."

"Don't go, Luke," Courtney whispered. "Daddy doesn't mean it."

Eric came forward and, biting his lip, took Courtney's hand possessively. "Yes, I do, Courtney. I mean every word."

Kristen fixed Eric with a scathing look, and he dropped her hand. She bent over and pressed a kiss on Courtney's head, and handed her the duffel bag she'd put on the table. "Honey, take this to your room, okay?"

"But am I going or staying?" the girl asked, her face clearly showing her distress.

"You're staying," Kristen said. "Just give us a minute."

Courtney took one last appraising look at her father, then she set her little hand on Luke's shoulder, patted him with a mature gesture meant to make him feel wanted and left the room.

Kristen tried to control her tears and she turned her furious eyes back to Eric. "I will not allow you to stand here and play tug-of-war with my daughter!" she said. "She's not a weapon, Eric. She's a child!"

"She's *my* child, too," he said. "And I'll be damned if he's going to try to influence her the way he's always tried to influence you."

"Me?" Kristen looked at Luke, who had risen again, and now glared at Eric with animosity that was rooted in something far deeper than Eric's demand today. "What are you talking about? I haven't seen him in eleven years!"

"Yeah, but it was those years before he got smart I'm talking about," Eric said. "Those years when he grilled every guy you went out with, like he had some right to declare himself your protector."

"He *did* have the right," Kristen said through her teeth. "I gave him the right."

"It didn't work, though, did it, pal?" Luke asked, his eyes murderously cutting into Eric's. "She still wound up with you, didn't she?"

"Why don't you just do everybody a favor and get out of her life?" Eric bit out. "You did it once before. You can do it again."

Luke grabbed the collar of Eric's designer shirt so fast that Kristen gasped, and he brought his face so close to Eric's that their noses almost touched. "The last time you asked me to get out of her life, I did it because I cared about *her*, not because I gave a rat's ass about you or the pathetic huffing and puffing that you considered a threat. If I walk out of here today, it'll be for the same reason."

Kristen smeared the tears across her face, and touched Luke's arm.

With a slight shove, he released Eric. The man stumbled back far enough to get his footing.

"Would you please excuse us for a minute, Eric?" she asked coldly.

Eric's face blazed red-hot through his gold tan, and he crossed his arms and shook his head. "I'm not leaving this room without Courtney."

Kristen felt as close to the breaking point as she'd ever been. "It's all very touching, Eric," she whispered harshly, so that Courtney wouldn't hear. "All this sudden parental concern. It makes me sick. Luke's a better influence on her than you'll ever be."

"Oh yeah? Sure," Eric said. "What's he influencing her into doing? Building bombs?"

"Get out!" Kristen cried. "I told you, I want to talk to Luke. What do you think I'm going to do? Sneak Courtney out the back door?"

Eric stood stock-still, assessing her for a long moment, and finally he sighed heavily and opened the door. "I'll be back in this house for Courtney in five minutes if I don't see him leave."

The door closed, leaving Kristen and Luke alone in the room, and Luke felt as if everything in his life had led up to this moment. Hadn't he known it would come to this? That she'd have to make a decision between her life and him? That she'd come out the loser if he chose to be a winner?

"Somebody always has to lose," Luke whispered through the vast silence that had suddenly overtaken them. "I'd rather it was me."

"Luke, don't let him blackmail us," Kristen said, stepping toward him with her arms extended for him. "Please. If we let him do it once, he'll keep doing it over and over."

"There won't be a second time," Luke said, his eyes as barren and empty as the surface of a dying planet. "Because he's absolutely right. The last thing Courtney needs in her life is some guy who's headed for prison."

"What about what *I* need?" Kristen asked, her voice wavering. "And what about what you need? And as for Courtney, I know firsthand that knowing you is a blessing, not some kind of stigma. You're a good man, Luke. And I *want* my daughter to know you and love you the way I do."

"So what do I do?" Luke asked, his composure cracking as his expression grew more desperate. "Am I supposed to just sit here, knowing that your ex-husband is going to take you back to court for custody of your daughter? Am I supposed to let you give up custody of her so you can have custody of me? Forget about me wrecking your job! Now I'm wrecking your family!"

"Luke, I can't let you go!" Kristen cried, reaching for his arm. "Don't you understand what my promise to Jack and the judge meant? I said I'd keep you in custody! I'm responsible!"

"Kristen, I'm not jumping bail, for God's sake. You know where to reach me." He jerked his arm away, put some distance between them and turned back to her, his hands in the air, grasping for some lifeline that just wasn't there. "All I know is that I can't stay here. I can't hurt you anymore. If you have a problem with that, turn me in and they can haul me back to jail. At this point, I really don't give a damn. At least then I'd have an airtight alibi for whatever those jackals out there decide to do next!''

He started back to the guest room to get his things, and Kristen leaned against the wall, letting warm tears trickle off her chin to wet her blouse.

''Is he going, Mommy?''

Courtney's voice came soft and timid from her bedroom, and Kristen turned around. ''Just for a little while,'' she whispered, trying not to let her pain come through in her voice.

Courtney began to cry, and she ran into Kristen's arms. ''It's all my fault, isn't it? I shouldn't have told Daddy.''

''No, honey, it's not your fault. We weren't trying to hide anything.'' Kristen squeezed Courtney tightly against her, and when Luke came out of the bedroom, she could see the torment on his face as he tried not to let the child's tears get the best of him.

He met Kristen's eyes, held her gaze for a moment, and finally, he managed to speak. ''You know where to reach me,'' he said.

She nodded and swallowed. ''Yeah. Wh-what about the case? We need to work—''

Luke dipped his head and rubbed the bridge of his nose, and she knew he was struggling with the words. ''That's another thing I was going talk to you about today.'' He looked up the hall, unable to focus on her.

''What, Luke?''

Courtney looked up at him, and he didn't meet her eyes. ''I was just in there a little while ago...thinking, and . . .'' He cleared his throat, took a deep breath. ''I think I need another lawyer, Kristen. This is turning out to be a lot more serious than I thought at first. I think I need someone a little more...experienced.''

"What?" Kristen sounded as if the wind had been knocked out of her.

"Nothing personal," Luke said, his voice thick and shaky as he went on. "It's just business. You understand."

"You're firing me?" she asked, astounded.

Luke breathed a heartless laugh. "That's not the word I'd use."

"I don't care about the *word*," Kristen said, glaring up at him. "Is that what you're doing?"

Luke looked at the ceiling, not at her, and after a moment, he started toward the kitchen. "Yeah," he said coldly as he reached the door to the garage. "That's about it. I'll call you later, okay?"

Before she could scream for him to stop and explain himself, Luke had banged out of the door. And as she heard his motorcycle starting and screeching out of the driveway, she felt strangely like that nineteen-year-old girl he'd left at the bus station eleven years ago.

Only this time, she feared, he needed her as much as she needed him. Kristen gave in to the tears overwhelming her, and Courtney hugged her, as if she knew instinctively that her mother needed comforting more than she ever had in her life.

FATIGUE, PAIN AND ANXIETY combined in Kristen's heart to make her mad at the world and everybody in it the next morning. And since Eric wasn't within lashing distance, and Luke wasn't answering his phone calls, Kristen walked with sprint-speed across the floor of the law offices and into the staff meeting where the partners and associates sat, discussing the cases the firm was engaged in.

The conversation hushed when Kristen burst through the conference room doors, her face blazing red as they looked at her.

"Well, well. Kristen decided to join us at last." Robert Broussard laced his fingers in front of his face, and John Norsworthy wrenched around in his chair and regarded Kristen with a smug look. The others sat quietly, waiting for whatever was to come.

"I've been busy," Kristen said, dropping her brief-case on the table at her place and remaining standing as she regarded each partner one by one. "I've been defending a client whom I made a commitment to defend, a commitment that I feel compelled to honor because of the example that each of you has set for me in the years that I've worked for this firm."

"Kristen, we've talked this over," Laura attempted, looking down the table at her. "We really feel it's in your best interest to reevaluate—"

"It's in *my* best interest to defend an innocent client," Kristen volleyed.

John shook his head and rubbed his temples as if he were already tired of the argument. "You're losing your grip, Kristen. Moving him into your house, taking responsibility for him with the judge—"

"My relationship with Luke Wade is not the issue here," Kristen said. "The issue is whether this firm trusts me to represent who I choose, or not."

"Then you admit you do have a so-called relationship with this man?" the firm's patriarch asked.

Kristen turned to Robert and leaned over the table, bracing her hands on the wood. "Yes, Robert. I do have a so-called relationship with this man. I have had since I was nine years old. He means a hell of a lot more to me than my colleagues or my new office or my title. And if it comes down to choosing, there's no contest."

A moment of breath-held silence passed as everyone in the room gaped at the young lawyer who had started with the firm right out of law school. In that moment, Kristen knew that her history with the firm, all the successes and achievements, all the mistakes and failures, held like a flimsy thread the weight of the case she had vowed to take and win—for Luke, and no one else.

Finally, the only man in the room with the authority to make a snap decision heaved a sigh. "We'll respect and trust your professional judgment in this matter," he said quietly. "We would truly hate to lose you."

Kristen felt as if a thousand pounds of burden had been lifted from her shoulders. But she still had another three thousand to discard. Taking a deep breath, she lifted her briefcase and started out of the room, knowing that if she didn't make a quick exit, she'd burst into tears in front of them all. "Thank you, Robert," she said brusquely. "Now all I have to do is convince him to let me represent him."

And before the partners could do more than gasp, she was almost to the elevator again.

LUKE SAT ALONE in his kitchen, scraps of torn paper sorted out in columns on his table as he squinted down at the facts he'd managed to assimilate. From the newspaper articles he and Kristen had found, he'd learned that Samuel Bates was in prison for shooting a city councilman. He had a younger brother in his early twenties, who'd been arrested several times for dealing cocaine. Could the brother be the one who had bought the bomb from Hank?

He thought for a moment, and decided that he needed to get a picture of the guy to take back to Hank and see if it was one of the men who had hired him to build the bombs. Quickly, he looked up the brother's name in the phone book, found an address.

It was a long shot, he thought, one that the police had no doubt tried already—unless, of course, they were so sure he'd done it that they'd stopped looking for anyone else.

Feeling as if he were taking charge of his life and getting back on the right track, Luke went outside to his bike. Pulling on the helmet that disguised his face—a face that had been plastered all over the local news—he rode off to find the man who had planted Hank's bomb.

LUKE'S HOUSE WAS the first place Kristen went when she left her office that morning, but no one was home. Frantic to find him, she drove to the hospital, hoping he was there.

The elevator crept to the fifth floor, stopping at every floor along the way. When she finally got off, she went to the waiting room where Hank or Nancy always seemed to be sitting, but no one was there.

Quickly, she went to the nursing station and confronted a small nurse with tired eyes and a trayful of medications in her hands. "Excuse me," she said.

"I'm looking for someone who might have been here to visit Sherry Gentry or her husband. A man wearing a green flight jacket, blue jeans. Dark hair and—"

"And smoky bedroom eyes?" the nurse asked with a smile.

Kristen let out a breath of relief. "Yes," she said. "That's Luke. Is he still here?"

"Lord, no," the nurse said, setting down her tray and looking at her watch. "Last time I saw him was Saturday night. Or should I say, Sunday morning?"

"Saturday night?" Kristen asked "When?"

"Must have been three-thirty or four," the nurse said. "I had just come back from break. I work eleven to eleven."

"Three-thirty or four *a.m.*?" Kristen asked. "Are you sure? What was he doing here at that hour?"

"Looking for Mr. Gentry," the nurse said. "He said it was an emergency."

Kristen looked back toward the waiting room, as if she could visualize the scene, and thereby understand it. "I see," she whispered, distracted. "Thank you."

The nurse trotted off to deliver the medication, and Kristen grabbed the desk to steady herself. Was this where Luke had really come that night? Did his secrecy have something to do with Hank?

Slowly, she started toward the elevator with more questions than she'd had before she came. The doors opened, and Hank stepped out.

Immediately, Kristen saw the swollen, cut place on his lip, and the bruise on the left side of his jaw. "Hank."

Hank gave her a defensive look, a look that told her she was the last one he wanted to see, and she allowed the doors to close without her.

"Hi," he said reluctantly.

"Hi. I was looking for Luke," she said. "Have you seen him today?"

"No." The answer was simple, no frills. "I haven't seen him since you were here with him Saturday."

Kristen schooled her features to not look surprised at the matter-of-fact lie, and nodded blandly. "Oh." Swallowing, she gestured to his lip. "What happened?"

Self-consciously, he touched it. "Nothing. I was tired, wasn't looking where I was going."

"Yeah?" Kristen asked, knowing instinctively that Hank was lying, as surely as he'd lied about seeing Luke. And somehow she knew that Luke was responsible for Hank's injuries.

"Well, I'll go look some more for him," she said. "He got a little upset yesterday and fired me. Then he left."

"Oh, no." Hank's words were laced with genuine concern and a slight note of alarm. Curious, she thought, if Luke had, indeed, hurt him. "He fired you? Why?"

Kristen breathed an empty laugh. "Said he wanted someone more experienced."

"Oh God." Hank raked his splayed fingers through his hair, cast his worried eyes on the ground, then regarded her again. "He didn't mean it. You know that, don't you?"

Kristen tried to fight the tears pushing into her eyes. "Yeah, I know."

"You haven't seen him since?" Hank asked.

Kristen shook her head and jabbed the elevator button again, the incongruity of Hank's concern against his lies making her feel sick.

"He'll turn up," he said. "He gave you his word, didn't he?"

Kristen nodded, took a deep breath and decided she couldn't deal with Hank's predictions anymore. "How's Sherry today?" she asked.

"Bad." Hank looked up the hall toward the room where Sherry lay dying.

"I'm sorry," she whispered, swallowing. It was all so mixed up, she thought. Her distrust of Hank one minute, and her pity for him the next. "I'll go down and give some more blood before I go. They said I could give it after two days."

Hank nodded, as if he didn't hold much hope in the gesture, but cherished it nonetheless. "Thanks, Kristen," he said.

The elevator doors opened, and Kristen stepped on. Just as they started to close, Hank reached out and stopped them. "Hey, don't give up on Luke, okay? He's about the most decent man I know. He needs you."

"I know he does," Kristen said. "Don't worry."

The doors closed, leaving Hank on the outside, looking as forlorn as an orphaned child who didn't know which way to turn. And as the elevator descended to the first floor, something jelled in Kristen's heart. No matter what it took to stand beside him, Luke wasn't going to shake her off again.

CHAPTER FOURTEEN

JEREMY BATES'S APARTMENT was in a broken-down complex with a rusty refrigerator and an old washing machine sitting on the front lawn. Because the phone book had failed to list his apartment number, Luke could do nothing but wait and watch, hoping for some clue to the man who was behind the bombing.

Luke parked his bike and took off his helmet, and sliding his camera inside his jacket, began to walk the parking lot, between the bondoed cars, some with their hoods left up. He saw a little boy with dirty legs scamper by chasing a puppy, and he watched for a moment, trying to look inconspicuous.

His eyes scanned the license plates, searching for a clue to which car could belong to the culprit, but nothing caught his eye.

After a moment, the puppy that had run by began to bark, and following the sound, Luke ambled around the wing of the building to another wing with more apartments. There, as if fate had led him to his booby prize, he saw a van with the words *Bates Plumbing* marked on the side.

"Bingo," he muttered under his breath, then looked around for a place to sit out of the sight of the tenants who might come and go. A place where he could take pictures unnoticed. A place where he could get what he'd come for.

He found a small playground in a park across the street, directly across from where the Bates van was parked. Sitting half-hidden by a small tree, he watched for someone to come out, anyone at all who might be the man he was looking for.

As he waited, he adjusted his telephoto lens on the camera, focused it and snapped an occasional old woman coming out of an apartment, just in case. An hour passed . . . an hour and a half . . .

Children came and went to play on the slide and the broken swing set, but no one gave him more than a glance as he sat idly on the bench, his relaxed attitude not giving away the fact that he was prepared to pounce as soon as someone got in that van.

Finally, when he'd almost told himself that Bates wasn't home, an upstairs apartment opened and three young men in their early twenties came out. Quickly, he leaned forward and brought the camera to his eye, and snapped the camera several times until they reached the parking lot.

Then, holding his breath, he watched as they got into the van.

Punching the air with victory, Luke secured his camera back in its pouch on his bike, pulled on his helmet and headed for the nearest one-hour photo shop to get the snapshots developed.

KRISTEN STOPPED in the lobby of the hospital after she'd given blood, trying to decide what to do next. She didn't have a clue where Luke could be, but she knew that she couldn't give up now. He'd be back; she knew he would. He wouldn't skip out when she was counting on him.

She thought of going back to the office, but decided that would be a waste of time, since all she could think of was finding Luke, anyway. Frustrated, she dropped onto one of the plush lobby couches and reached for the telephone on the end table. Quickly, she dialed her office and asked her secretary for her messages. None was from Luke.

Pushing down the button to cut her off the law firm's line, she got the dial tone and started to dial Luke's number again, and glanced toward the front doors as the phone began to ring.

As if on an urgent mission, Luke Wade dashed in, carrying a small bag in his hand, and headed for the elevator doors, which were already open. The doors closed before she could stop him.

Grabbing her things and jamming them back into her case, Kristen darted to the next elevator, which was just opening, and got on, pressing the button for the fifth floor.

It took an eternity for the elevator to reach her destination, but when it did, Kristen got out and looked for Luke. She saw him standing up the hall, close to Sherry's room, talking to a nurse.

Something about his manner, his harnessed energy, his expression, told Kristen not to approach him just yet. Instead, she lingered where she was, watching.

In a moment, she saw Hank come out of Sherry's room, his eyes defensive and cool as he confronted Luke. She watched as Luke reached into the yellow bag he carried, pulled out some snapshots and handed them to Hank.

And finally, she started toward them.

"JUST ANSWER the question," Luke said. "Are any of these the guys you sold it to?"

Hank looked around to see if anyone had heard, then frowned and took the snapshot. "Yeah," he said, nodding. "Two of these guys. These two on the left."

"I thought so," Luke said, jerking the photo out of his hand and sticking it in his coat pocket. "Now these bastards are gonna pay."

Hank grabbed Luke's arm as he started to turn away, and met his eyes directly. "Be careful, okay? Don't try to handle this yourself."

Luke laughed bitterly. "No?" he whispered so no one else could hear. "Then just what do you suggest? We've already established that I can't go to the cops."

Hank dropped Luke's arm, letting his own hands fall helplessly to his sides. "I just mean...don't go off half-cocked and start pulling any heroics. Kristen was here a little while ago. She said you'd fired her."

"Don't worry about it, pal," Luke said. "I can take care of myself."

"She's worried about you," Hank pressed. "Don't shut her out. She can help you, man!"

Luke's face flashed murderously red as he leaned over to Hank. "*Nobody* can help me but you," he said.

Hank bowed his head, rubbed his tired eyes. "I know, man. I'm sorry."

Luke made a disgusted face at his friend, then turned away and started back up the hall. The sight of Kristen made him freeze.

"Hi, Luke," she said, her voice wobbly. "I've been looking for you all morning."

Luke swallowed and tossed a look at Hank over his shoulder, wondering just how much she had heard. "Yeah, well, I've been busy."

Kristen nodded and looked at the floor. "Look, could we go back to your place? We need to talk."

Luke tried not to notice that she was wearing his favorite color, a deep aqua that highlighted the color of her eyes...her tired, red eyes. "Kristy, there's really nothing to say."

She wet her lips, and he saw the glitter of tears forming in her eyes. "Luke, please..."

Miserably, he turned away from her and punched the elevator button. No matter how he tried, there was really no way he could turn her down. All she ever had to do was ask. Finally, he gave her a sad, accepting look, and whispered, "Okay, follow me home."

THE WAY LUKE DROVE through town like a maverick with nothing left to lose made Kristen's heart swell in fear. Something was terribly wrong, she thought. Whatever he was keeping from her was more serious than she had imagined.

She tried to organize the facts in her mind. Hank's bruised jaw, the pictures Luke was showing him, the new animosity between them, Luke's disappearance the other night and his winding up at the hospital in the wee hours of morning. Everything seemed to point to Hank. But why?

She followed Luke up his street and pulled into his driveway, turning off her engine as he yanked off his helmet and left it lying on his bike. Then, not waiting for her, he went to the house and unlocked the door.

He pulled off his jacket and dropped it over a chair as Kristen came in behind him, and she glanced down and saw the photograph in the inside pocket, bearing the faces of three men she didn't recognize. She moved her eyes back to Luke, to the T-shirt stretched across his chest and biceps, and she wanted to fall into his arms and beg him to open those gates that were locking her out, to be honest with her and stop playing those noble games of his.

He bent over his jacket, reached into the pocket and pulled out an unwrapped pack of Marlboros. He gave a deliberate glance at her as he tapped the pack against his palm, as if waiting for some reaction. She stood quietly watching as he pulled the ribbon at the top, peeled back the cellophane and wrinkled it in his hand. "So you wanted to talk," he said. He started into the kitchen, knowing she would follow, and dropped the cellophane into a wastebasket. "Talk."

Kristen didn't let his tight attitude daunt her, for she knew that it and the cigarettes, as well as his dismissal of her yesterday, were all part of some small act of defiance. Defiance of what, she wasn't sure. Suddenly, she felt as if he had placed her in that authority-figure category of people he had spent a lifetime trying to shock. That, more than anything else he'd done, hurt her.

Quickly, she opened her purse, rummaged through it for the book of matches she kept there for the occasional client who needed a light and tossed it to him.

He caught it reflexively, looked at it with a glint of surprise and muttered, "Thanks."

"Don't mention it," she said, schooling her expression to remain as cool as his. She pulled out a chair, sat down at the table and saw the torn pieces of paper lined up in columns, the scattered bits of facts in the case laid out like quotes on a term paper. More questions rose to her mind. More answers flitted through her heart. After a moment, her gaze returned to Luke.

"I'm not letting you fire me," she said, her words as matter-of-fact as her manner.

"Well, you don't have a choice in the matter," Luke said, placing the cigarette between his lips and fingering the book of matches.

Kristen snapped up her chin and fixed her piercing gaze on him. "Because I'm too inexperienced?" she asked, stressing the last word with sarcasm. "Because I don't know what I'm doing? Because you want someone who can do a better job for you? Because I'm in your way?"

The questions were point-blank, requiring a yes-or-no answer, but Luke couldn't give her either. He also couldn't look her in the eye. Instead, he took the unlit cigarette out of his mouth, stared down at it. "Maybe."

"And maybe not," she said. "Maybe it's all just a smoke screen for that incorrigible protective sense you've always felt toward me. Maybe you think you're doing me a favor."

"Kristen, you don't understand," he said through his teeth, his struggle with the truth—his truth, her truth—apparent on his face.

"I understand," Kristen said, coming to her feet. "This time I understand. Damn it, I bought into your martyr act eleven years ago and let you walk out on me then. But I'm not going to let it happen again."

Luke whispered a curse and slung the cigarette into the trash can, then kicked the can until it fell over, its contents rolling out onto the floor. "For God's sake, Kristy!" he said, whirling around to face her with eyes that were red with fatigue. "I've given you every reason in the world not to trust me!"

Kristen shook her head in frustration. "Just because you sneaked out in the middle of the night, lied to me about where you went, beat Hank up for heaven knows what reason, disappeared for half of today—"

Luke's face went slack, and she could see that her knowledge of more than he had expected surprised him. He started to speak, caught himself, then turned to the refrigerator and opened the door, and stared with vacant eyes at its sparse contents.

"Despite all the pieces flying around in my head, not fitting together, not adding up, I still know that you did not commit those crimes," she said. "Why can't you be honest with me, Luke? Why can't you trust *me*?"

Luke flung the door shut, knocking over the bottles on the door shelves, and settled his turbulent eyes on her again. "Because I don't want to drag you down with me!" he shouted. "Don't you understand what that's doing to me? It's worse than jail. It's worse than anything—"

"You won't drag me down!" she shouted back, her voice overpowering his. "Listen to me! I met with the partners this morning and set them straight about my representing you. Once they realized how determined I was, they backed down. My job's not on the line anymore, so your excuses don't wash, Luke! You're stuck with me!''

Luke shook his head violently, not accepting her explanation. He started out of the kitchen into the living room, and she followed him. "It doesn't matter," he said. "They'll change their minds again when they see the evidence stacking up against me."

"Evidence like those pictures in your jacket?" she asked. "Evidence like Hank's black eye? Evidence like your showing up at the hospital in the early hours of the morning?"

He swung around and confronted her, his face raging red. "Kristy, I don't know what you think you know, but I'm not hiding anything. I just went to the hospital that night to check on Sherry. I was worried about her."

"At 3:00 a.m.?" she asked, not letting him off that easily. "And your worry made you wind up hitting Hank?"

He set his hands on his hips, and she could see in his shallow breathing and the strain on his face that he was lying. "I went out for air and ended up there," he said again, as if saying it enough would make it true. "Hank and I got into a little argument, and I flew off the handle."

"Luke Wade does not fly off the handle," she said. "For you to hit your best friend, you had to be foaming mad."

Luke brought both hands to his head, held it, as if it might split right down the middle if he let it go. "Kristy, don't do this."

"Don't do what, Luke?" she asked, coming closer to him. "Don't make you tell the truth? You're covering for someone, aren't you?"

Luke's hands dropped to his sides, and he glared at her, guilt and blame in his eyes.

"Is it Hank?" she asked. "Is he involved in this somehow?"

"No!" Luke shouted. "No, it's not Hank. I'm not covering for anybody, okay? I don't know anything!"

Kristen knew she was pushing him too far, but it was the closest she'd gotten to the truth. "What about the pictures I saw you showing to Hank this morning?" she asked. "And those papers all over the table in there? Samuel Bates, Jeremy Bates..."

Luke punched at some invisible object in the air and uttered a soundless curse, then covered his face with his shaking hands. "I read in one of those articles that Bates has a brother," he said through his teeth. "I thought if I could find him, maybe I could figure out if he's the one who planted that bomb. I found out where he lived and took some pictures of him this morning, and I wanted to show one to Hank in case the faces rang a bell."

Kristen issued a heavy sigh, for his explanation sounded like the truth. Still, she couldn't be sure. She watched his hands slide down his face, leaving it red, though his fight seemed to be depleting. In her mind, she tried to picture the scene she'd witnessed at the hospital. Luke showing the photo to Hank. Hank nodding yes. Luke jerking it angrily away, then saying something to Hank through his teeth, as if he would strike him again if he was provoked far enough.

"Did Hank recognize them?" she asked.

Luke shook his head. "No. He's never seen them."

It was at that moment that Kristen knew, without a doubt, that Hank *was* the one Luke was covering for. He wasn't lying to protect himself. He was lying to protect his friend.

His best friend... his wife is dying....

She thought of calling him on it, letting him know that the pieces were beginning to form into a solid picture, but somehow, she knew it would only make him shut those doors again. She'd pushed him far enough.

So instead of fighting him again, she chose to slide her arms around his waist. She felt his resolve melting as his muscles lost their tension, felt his hands sliding up her arms. "Luke, please don't shut me out again," she whispered. "I know how hard this is for you. We can fight this together. Tell me that you won't shut me out."

Suddenly his trembling arms were around her, and he was crushing her against him, burying his face in her hair. "I feel...so out of control..." he whispered. "I feel so helpless."

"I know," she said, rising on her tiptoes and pressing soft kisses along his neck. "I know."

"And somehow just getting you out of this mess felt like I was doing something positive again, like I was getting back in control."

"I don't want out of this mess, Luke," she whispered. "Please. I love you."

His mouth found hers, and his kiss was hard, desperate, ravaging. His breath grew heavy, and she felt his heart tripping against her breast, felt his manhood hardening against her belly. His hand moved down to her hips, wadding her skirt in handfuls until the hem was in his reach. Urgently, he molded his hands to her, arching her against him. His other hand foraged through her hair, finding and discarding pins, letting ringlets tumble around her shoulders.

He left her lips and found her neck, bit and nuzzled, his breath creating a shiver over her flesh as his hands groped for buttons and zippers and clasps. Deftly he opened the front of her dress and released the hook of her bra, then slipped his hands over the sensitive swells of her nipples.

Desperate for a union, she tugged his T-shirt from his jeans and slid her hands over the hard plane of his abdomen, moving his zipper down, down, until she confronted the full force of his desire.

He drew in a sharp breath. "Last night...was the most...miserable night of my life," he whispered.

"Mine, too," she gasped.

He bent down and lifted her and in quick strides carried her to his bedroom. He laid her on the mattress, and peeled off her panty hose. Before she knew what had happened, he had discarded his clothes and was above her, joining her with a thrust so deep that it reached right into her soul.

They flew through a dark galaxy, Luke the only beacon Kristen had to guide her. Blindly, completely, she followed, until their desperate explosion consumed her absolutely, leaving her limp and weak in Luke's strong arms.

Afterward, they lay side by side, letting their breathing return to normal, letting their heartbeats find their common pace.

"That's better than a cigarette any day," Luke whispered against her neck.

Kristen couldn't laugh. Instead she wanted to cry, for the time that was slowly being drained away from them, the time they would have to spend keeping Luke out of prison. But as sure as she was that he held a secret from her, Kristen was just as sure that Luke's secret would not be a source of shame. She knew his deception was a selfless act of love, of honor, and for that she could not be angry.

It only made her love him more.

CHAPTER FIFTEEN

IT WAS MIDAFTERNOON, after Kristen had pulled some strings at the police department to get information on Jeremy Bates and the other two men in Luke's snapshots, that Luke gave her another accidental clue.

"Well, at least we've established that they each have a long record of arrests," he said, gazing out her car window as he spoke. "The drug dealing probably explains where they got the money for the bombs."

"What money?" Kristen came to a red light and looked over at Luke. "How do you know they bought the bombs? I assumed they'd made them themselves."

Luke rallied quickly. "I mean for the stuff to make the bombs."

"But they stole it," Kristen said. "The explosives from the ammunitions plant."

"Right." Luke shifted uncomfortably in his seat and looked out the window. "I just meant—you can go, the light's green."

Kristen moved her eyes back to the road and pressed the accelerator as an uneasy feeling began to ripple inside her. Luke didn't think they had stolen the explosives. He thought they had bought them. But if that was the case, who had sold them? And more important, who had planted them in his car?

"I just meant that there are other things that go into making bombs," Luke tried again, his voice containing little conviction. "Expensive things. They had to have money."

Kristen drove in silence for a moment, more aware than she'd ever been in her life that what Luke had said moments earlier was an unintentional slip—one he counted important enough to carefully explain away. Quietly, she added the new information to the file in her mind marked "Luke's secrets." Money. They had bought the bombs. Which meant someone else had sold them to them. And Luke knew who that someone was.

As much as Kristen wished it weren't so, she feared that she knew, as well. *Hank...money...his wife is dying....*

She glanced over at Luke, saw that he nursed his thoughts, too, probably cursing himself for getting too loose with his mouth. Finally, she pulled into his driveway, but she kept her car running. "Luke, I really want you to come back to my house," she said. "I wouldn't be surprised if you were being watched until the hearing, and I don't want them to think that you're bucking authority by moving back home."

"Bucking authority?" He almost laughed. "Is that what you are, Kristy? Authority?"

She gave him a grin. "I meant the judge."

Luke's smile faded, and he looked down at his hands. "I can't go back there, Kristy. I'm not going to jeopardize your family. Eric would be over there in five minutes with some kind of court order."

Kristen shook her head. "You don't know him, Luke. He's not interested in taking Courtney full-time.

She knows that as well as anyone. He just wants to get at me, because in his heart, he knows I've always loved you."

Luke took her hand and smoothed his rough fingers over it. "Still, I don't think you want to take the chance any more than I do. Courtney's too precious. I'm staying here. If I'm being watched, then it should be clear pretty quickly that I'm not going anywhere." He sighed, let go of her hand and rubbed his face. "Besides, I have to sit down with my books and figure out how I'm going to make a living from now on. Even if I get out of this somehow, I'd say my future in the securities business has gone to pot. Anybody'd be a fool to hire an accused criminal to install a security system in their business."

Kristen wished she had an answer for that, but sadly, she didn't. She took his hand, pressed a kiss on his knuckle. He turned his hand over and stroked her cheek. "It's not just the fact that you might be watched that bothers me," Kristen said. "If you're at home alone, you might get set up again. There could be another bombing, and you'd be caught without an alibi, or someone else might plant something...."

"It won't happen," Luke said with a certainty that made her uneasy. "I don't think I'll be set up again. Besides, I could be set up just as easily at your place as I could here. And if the cops are watching me, then they'll know I'm not involved in anything else that might happen. I really think it'll be all right."

Kristen nodded blandly, and looked down at the clock on her dashboard. "Well, I have some things to do back at the office," she said. "I'll call you tonight, okay?"

"Sure," he whispered. "Take care of that little girl. Give her a kiss for me, okay? Tell her I didn't let that cigarette this morning defeat me."

Kristen's heart swelled with regrets and sadness. "Oh, Luke," she whispered. "If only you had been her father."

Luke's grin was vulnerable and a little surprised. "Me, a father? Now that's hard to picture."

"Not for me," Kristen said. "It's easy. I saw you with her the other night."

"That wasn't fathering," he said. "That was fun. It's easy with Courtney."

Kristen leaned her head back on her seat and sighed. "If Eric would say something like that just once, I might be a little more tolerant of him."

"It's not what he says," Luke said. "It's what he feels. I can tell he loves her."

Kristen's gaze drifted out the window. "Yeah, I guess he does. It's just his means of showing it that drives me crazy. I wish he could be more like you."

Luke leaned over and caught her lips in a quick kiss, then pulled back slightly, his eyes smiling with the tenderest love she'd ever known. "Only you could look at a man going down for terrorism and tell him that you wish your stockbroker ex-husband was more like him. Incredible."

Kristen's smile mirrored his. "Not so incredible to me," she said.

Luke slid back across the seat and opened the door. "I'll talk to you later, babe."

Kristen watched with tears in her throat as he walked inside. But the moment he disappeared from her sight, a piercing sense of purpose filled her. She had to go see Hank. And if she'd ever had any talent as a lawyer who could cross-examine a witness and make him tell whatever he knew, she would use it on Hank today. If it was the last thing she did, she would find out what Hank had to do with this situation. She wouldn't sit by and let Luke take the fall for someone else.

Not even for someone he loved.

THE BLINDS TO THE WINDOW overlooking Sherry's laminar airflow room were open when Kristen got to the hospital. Looking in, she saw Hank sitting with her, wearing a sterile hat and gown, her limp hand clasped firmly in his. Over his mask, she saw the despair in his exhausted eyes as he spoke to Sherry, and the death pallor of Sherry's face as she answered.

"May I help you?"

Kristen glanced at the nurse who had come up behind her and shook her head.

"I'm waiting to speak to Hank," she whispered, blinking back the tears in her eyes, "but don't disturb him. I'll wait until he comes out." Her gaze gravitated back to the frail woman lying on the bed beneath tubes and wires that monitored every last thread that kept her hanging on to life. "How is she?"

The nurse seemed more like a worried friend than a health care professional when she stepped up beside Kristen and regarded Sherry through the glass. "It's hard to say. She came out of coma this morning, but her fever's still dangerously high."

"But the chemotherapy," Kristen said, groping for some hope. "Won't it help? I mean, isn't it just a matter of time before she starts getting better?"

The nurse leaned back against the wall beside the window and faced Kristen with troubled eyes. "That's the thing about chemotherapy. It kills the bad cells, but it also kills the good ones. Any kind of infection at this point can be fatal, and it looks like Sherry's in a lot of danger. We're pumping antibiotics into her, but so far she just isn't responding."

Kristen's heart plummeted further, and she felt her purpose slipping away. Maybe it wasn't that important that she confront Hank right now.

But just as soon as the thoughts entered her heart, she remembered how quickly Luke's time was slipping away from him. And his life was as precious as Sherry's. She wiped the mist from her eyes, took a deep breath and looked at the nurse again. "I'll be in the waiting room," she said after a moment. "When Hank comes out would you tell him I'd like to see him?"

IN SHERRY'S ROOM, Hank stroked his rubber-gloved fingers along her cheek, and looked into the hazy-sick glaze of her eyes, searching for the woman who had once exuded such vibrant life.

"Tired..." she whispered. "Need to rest...."

A tear rolled down his cheek, and he smeared it away. "Okay, love. Go ahead and rest."

"...love you...don't be angry...."

He almost didn't hear the endearment, her whisper was delivered on such a thin wisp of breath, but when he realized what she'd said, an alarm went off in his heart. "Why would I be angry?" he asked.

"Tired," she whispered again. "So tired."

Her eyes closed as she drifted into a shallow sleep, and he held his breath, trying not to suck in the sob lingering in his throat. Was she telling him that she was too tired to fight? Was that why he would be angry? Because she was ready to let go?

He bowed his head as tears squeezed out of his eyes, and he fought the urge to shake her and force her to wake up. Sleep was a powerful drug, one that she needed right now. But death was even more powerful, and like a narcotic that promised peace and numbness, it called to her.

And its voice was stronger than his.

Knowing that she would be asleep for a while and that he was too weak to keep his emotions quietly contained, he stood and started out of the room, discarding his sterile clothing with vicious rips and wads once he was past the plastic that was supposed to protect Sherry from the evils of the world.

He looked up and saw one of Sherry's nurses watching him with sad eyes. They all seemed like family, he thought, and some had long ago lost their objectivity where Sherry was concerned. He was glad she wasn't surrounded by strangers now. "She's just sleeping," he said in a shaky voice, as if to reassure them that she'd be back.

The nurse tried to smile. "We've really gotten attached to her," she whispered.

Hank shrugged. "Sherry does that to people." He sighed and rubbed his face. "How do you do it? Day after day, one patient after another? How do you keep going?"

The nurse turned back to her monitor, adjusted a button, then brought her eyes back to Hank. "I guess we just concentrate on the miracles. There are a lot of them on this floor, you know."

"Yeah, I know." Hank frowned and tried not to choke up as he looked back into the room. Had Sherry used up all her miracles, he wondered, or was there one hovering over her even now, waiting to pull her back?

"Oh, I forgot," the nurse said. "There's someone in the waiting room to see you, Hank. Kristen Jordan."

That beaten look on Hank's face hardened with a defensive edge as his startled eyes met hers. "Is Luke with her?"

"She's alone," the nurse said.

Alone? Hank wiped the tears from his face, telling himself his breakdown would have to wait, and started toward the waiting room. Why would she want to see him alone, unless it was about Luke? Had he told her? Had he broken his promise?

Like a prisoner walking to meet his executioner, he went down the corridor to the small waiting room. Cautiously, he stepped into the room, and Kristen came to her feet at once. "Hank, hi. I didn't want to disturb your time with Sherry—"

"It's okay," he said, raking back his hair. "She's sleeping." He came into the room, kept standing. "Where's Luke?"

"At home," she said. "He doesn't know I'm here."

Hank swallowed the sudden dryness in his throat, and dug into his pocket for some change. "Want a soda?" he asked.

Kristen sat back down. "No thanks. You go ahead." She watched the meticulous way he sorted through his coins, inserted them, made his selection and retrieved the can that rolled out with a tumble that seemed much too loud. "Hank, I need to talk to you about Luke's case. I think he knows something he's not telling me. And I think it has to do with you."

The look on Hank's face told Kristen instantly that she'd hit home, but he quickly rallied and sat down, and took a long time sipping the drink, as if it were Scotch rather than soda. "I don't know what you're talking about," he said at last.

Kristen had expected no less, but she was prepared. She leaned forward, fixing stubborn eyes on him. "Hank, I've given this a lot of thought, and I've put a lot of things together. You're Luke's best friend. He's just the kind of person to take a fall for a friend, especially when that friend is going through a tough time, anyway." She paused, waited for Hank's reaction.

Hank stood up and went to the window, turned his back to her, and she could see that he held his breath. His shoulders didn't move as he stared rigidly out at the parking lot, and she knew that she was getting warmer.

"I have this scenario in my mind," she went on, "that someone...whoever actually stole the explosives...might not be the same one who planted the bomb in the building. Maybe he was just some kind of middleman. Maybe he thought he had a good reason for doing whatever he did."

Hank still didn't move, and Kristen went on. "I can't see any good reason why that person would set Luke up the way he did, but if Luke knows about it and is willing to take the heat, then there must be one." Her voice cracked, and she swallowed and looked at the floor. "The thing is, if Luke cares enough for that person to risk prison, I don't understand how that person can care so little for Luke."

Hank turned around, his granite face expressionless, though a muscle in his temple twitched. "I told you, I don't know what you're talking about."

Kristen nodded her head without conviction, and she stood up and faced him with less compassion and more accusation. "Fine, Hank. Maybe it'll become clear to you by the time I subpoena you to testify in court."

"It won't come to that," Hank said. "He won't even be indicted."

Kristen glared at him in disbelief. "How can you say that? When that grand jury sees all the evidence the government has against Luke, they'll want to hang him on the spot."

"But I told you, it won't come to that," Hank said, his lips hardening into two unwavering lines. "I won't let it."

His words hit her like a rush of icy air, and she caught her breath and stood quietly, their eyes locked in silent combat. After a moment, she swallowed, anger and relief moving through her in alternate waves. "Then you admit it," she whispered.

Hank's stony facade cracked, and he walked to the doorway of the waiting room, looked out into the hall. Satisfied that no one was nearby, he turned back to Kristen, tears reddening his raw eyes. "You have to understand how desperate I was," he said, that same desperation undulating his voice. "I only did it to get the money for her treatment."

Kristen dropped her face in her hand, slumping under the heat and the ache of hope and dread, of gratitude and fury.

"And when the ATF started snooping around..." His voice broke, and he stepped out into the hall, looked in the direction of Sherry's room. "She's dying in there, Kristen. She's given up. Luke has the rest of his life, but Sherry might only have a few more days...and only then if she has the strength to fight that long."

Kristen lifted her face to look at Hank, and found that he was blurry through her own haze of tears. "Hank, I am so sorry for what you're going through with Sherry. I can see how much she means to you and I know how much Luke loves her, too. If there were anything I could do to help, I would. But Hank, one thing has nothing to do with the other."

"Yes, it does!" Hank whispered. "If I turn myself in, sure, it'll get Luke off the hook. But then they'll haul me to jail! What will they tell Sherry?" He fell to the couch, pinching the bridge of his nose and squeezing his eyes shut. "Kristen, I have to be there for her. I have to be with her when she lets go, so she won't be afraid." His voice broke on the last word, and he began to weep harder, so hard that Kristen moved closer, put her arm around him and rested her forehead on his shoulder. For a moment, she held him like a little boy who'd met with his first taste of life's unfairness. Then she released him and sat back, her own tears uniting them in kindred sorrow.

When he could manage his voice again, he set his elbows on his knees and looked at the floor between his feet. "I just want a few more days," he said. "I

swear to God, I'll turn myself in before Luke gets indicted. Just don't take these last few days from me. I
might deserve it, but Sherry doesn't.''

Kristen swallowed the pain in her throat, and told
herself that Hank was right. Sherry didn't deserve to
die alone, with only a team of nurses to help her
through the pain and despair, or the guilt she might
feel for being the innocent cause of Hank's criminal
acts. She didn't deserve to know that her husband had
committed a crime as serious as this.

''For what it's worth,'' Hank went on after a moment, ''I didn't plant that bomb. I stole the explosives, assembled the bomb and sold it to two of those
guys in Luke's snapshot. But I did *not* mean for anyone to get hurt!''

Kristen drew in a deep breath that fed her very soul.
''Did Luke make a promise to keep quiet for you until
you came forward?'' she asked wearily.

''Yes,'' he said. ''He knows how important this is.
He's doing it for Sherry. Please, Kristen, just a few
more days.''

The facts twisted in Kristen's stomach, creating a
tangled knot that brought her close to nausea. ''Hank,
I'm an officer of the court. And as Luke's attorney,
and someone who loves him as much as you love
Sherry, I don't think I can keep quiet about this. I
won't let Luke risk prison for you.''

Hank shook his head adamantly, and when he
looked at her, she could see the pain right down to his
soul. ''I would never let Luke do that for me,'' he said.
''I'm not asking for a ticket out of the country. I'm
asking for a couple of days. And if you give it to me,
I swear I won't let Luke down again.''

Then, not waiting for her answer, Hank left her in the waiting room, and, looking as if he carried the weight of both heaven and hell on his shoulders, he went back to watch Sherry sleep.

LUKE'S LIVING ROOM grew darker in the late-afternoon sunset, but he didn't move to turn on the light. Instead, he sat motionless on the couch, his head resting against the cushions, staring pensively at the videotape he'd taken years earlier.

Sherry Gentry ran across the television screen in a pair of jogging shorts, her long dancer's legs prancing for the camera. She turned around as Hank grabbed her, and giggling, wrestled him to the ground. "I'll get you, Gentry!" she screamed as he tickled her.

Luke picked up his remote control, aimed it at the VCR and fast-forwarded to the next scene with Sherry. Slowing the tape to normal speed, he smiled as her nine-month-pregnant belly—so big that it made his own stomach hurt—dominated the screen.

Hank was on his knees in front of the camera, which was balanced on the tripod, and Luke chuckled lightly as he watched himself step into the picture. Mischievously, Hank lifted Sherry's maternity shirt, exposing her bare stomach.

"I'd rather not have my gut exposed for posterity, thank you," she told her husband, pulling her shirt back down.

But Hank hadn't listened. Luke laughed now as he watched Hank produce two crayon markers—the washable nontoxic kind, Hank assured them both— offered one to Luke, and began to sketch a face on Sherry's stomach.

It hadn't taken long for Luke to join in the fun, sketching ears and freckles and a big nose that covered her navel.

On the screen, he watched Sherry laugh harder than he remembered her ever laughing, shaking her silky brown hair around as she did. And Luke had laughed, too.

And then the tape progressed to the scene of the two tiny babies just hours after their birth, and Sherry lying in her hospital gown, completely exhausted, but euphoric with pride over the perfection of those two little boys.

"Uncle Luke, meet Jake and Josh, the first set of co-Presidents in the history of the United States."

On tape, Luke leaned over and shook one of their tiny fists. "Nice to meet you, Mr. President."

Funny how things changed, he thought. What was to become of those babies now, with their mother dying and their father facing a prison sentence? Somehow, for some asinine reason that he told himself was completely irrational, he felt responsible.

The doorbell rang, and wearily, Luke got up and went to the door. Kristen stood there, her face sober and her eyes direct, and he knew she'd found him out.

"Can I come in?" she asked.

Luke nodded, and she stepped inside and saw the videotape playing on the screen. He closed the door and followed her farther into the living room. "I was just watching some old tapes," he said. "Remembering how it used to be."

Kristen sat down on the edge of the couch and stared at the face of the bright, happy woman on the screen, heard her quick wit and her even quicker laugh and saw instantly why Hank loved her so. "Is that Sherry?"

Mutely, Luke nodded.

"Oh, Luke," she whispered, her voice as distraught as the expression on her face. "She's beautiful."

It was a scene after the babies had come home, and Sherry was swearing that she looked her worst. On tape, she lamented the appearance of some "cellulite pockets" on her thighs.

"Where?" Hank asked doubtfully.

"Here," she said, pinching her flesh to show him. "See that?"

"That's not a dimple," Hank teased. "That's a mole."

"Not there, fool. Here!" she said.

"Oh, I see it," Luke had piped in from off screen, and the camera had zoomed in to Sherry's leg, as smooth as the day he'd met her dancing in Las Vegas. "Wow, Sherry. That's really disgusting. You should do something about that."

The pillow she threw at him had made the screen go black momentarily, and Kristen glanced at Luke. He wore a sad, nostalgic smile.

"I saw her today," Kristen whispered.

Luke moved his startled eyes from the screen and looked at her. "When?"

"When I left here," she said. "I went to the hospital to talk to Hank, and I saw her through the window." She looked back at the television screen, her eyes glossing with sadness. "She didn't look like the same person. She looks so healthy there. So strong."

"She is strong," Luke said quietly. "She's fought for a long time."

Kristen leaned back on the couch and reached for Luke's hand. "Hank thinks she's going to die."

Luke met her eyes quietly, waiting for her to tell him what she knew.

"He told me everything," she said.

Luke didn't believe her. "What everything?"

Kristen's eyes filled with tears, and she squeezed his hand and brought it to her mouth. "About how he's the one who set you up, and how you agreed to take the heat so he could be with her."

Luke muttered a curse and withdrew his hand. Leaning forward, he braced his elbows on his knees and flipped off the remote control. Sherry disappeared from the screen.

"He told me because I guessed it," she said. "There were too many questions, and I could see you hiding all those secrets. After a while, it all added up."

Luke dropped his face, pressed his fingers to his eyes. "So... are you going to go along with it?"

Kristen propped her cheek on her hand and wished she could tell him that she'd do whatever he wanted. But she couldn't. "I don't think I can, Luke. If I keep my mouth shut and let you do this, you'll probably wind up being indicted, and they'll keep you in jail until the trial. Even if Hank confesses before the trial, that indictment and your jail time will always hang over you. You can't escape something like that, Luke. It alters the rest of your life. Your business will be ruined, people will doubt you...." She sighed heavily. "Besides, keeping quiet makes you an accomplice—and me, too."

Luke stood up and paced across the room, his face a study in torment. "So what are we supposed to do, Kristen? Turn him in and let them drag him to jail? He just wants a few more days."

"That's all he wants now," Kristen said, carefully choosing her words. "But what if Sherry hangs on? What do we do then? Continue to spare Hank for her sake? And if she dies, will he then use the kids as his scapegoat? We can't incriminate Jeremy Bates without Hank's confession. Where does it stop, Luke?"

"I don't know!" he shouted. "I just know that Sherry doesn't deserve to check out knowing that the man she loves most in the whole world is a jerk!"

He stooped in front of her, took her shoulders and forced his voice back to a lower cadence. "You know, as much as I'd like to grab him by the throat and drag him to the cops myself, I almost understand why he did it," he whispered. "If it were you lying in that bed dying...I don't know...I might do the same thing."

More tears came to Kristen's eyes, and she raised her hand to gently stroke Luke's cheek. "No, Luke. You'd never set up a friend to go to jail for any reason. You'd find another way."

Luke let out a rugged breath and laid his hand over hers. "Maybe," he whispered, not certain. "All I know is that I can't help but do what Hank asked. I can't let Sherry down right now."

"*You* wouldn't be letting her down!" Kristen cried. "Hank let her down already!"

"But she needs Hank," he said. "She doesn't need me. I'm her friend, but he's her knight in shining armor. I can't be the one to take that away from her when she needs it most."

Kristen wiped a lone tear from her face. "*You're* the knight in shining armor," she whispered. "But once that indictment is handed down, I might be the only one who can see it."

Luke got to his feet. His eyes were longing and full of pain, and they broke her heart. "You'd see it no matter what I did," he said softly. "But damn it, you deserve so much more."

"More?" she murmured, a tremor in her voice. She stood up and took his hand. "Luke, what more is there, than a man so good that he can take a fall like this for his friend? I could look for a million years and never find anyone better for me than you."

She saw his eyes mist over with tears, and when he pulled her into his arms, his kiss was so tender, so soft, so heart-melding, that she realized he could have asked her to climb a stepladder to the moon, and she would have tried.

When the kiss broke, Luke held her close. "Just a few more days?" he whispered. "Please, Kristy. For me?"

Kristen clung to him with all her might, knowing she could be making the mistake of her life—of *his* life. "As long as he comes forward before the hearing," she said. "If he doesn't, Luke, I swear, I'm going to the U.S. Attorney. I won't let you be indicted for anybody."

"All right," Luke whispered, his grim victory not inspiring much joy. "It's a deal."

CHAPTER SIXTEEN

SHERRY'S DEATH CAME so peacefully that Hank wasn't aware of it until the nurse who'd been watching her monitor stepped into the room and met his eyes with silent, soul-deep sorrow. Just the day before, he and Nancy had promised Sherry they would not allow a code blue if she died—she didn't want to be dragged back once she crossed that threshold she'd lingered on for so long. She'd wanted to go with peace and dignity, not with a team of doctors shocking her heart, trying to revive her for yet another agonizing round with inevitable death. She had asked them to let her rest, and Hank had told her they would.

The nurses had all been told of the decision, but now that the time had come, a sense of incompleteness hung in the air. It couldn't be over that quietly, Hank thought. It couldn't.

He looked up at the nurse, his eyes denying what his heart couldn't accept. The nurse wiped a tear from her eye, and suddenly his heart absorbed the truth. Sherry was gone.

"Oh, no," he whispered, a sob catching in his throat. "I thought she was sleeping."

"She was," the nurse said, her voice trembling. "She went quietly."

He looked up through his tears, and saw Sherry's mother standing outside the room, pulling on a sterile gown, preparing to come in. But when Nancy saw Hank's eyes through the plastic and glass, her face distorted into a miserable twist of despair. Discarding the gown and letting it fall to the floor, she pushed into the room, her eyes leveled on the only child she had ever had. "Oh, God," she whispered on a high-pitched sob. "Don't tell me...."

Hank drew her into his arms and held her as she wept out the regrets of a mother who'd outlived her daughter. "So many things I meant to say..." she whispered. "I always thought there was still time."

They wept together in the room for a little longer, until the nurses and orderlies, with their own eyes misty and faces somber, came to take Sherry's body away.

It was an hour or more later, in the waiting room, that Hank and Nancy began to talk more rationally, more objectively, about what was to happen next.

"Hank, leave the boys with me for a while," Nancy said cautiously, drying her eyes with a handkerchief that had been constantly damp the past few days. "They're used to me, and they've got their little room in my house. Sherry's been in the hospital for so long now, that if we can keep their lives as stable as possible... it might be easier for them. I know it would be easier for me. You could move in, too."

Hank's eyes were raw with grief, and his heart felt like an open wound. "You're right," he said. "They don't need to be moved right now. And they need you. I think in the past few months, I've sort of lost touch with them. It's you they depend on most." He dropped his face, frowned and decided that there were things that needed to be said . . . plans that had to be made. His voice broke as he added, "But I don't think I'll be able to move in with you."

The question in Nancy's eyes made him want to die, but he told himself she deserved to know what had happened. She would understand, he thought, because she loved Sherry, too. And they had both done whatever it took to keep her alive as long as they had.

"I WANT TO TESTIFY for the grand jury." Luke's statement came with finality, and the U.S. Attorney looked as surprised as Kristen did.

"You're not required to do that," Bill Dothers said. "Has Kristen explained to you that this is a closed hearing, and that it's not for defense, but for me to lay out my evidence to prove I have enough to make a case?"

"Yes, of course," Luke said. "And I'm aware that she wouldn't even be allowed in the courtroom with me. But I've got to be there to tell my side. I can't just sit still and let this happen."

Kristen sat at the table in her office next to Luke, aware that he felt the urgency of time slipping away. The hearing was tomorrow, and still Hank had done nothing. She intended to keep her vow to expose Hank *before* the hearing took place, but she had no guarantee that her word would be enough to stop the hearing without the word of either Luke or Hank. Luke seemed to be preparing himself for the hearing, as well as the indictment, with no plans to break his oath of silence. Still, he fought the only way he could. Perhaps the worst way, Kristen thought.

"Luke, don't do it," she said. "It won't help. That's the only reason he'd consider letting you do it."

The prosecutor lacked sympathy as he flipped through his files. "I must admit, it wouldn't hurt my case a bit to have you tell your side. You have absolutely no proof that you didn't put those explosives in your trunk yourself, or that you didn't plant that bomb, or that you didn't phone in those demands."

"Proof?" Luke asked, his face reddening. "Whatever happened to 'innocent until proven guilty?' "

"As far as the grand jury is concerned, all I have to do is present the evidence I have." Dothers flicked his lighter, ignited a cigarette, and blew the smoke across the table. "If they think there are reasonable grounds to believe that you committed these crimes, then they're required to indict you. Unless you have some shocking bit of evidence you intend to spring on us at the last minute, nothing you can say will help your case at this point."

Luke lowered his face into his hands, then quickly looked back up. "I don't care," he said. "I want to be there. I have to be."

"Very well, but I warned you." The attorney shrugged and jotted a note on his papers. The satisfaction in his eyes set off an alarm in Kristen's heart. If Dothers got Luke on the stand, and Luke still didn't tell the truth, he'd fry him.

When the U.S. Attorney had picked up his briefcase, bade cool goodbyes and left the office, Kristen closed the door and turned back to Luke. His face was in his hands again, but she could see that his slump was born more of fatigue than of defeat. "Do you remember that Monty Python movie we saw together before you joined the Army?'' she asked.

Luke nodded. *''Monty Python and the Holy Grail?''*

''Remember the scene where that knight was guarding a bridge, and he got in a confrontation with Arthur?''

''Yeah.'' A dry grin took hold of Luke's face, and he looked up at her. ''Arthur cut off his arms, and the knight started kicking him. So he cut off his legs, and he started biting and spitting.''

''And he kept yelling for Arthur to come back and get what was coming to him.''

Luke couldn't seem to laugh at the comical scene replaying in his mind. Instead, the humor left his eyes and he fixed her with a dull, lusterless stare. ''What's your point, Kristy?''

''You're just like that knight,'' she said, sitting down behind her desk and leaning forward. ''You've allowed Hank to cut off every bit of your defense, and you're still trying to fight anyway. All you have to do is open your mouth and tell what you know, and you'll be vindicated.''

''I can't do it.'' Luke's tone brooked no debate.

The buzzer on Kristen's desk sounded, and sighing, she picked up the phone. ''Yes, Linda?''

Luke watched her as her eyes changed from frustration to apprehension, and she held out the phone to Luke. ''It's Hank,'' she said quietly. ''He asked for you.''

She saw Luke's adam's apple move as he swallowed hard, and getting up, he took the phone. Kristen pressed the button to put Hank on the line.

"Hank?" Luke's voice was shaky with dread.

He could hear the stopped-up hollowness in Hank's voice the moment he spoke. "It's over, buddy," he said quietly. "Sherry died a little while ago."

Luke didn't say anything for a moment. Instead, he stood looking at Kristen, limp with disbelief, his eyes misting over with despair. Letting out a ragged breath, he said, "I'm sorry, man."

Hank cleared his throat and went on. "It was peaceful," he said. "She was sleeping...and then, she just wasn't anymore."

Luke closed his eyes and pressed his thumb and forefinger against his lids, and Kristen came around her desk and put her arms around him, knowing intuitively that Sherry's battle was over.

"I...I told Nancy what I did," Hank said, then cleared his throat again. "She...she's going to keep the kids." His voice wobbled, and his swallow was audible over the line. "She understood," he said, as if that made everything so much easier. "She said she even appreciated that I did it to buy Sherry some time."

His voice cracked, and Luke could hear him muffling the phone, trying to restrain his emotion.

"That's good, man," he said. "Sherry...she would have understood, too."

"Yeah," Hank whispered. "Maybe so. But I appreciate her not having to. Thanks for giving me the extra time."

Luke nodded, but he couldn't speak. An enormous lump was lodged in his throat.

"The thing is, I wanted to ask you one more favor."

Apprehension began to tighten Luke's muscles by degrees. *No more favors, Hank,* he thought. *Please don't ask any more of me.* Finally, Luke swallowed and made himself, ask, "What?"

"Oh, God, I hate to ask," Hank said. "I need more time, Luke. Just another day or two. I need time to get a hold on things, time to take care of—the arrangements . . . and be with the kids. . . ."

"Hank, the hearing is tomorrow," Luke said as gently as he could. "My time is running out."

Kristen dropped her hold on Luke and stepped back, her grim expression hardening.

"I know," Hank said. "I'm still going to turn myself in. I told you—"

Luke drew in a deep breath and felt his face reddening.

Kristen began shaking her head furiously. "Tell him no," she whispered through her teeth.

"Hank, I'll be indicted. There's no doubt about it. You're making me into an accomplice."

Kristen grabbed the phone out of Luke's hand and brought it to her ear, as Luke sank down into the chair behind her desk.

"But you'll be vindicated after I confess," Hank was saying. "The indictment won't mean anything."

"It means something to him!" Kristen said, her voice firm but calm. "And it means something to me. Don't do this to him, Hank. He gave you what you asked for. It's your turn now."

"I told you," Hank said, his tone unyielding. "I'll turn myself in. Just not yet."'

"Then when?" Kristen shouted into the phone. "What guarantee do we have that you'll turn yourself in at all?"

A long pause passed between them, and when Hank spoke, his voice was hoarse and carefully controlled. "You don't have a guarantee," he said. "You'll just have to trust me to do the right thing."

"Hank!"

The phone went dead in her hand, and Kristen stood clutching it, staring at Luke. "He hung up!" she said, her face as panicked as the emotion in her voice. "He's going to let you be indicted, Luke."

Luke didn't answer. Instead, he sat staring into space, disappointment coloring his dark eyes.

"This has gone on long enough." Kristen bent over his chair, putting her face only inches from his. "Luke, I can't keep quiet any longer. I have to tell Bill Dothers."

"Don't please," Luke whispered. "He's still reeling from Sherry's death. Give him a few hours. Maybe he'll come around."

"Yeah, and maybe he'll leave town," Kristen said, her eyes glinting with rage. "Maybe he'll disappear and leave you holding the bag."

Luke came to his feet, his muscles moving wearily beneath his weight. "Just let me go find him. I'll talk to him. Just give me a couple of hours."

Kristen threw up her hands. "I can't believe this! You're still covering for him, aren't you? You're still willing to carry this load. Don't you understand that if he disappears, no one on God's green earth is going to believe that he did it? They'll think it's your last-ditch effort to get off the hook. Unless they get him and hear his confession, you're going to prison, Luke!" She spun around and headed for the phone. "I'm calling the police right now."

Luke started across the room, his face a mask of dazed confusion, but with one clear purpose in mind. "If it's in my power, Kristy, I'm going to find him first. Hank's gonna turn himself in. We've come too far to throw him to the wolves now."

Kristen watched as he left her office, leaving her with the easiest and most difficult decision she'd ever had to make. But as sorry as she was for Hank's grief over Sherry, the choice was clear. Kristen wasn't going to let Luke pay for Hank's mistake. The police had to know.

LUKE LOOKED FOR Hank at home, then at Nancy's. Finding no one home at either house, except for the baby-sitter who was watching the twins, he tried the hospital.

It was funny, he thought, how little things changed after someone died. The sun still came up in the morning; the wind still whisked undaunted over the city. People still ate breakfast and went to work, appointments were kept, and the nurses and doctors on the fifth floor went on with business as usual.

But Sherry was gone.

A strange emptiness yawned inside Luke, as if some vital part of himself was missing. His friendship with Sherry had been the first real friendship he'd had with a woman after Kristen. It seemed he was always losing these days.

Slowly, he started up the hall toward the room where Sherry had been, knowing she wasn't there, but feeling strangely as if he needed to go there, to see the empty room, the fresh sheets, the machinery that sat unplugged and disconnected. In his way, he needed to say good-bye.

The miniblinds over the window were open, and he looked with dull eyes into the sterile room, so stripped and clean that the new patient who would be brought in today to struggle for his or her life might never know that the one who was there before had lost her war.

Tears came to his eyes, and he touched the window with his fingers, and rested his forehead against the pane of glass. This wasn't supposed to happen, he thought miserably. Back in basic training, when the only thing he and Hank had had to worry about was getting through the regimen, no one told them how painful life could turn out to be. Hank wasn't supposed to fall in love with a great girl and lose her to some elusive disease that no one knew how to cure. And he wasn't supposed to screw up so badly that he faced prison. And he wasn't supposed to be put in a position where he had to betray his best friend.

Strangely, Luke wasn't angry anymore.

His hand trembled as he brought it to his eye and wiped the mist away before it formed into tears.

"You're a good man, Luke Wade."

Luke spun around and saw Sherry's mother standing behind him, her eyes red and swollen, and her nose looking as raw from crying as if she'd had the flu.

"Hank told me what you've done for him."

Luke dragged in a broken breath and averted his eyes, unable to accept the gratitude in hers. "I didn't have a whole lot of choice," he said.

"Yes, you did," Nancy argued. "You could have turned him in any time. But you didn't."

Luke lowered his blurred focus to the floor, and fresh tears worked into his eyes, but he blinked them back. "Nancy, I'm really sorry about Sherry. You must be..."

Nancy nodded and touched Luke's chest, stopping him before he had to rip out the words. "I had to wait here to take care of some things." She looked toward the empty room, where hours before her daughter had lain in agony. "She's at peace now."

"Yeah." A moment of silence followed, but finally Luke rubbed his hand over his jaw and forced himself to remember the urgency of why he'd come. "Look, I have to find Hank. I know how torn up he is, but I can't hold Kristy off any longer. The hearing is tomorrow, and he doesn't sound like he's coming around."

Nancy wiped her eyes and peered into the empty room. "I know. It's really hard for him. Most men, when they lose their wives, don't have to turn right around and let the police lock them up." She brought her eyes back to Luke, searching his face for understanding. "He only did it for her, you know. He was desperate."

"I know, Nancy," Luke said. He slid his hands into the pockets of his flight jacket. "Do you know where is is? I need to find him before the cops do. It'll be so much better for him if he turns himself in."

Nancy shook her head wearily. "No, he said he had to go think, and he just walked out. He's had so much on him, Luke."

"I know," Luke said. "And if I could make this all go away, I would. But I can't." He looked past her, trying desperately to find a way to put his feelings into just the right words. "See, if it were just me, I wouldn't care so much. I could hang on a little longer, accept the indictment. Hell, I never cared before what people thought of me." He took a few steps, measuring the words that didn't come easily. When he turned back to her, his eyes were rife with emotion. Clenching his fist in front of him, he added, "But there's Kristy now, and her daughter. I love her, Nance, just like Hank loved Sherry. But the longer this goes on, the deeper it gets. I'm dragging her down with this, just like I always knew I would. I can't let that happen. I'd rather never see her again than ruin her life over this."

His face twisted in pain, and he rammed his fist at the air. "But, damn it, I want to marry her. I want to spend the rest of my life with her. I want to have what Hank and Sherry had."

Nancy's eyes welled and she stepped toward him, her hands extended in love. Luke allowed her to pull him into her arms, just as a mother would have done, just as his own might have done had she lived. Awkwardly, he returned her embrace.

"I want to be more for her than some bum with a record, Nancy. I want to be somebody she can be proud of. For most of my life, I've watched other people being loved. I've always been the spectator. Just this once, I have the chance to have it for my own." He took Nancy's shoulders and stepped back. "I know it's selfish, but I don't want to give it up for Hank."

Nancy looked at him and, reaching up, she wiped a lone tear from under Luke's eye. "Then go and find him," she whispered. "And tell him that. Hank's a good man, too. He'll do the right thing."

She dropped her arms as Luke stepped back, and slowly started to walk away. "Luke?"

He turned around, his face a portrait of misery.

"Try the lake," she said. "I think he may be there."

IT TOOK FORTY MINUTES for Luke to reach the lake, then another ten to negotiate his bike through the woods that led to the private little spot he and Hank had found so long ago. When he reached the clearing where they'd always parked their cars, he saw Hank's sitting there, abandoned.

Slowly, Luke got off the bike and pulled off his helmet. Shrugging out of his jacket, he tossed it over the seat, then scanned the bank as far as he could see. Hank was nowhere to be seen.

Wishing to heaven he hadn't thrown that pack of cigarettes away the other day, Luke started up the hill toward the water, looked up and down the bank. Finally, he saw a small figure hunched over several yards from where he stood, and he knew that it was Hank.

Swallowing the emotion in his throat at the sight of his best friend, sitting alone with his arms hugging his knees and his face tucked between his elbows, Luke slowly walked toward Hank without saying a word.

Hank heard his footsteps and looked up, his eyes wet and swollen. Not uttering a sound, he drew in a cleansing breath and looked out over the water.

Luke sat down on the grass beside him, leaned back on his elbows. For a long time, neither of them spoke.

"Do you remember that day we brought Sherry with us to fish out here?" Luke asked finally, his voice quiet against the natural orchestration around them. "Remember how excited she was when she caught her first fish?"

Hank wiped his eyes and nodded. "Yeah. She almost fell in the water, jumping up and down."

"Remember she wanted her picture taken with it? It must have been four inches long, but you would have thought it was a monster bass."

Hank smiled. "Yeah. When I told her she'd have to clean it, she threw it back in."

They laughed, a soft sound of relief and surrender, but the laughter died on a sad note.

"I wish I'd brought her out here again before we checked her into the hospital this time," Hank said, his red eyes skimming the surface of the water. "But I always thought we had time."

Luke sat up and propped his wrists on his knees. Idly, he tore a blade of grass out of the ground.

"The damnedest thing," Hank went on, his voice growing angrier the more he spoke, "is that all that stupid-ass stuff I did to get in such deep trouble was all for nothing. No matter how much money I had, it couldn't keep her alive." His wounded eyes met Luke's. "But you know something, man? I wouldn't give up one minute I had with her to erase what I did. Every day with her was precious."

Luke squinted in the breeze and tried to keep his voice from breaking. "You know how Sherry always looked at you with that smile in her eyes, like you lit up the world all by yourself?"

Hank sighed. "Yeah. Somehow she always made me feel like I could."

"That's the way Kristy looks at me," Luke said. "It's like she can't see all the flaws and blemishes. And when she looks at me like that, I feel so...right." He met Hank's eyes, pleading for him to understand his point. "I never thought that I could have what you and Sherry had."

Hank cocked a sad half grin and shrugged. "I guess this mess was good for something, huh? I mean, if I hadn't set you up, you never would have called Kristen."

Luke smiled, but there was no joy in his heart. "I guess that's one way of looking at it."

Hank dropped his gaze, leveling his eyes on the ground. "Sherry always said she was going to dance at your wedding."

Luke's smile faded again, and a deep frown cleaved his brow. "Who knows," he whispered. "If there's a wedding, maybe she will. I still feel like she's here."

"Yeah," Hank whispered. "Me too. And she'd die all over again if she knew what I was doing to you."

Luke picked up a rock, tossed it into the water, watched it plop and ripple in concentric circles, disappearing from sight.

"Do you think if I turn myself in now, they'll let me go to her funeral?" Hank asked.

Luke shook his head. "I have no idea, Hank. But you can ask."

"Yeah," Hank said. "I guess I can."

They sat still for a moment, both pairs of eyes fixed on the water, both their spirits as low as the rock that had sunk to the lake's murky floor.

Finally, Hank got to his feet and held out a hand to help Luke up. "Let's go, buddy," he said. "It's time I set things right."

IT WAS LATE THAT AFTERNOON, as Luke sat hidden away from the press in Kristen's office, when the U.S. Attorney at last made the appearance they'd been hoping for. The reporters stopped him in the hall just outside Broussard, Street and Devereux and, humoring them, he gave them a prepared statement.

"Mr. Hank Gentry has confessed to stealing explosives from the ammunitions plant and assembling them into bombs, which he subsequently sold. Based on Mr. Gentry's identification, we have two suspects in custody at this time, and their names will be released later today."

"What about Luke Wade?" someone shouted from the crowd of flashing cameras and microphones.

"The charges against Mr. Wade have been dropped. Mr. Gentry confessed to planting the explosives in his car to divert investigators."

"We understand Mr. Gentry's wife died this morning," someone else shouted. "Will he be allowed to attend her funeral?"

"We're not sure yet," Dothers said. "The judge is taking it under advisement."

AN HOUR LATER, Luke emerged from the office finally feeling like a free man, with Kristen on one side of him, and the U.S. Attorney on the other. But his expression was far from victorious.

"I don't want to talk to the press," he told Kristen when he saw them hovering around the outer office, waiting for a statement. "I really don't have anything to say."

Kristen touched his arm and tried to smile. "I'll go out and answer some questions," she said. "You can wait for me here. We'll leave through the back way."

He watched, feeling oddly empty, as the crowd of reporters enveloped her. Leaning back against a copy machine, he tried to relax, but found he couldn't. So what did he do now? He was tired . . . so tired, and he was worried about Hank. He still had Sherry's funeral to attend, and 101 matters to take care of with his business. He'd probably close it down, he thought. With Hank's involvement and Luke's reputation, it was dead in the water, anyway.

"Looks like you're something of a hero today." Luke turned to see John Norsworthy approaching him.

"Seems you just got out by the skin of your teeth."

"Yeah," Luke said, crossing his arms. "Sorry I had to disappoint you."

John laughed cynically and looked in Kristen's direction. "You know, she came this close to losing her job," he said, indicating a narrow distance between his thumb and forefinger. "She's a lucky lady."

"Luck has nothing to do with it," Luke said. "She's good at what she does."

"Yes, that she is," John said, moving his eyes back to Luke. "But there are all kinds of things that can get in her way."

"Things like what?" Luke asked, not disguising the antagonism in his voice.

"Things like who she's involved with, what people think of him, how many rules he causes her to break.

You know, already the partners have lost a little respect for her. Dothers may not know it, but it's pretty obvious to us that she knew about Hank Gentry's involvement before she went to the police. She compromised on too many things for you, Wade, and when a lawyer begins compromising, that's when she starts to lose her edge.''

"What's the matter, Norsworthy?" Luke asked quietly. "Are you afraid you'll lose your divine power over her if I stay in the picture? Maybe she'll go on thinking for herself?''

John took on the hard edges of a man who'd made a career out of winning his fights. "Sometimes thinking for yourself is precisely what gets you into trouble," he said. "And I'll tell you something. You may have been vindicated on this, but as far as I'm concerned you're still just as bad for Kristen as you ever were.''

John walked away before Luke could fling a retort, and Luke told himself that it wouldn't pay to drag him back and beat the hell out of him in front of the press, who would be watching through the glass. Besides, he thought, maybe the man was right. Maybe he knew what Aunt Margaret had known all along.

He was still Luke Wade, after all.

LATE THAT NIGHT, they sat in front of Kristen's television, watching the account of Hank's confession and Luke's vindication. Courtney was asleep on the couch, and Kristen was curled up next to Luke with her head on his shoulder. It felt so right that one part of him ached to declare that all was right with the world. But another part of him knew better.

"How does it feel to be free?" Kristen asked when the report was over, and she'd turned the volume down.

That haunted look returned to Luke's eyes, and she noted it at once. "I don't know," he whispered. "Maybe a guy like me can't ever really be free."

He saw that Kristen looked ready to dig into his comment, when he leaned over and scooped Courtney up in his arms. "I'll take her to bed," he said.

Kristen waited quietly on the couch, wondering at the strange sad expression he wore, the pensive attitude in his posture, the quiet that had hovered over him all evening. It was as if he still had something on his mind, something she wasn't going to like.

He came back in, a soft half smile playing on his face. "She didn't wake up," he said. "I pulled that quilt at the end of her bed over her." He sat down next to Kristen again, took her hand and seemed to study it. "I shouldn't be here with her. Eric might start trouble again."

"No, it's okay," Kristen assured him. "I told him you were coming tonight and asked him if he wanted to keep Courtney with him. He had a date, and couldn't spare the time, so he had to compromise his principles just a little."

Somehow, the way that loophole had come about didn't make Luke feel better. He shook his head grimly, but didn't utter a word.

Kristen pulled her feet beneath her and raised up slightly on her knees. Leaning over, she framed Luke's face with her hands and pressed a soft kiss on his eyelid. "You're tired," she whispered.

"Um-hmm."

Her lips trailed down to his cheekbone, then followed the line leading to his mouth. His lips parted as she met them, and he rose up to meet her kiss.

"I love you, Luke," she whispered.

Luke didn't answer. There was a lump of emotion in his throat that he couldn't seem to get past.

"I want you to stay with me tonight," she said, her lips grazing his as she spoke. "I want you here every night. I want Courtney to grow up with you around."

He lost himself in her sweet kiss, melting into a thousand different pockets of desire, but his thoughts were too vivid to concede to his yearning. He opened his eyes and beheld her as she pulled back again. She was so beautiful, so precious, so innocent still to the ways of the world.

"I want to be your wife, Luke," she whispered. "I want everyone to know that we belong to each other."

He caught his breath as a ribbon of joy slid up inside him, but something stronger—that incessant doubt that robbed him of the best moments of his life—told him it could never be.

You'll never amount to anything. Aunt Margaret's angry words flew back through his mind, and he had to remind himself that she was right. Here he was, a grown man with no job, no income, and a reputation that would keep him from getting one. From those who had shot questions at him today, he knew there was enough doubt around about his having been in cahoots with Hank that he'd never really be free of the stigma.

And now Kristen wanted to marry him. He swallowed and looked up at her, waiting nervously for an answer, and he could see that it had taken great effort for her to ask.

His hand came up to cup her face, but he couldn't seem to find his voice.

"Did you hear me?" she asked, her voice trembling.

He swallowed. "I heard you. I . . . I just don't know what to say. . . ."

"Say that loving me means something to you," she pleaded. "That you aren't getting ready to saddle up and ride off into the sunset again."

He pulled away from her—from those soft, heart-melding eyes that made his heart want to abandon his head—and stood up. "I don't think you really know what you're asking," he whispered. "What marriage to me would mean, Kristy. I don't think you realize—"

"I realize everything," Kristen said, her voice wobbling as her lips quivered with emotion. "That I've loved you most of my life, and that you love me. That we need each other."

"But that's not enough," he said. He looked at her, and she saw misty sadness glistening in his eyes. "Look at me. I'm going to have to close my business down, because half of the world still thinks I had something to do with Hank's crimes. That means I don't have a job. It means I don't have an income. It means I don't really have anything at all to offer you except a lot of bad luck."

"You'll get back on your feet, Luke," Kristen said. "You've been down before, but you always make it."

"Yeah," he said with a mirthless laugh. "Old Luke always lands on his feet, right? Well, maybe it's not that simple! Maybe this thing has brought me to my knees! Maybe this time I won't be able to make it. How would somebody like me fit into the corporate image of a spouse? I'm not a college man, or a professional, or a six-figure earner, Kristy. As far as your reputation is concerned, I'm like an albatross around your neck."

Kristen came to her feet, face-to-face with him. "I've had all that," Kristen said. "And it didn't work for me. Luke, the only albatross hanging around my neck is the image you have of yourself. That's *always* stood between us. Don't let it ruin us now."

Luke took her shoulders and peered down into her eyes. "You have to understand," he whispered, "that I can't take you for my wife until I *feel* in my heart that you'll be better off. I have to believe that I'm bringing something into this marriage, not just taking."

"Then what do I have to do to make you believe that?" she asked, her voice rising in fear. "Because *I* believe it!"

He dropped his hands helplessly and turned away from her. In his stance, she could see the battle being waged in his heart. "I've tried to protect you from the wrong people and the wrong situations since you were a little girl," he said. "And those wrong things have always included me. It's not easy for me, Kristen, to just throw out all that, and say, 'what the hell?' You mean too much to me."

"Oh, boy," Kristen whispered, and she sank onto the couch and lowered her forehead into her hands. "You're doing it again, aren't you? The martyr routine? You're going to walk out on me again, aren't you?"

Luke came to her, stooped in front of her. "Kristen, you have to understand—"

"Just go," she said, angry tears leaving tracks down her face. "You don't have to make excuses to me, or pretend that it's something noble you're doing. I'm a grown woman, Luke, and I don't need you making my decisions for me. The bottom line is that I want you and you want me, but that can't happen until you learn something about yourself that I learned a long time ago."

"What?" he asked.

She looked up at him, one last poignant plea in her angry eyes. "That if the truth were known, I'm the one who's probably not good enough for you! I have never in my life met a man who has nobler ideals. But when those ideals start to become your prison, as real a prison as the one Hank almost sent you to, then maybe it's time to ask yourself if they're not just safe little excuses to keep you from facing your fears."

"Kristy, I just need some time," he said, clutching his head in misery. "Try to understand."

"I understand, all right." Kristen slapped the tears from her face and stood up. "Just go, Luke. Run, and don't look back, just like you did when I was nineteen and you left me at the train station with a broken heart. Keep running, and if you're real lucky, maybe you won't ever really have to face it."

With a look as turbulent as she'd ever seen, Luke reached up to touch her face, but his hand didn't connect. Instead, it closed into a fist as his teeth came together. "I love you," he whispered harshly.

"Well, like you said, sometimes love just isn't enough. Sometimes it takes a little effort . . . and even a little risk."

Luke dropped his fist to his side, hovered there a moment, then quickly turned and started through the door. It closed with a dull thud, its finality crashing in Kristen's heart.

As he cranked his motorcycle outside, she leaned against the door, throwing her hands over her mouth to muffle her despair. "Damn you, Luke Wade," she whispered to the darkness ebbing in her soul.

But who she really damned, were all the people in Luke's life who had failed to love him, making it that much harder for him to believe anyone could.

CHAPTER SEVENTEEN

THE NIGHT WAS LONG, for Luke hadn't meant to spend it alone. He lay awake in his bed, trying to feel the breeze of freedom blowing in through his window, but instead he felt the new prison of martyrdom he had created.

"Run and don't look back," she'd said last night. But he couldn't seem to make himself do it. It wasn't as easy this time.

He got up and showered, then pulling on a robe, wandered aimlessly through his house, amazed at the methodical way he dressed and prepared for Sherry's funeral. Nancy had called last night to tell him that Hank was being allowed to attend the service, escorted by several police officers, and that it was scheduled for two in the afternoon. Visitation at the funeral home would start at ten, though, and she had wondered if Luke would mind being there with her, since Hank couldn't be.

The request made him feel, in some small measure, as if he belonged in the circle of family he had created in Hank and Sherry. But they were both gone now.

As he sat at his kitchen table sipping a cup of luke-warm coffee, it hit him just how dreadfully alone he had become. Sherry had died, and he'd never hear her laughter or see her teasing eyes again. Hank was locked away, and except for the funeral today, was not even being released on bond. He had lied and betrayed his best friend, the judge had said, so he couldn't be trusted to await his trial outside the confines of jail.

And now, following the inevitable pattern Luke seemed to have set for himself, Kristen wasn't there, either.

With no stomach for food, Luke dressed in a suit and made ready to stand in for his friend once again. His car, still being held as evidence in Hank's case, wasn't there, so he went out to his motorcycle and straddled it, pulled on the helmet and headed for the funeral home.

Set back from the road in a grove of pine trees, the building seemed like a peaceful sanctuary from the rat race of everyday life. As he pulled into the parking lot, the sight of the place struck his heart in an old, tender spot he hadn't expected to feel. He had forgotten that he'd been here once before. Years ago, when his parents died.

He pulled the motorcycle into a parking space and cut off the engine, slid off the helmet and stared straight ahead at the doors through which he'd gone so many years ago. He'd held back his tears that day, he thought, and had tried his thirteen-year-old best to buck up and be a man. He remembered that his rigid exterior hadn't even crumbled when he saw his parents lying in their coffins, patched up and painted to hide the injuries of the car accident that had taken their lives, injuries that were never given the chance to heal.

It wasn't until the coffins were closed that he'd lost himself, and he remembered running out of the room and hiding in the bathroom and crying his heart out until he'd had to make himself go back and join the others. Uncle Ed had come in after him, and in as patient a voice as the man had ever used in his life he had warned Luke that the procession would leave without him if he didn't come on.

It was then that Luke had realized that from that moment on, he was on his own. Oh, he'd always have a place to sleep at night, food to eat, clothes to wear. But he wouldn't really belong.

Funny how life worked in cycles, he thought. Funny that he'd wound up here again, still just as alone....

He heaved a deep sigh and started up the steps to the funeral home. Unable to go in just yet, he diverted his steps and walked around the building to the trees skirting it. He sat down on a bench for a moment, and stared through the trees as another, stronger memory tugged at his heart.

He hadn't always been alone. Before that funeral that changed his life, he had been loved. He gazed through the trees and imagined the little house where he'd lived with his parents, so unpretentious and rustic, set in a grove of trees just like these. His aunt had called his mother a hippie, and he supposed, in her time, that was exactly what she was. But what *he* remembered was the simple way she had looked at life, and the passionate way she had embraced it.

He still remembered her scent, and the soft feel of her lips on his face after he'd grown too old to kiss her back. He still remembered, too, the respect with which his father had treated him, as if he were a little adult rather than a child. Carefully, they had taught him and nurtured him, as if they knew instinctively that those years would have to last Luke the rest of his life.

And there had been no price tag attached to their love, no contract, no explanation. It simply had been. It wasn't until it disappeared that he realized how special that was.

As special as Kristen's love for him.

He swallowed the pain in his throat, struggled with his sense of helplessness and made himself face the doors of the funeral home again.

Nancy was waiting just inside the front lobby. The twins were with a baby-sitter.

"We're keeping her coffin closed," she said with tears in her eyes. "Is . . . is that all right with you?"

Luke frowned and tried to blink back the mist in his eyes. "Of course. Whatever you and Hank want. I'm not even family."

"Yes, you are," Nancy said. "Sherry loved you, and to me, your feelings are as important as anyone's." She had hooked her arm through Luke's, and escorted him into the room where the coffin lay, draped in flowers that had already arrived. "I just wanted everyone to remember her as she was," she whispered. She pulled him closer and pressed her forehead against his shoulder. "Thank you for being here with me, Luke. I'll never forget it."

Luke set his eyes on the coffin and nodded, unable to speak. For being asked to come meant as much to him as his coming meant to Nancy.

BECAUSE SHE WAS SO YOUNG and had made so many friends over the years she'd lived in Atlanta, more than two hundred people turned out at Sherry's funeral. Luke stayed in the forefront with the family, but through the crowd at the burial site, his eyes collided with Kristen's. He wondered why he was surprised that she had come, for he had known in his heart that she cared for the woman she'd never had the chance to meet. Kristen wasn't wearing black, he saw with some pleasure. Instead, her dress was a pale blue that reminded him of peace. Sherry would have liked that, he thought. She had always hated black.

He took a step toward her, not knowing what to say as the memory of yesterday's goodbyes played over in his mind again. After all the goodbyes he'd said in his life, he would have thought he'd be better at it by now.

He took another step toward her, just to thank her for coming, for wearing blue instead of black, for looking like a ray of sunlight on such a dark day....

But as if she sensed his approach, Kristen looked away, wiped at her eyes with a handkerchief, then turned and slipped deeper into the crowd. And Luke lost sight of her for the rest of the day.

Hank held up well, and Nancy seemed comforted by the kind memories and sympathy of those who had come to pay their respects. It seemed hours before the whole ordeal was over, but finally the grounds were cleared, and Luke found himself lingering behind with only Nancy, Hank and his guards.

Just before the officers escorted him back to the squad car that had delivered him, Hank regarded Luke, his eyes welling with tears as he tried to speak. "You've been the best friend I've ever had," he said. "I know Sherry felt that way, too."

Luke looked at the ground, uncomfortable with the idea of being anything but a first-class jerk when his friend was heading off to prison.

Hank patted his shoulder, his touch more eloquent than words. "I plan to plead guilty," he said, "but I thought you should know that Kristen's representing me."

Luke's eyes flashed up to Hank's. "She is? What about her firm? Are they letting her?"

Hank shook his head. "I don't know anything about the firm. All I know is that she showed up early this morning and told me that she wanted to represent me."

Feeling as if the wind had been knocked out of him, Luke glanced in the direction in which she had disappeared some time ago.

"I'm grateful," Hank went on. "She, more than anyone, understands why I did what I did. And it means a lot that she's willing to take a stand for me. She's a good lady, Luke."

Luke's frown etched itself so deeply in his face that Hank doubted it could ever be erased. "You don't have to tell me that," Luke said. "I know how good a lady she is."

Hank wiped his damp eyes and let his hand slide down Luke's arm. "She told me you two had sort of split up last night."

Luke stepped back, disengaging his arm from Hank's grip, and started to turn away. "Man, I don't want to talk about it, okay?"

"Don't you think you've suffered enough?"

Luke turned back to Hank, his face tight with denial. "Come on, Hank—"

"No," Hank said, his voice growing louder. "It's your turn, Luke. Just like you told me yesterday out at the lake. You've been alone long enough. It's time you had what Sherry and I had."

"It's not that simple!" Luke shot back. He took a few steps away, placed his hands on his hips and stared off over the groomed graves plotted like neat decorations over the landscape.

"It is that simple," Hank said. "It's so simple, it's scary. All you have to do is let it happen. What have you got to lose?"

"Maybe nothing," Luke said. "But Kristen does. I don't want to be the weak link in her life."

Hank managed to utter a soft laugh. "I don't think you have to worry about Kristen. She can take care of herself. And it isn't you who's the weak link. It's your faith in what you feel. Just go with it, Luke."

When Luke didn't answer, Hank finally turned back to the guards and said, "Just one more minute." Luke watched, then, as Hank went to the grave one last time, stood alone there for a few minutes and finally went back to the guards who waited to lock him back in the car.

Dazed and mournful, Nancy said goodbye to Luke, too, leaving him standing alone at the grave of one of his closest friends.

He looked around at the pampered plots of other people who had loved and lived and left behind people who grieved. His parents had been buried at his grandparents' grave site in a nearby town, and he had rarely had occasion to go there. But they weren't really there, he thought, reaching down and righting a vase of flowers that had fallen over. Just as Sherry wasn't really here. The real Sherry was in his heart, in his mind, on his videotape, in his memory....

"You'll make some girl a great husband," she'd said more than once, *"if you ever manage to find one who can get under your skin."*

She hadn't known it then, but that girl had gotten under his skin long before he'd been a man. And he'd never gotten her out of his heart.

He went to his motorcycle, which he'd ridden to the cemetery at the end of the procession, and pulled on his helmet. Before getting on his bike, he took off his jacket, pulled off his tie and rolled up his sleeves. Tucking the garments into the small pack on the side of his bike, he threw his leg over and pulled the bike off the kickstand. Then he drove off into the wind.

He drove without destination, without thought, until finally he ended up at the street where he and Kristen were raised, the street where he'd fallen in love with her, the street where he'd watched her dates come and go and had forced himself to leave her alone.

He slowed to a crawl when he grew closer to the house where he had lived, the house where he had never belonged.

Aunt Margaret had kept it up well, he thought, even without Ed. The garden was carefully tended, and the house looked as if it had been freshly painted. It was obviously a source of pride to her, he thought, unlike her nephew, who hadn't warranted that much of her care.

He cut off his engine and sat still on the curb, wondering why he had come here. He had no desire to see Aunt Margaret and hear her reprimands, or experience her shame. And yet he had come, like a little boy seeking his mommy's approval.

He heard a child's voice, and looked across the street to Kristen's mother's house. In the side yard, where he and Kristen had often sat in the large oak tree and talked, were Courtney and two of her friends, a boy and a girl. Courtney was hanging from a tire swing, and the boy was turning it, letting the rope twist so that she'd spin when he let it go.

Luke watched as the boy gave the tire one last shove and stepped back. The swing began to twirl, and Courtney screamed. Suddenly, he saw her fall, and before he had time to think, he was off his bike and dashing across the street.

"I didn't mean to do it!" the boy was shouting over Courtney's screams. When they saw Luke, the two children started to run away, fearing for their safety once his anger became directed at them.

Luke bent and picked up Courtney, who was still screaming. He saw that her hands were skinned where they'd broken her fall. The little girl's arms went around his neck, and she buried her face in his shoulder. He held her close until her wails, loud enough to alert the entire neighborhood, abated.

Kristen's mother came running out, but her steps slowed when she saw Luke holding her granddaughter like a cherished treasure.

"Feel better?" he asked Courtney tenderly.

She hiccuped a sob and wiped her face.

Luke glanced aside and saw Kristen's mother...and someone else behind her. His heart caught and stumbled when he realized that Aunt Margaret was watching him.

"Hello, Aunt Margaret," he said quietly.

Margaret nodded her head, like a casual acquaintance who hadn't seen him in a while. "Luke."

Kristen's mother took the whimpering Courtney from Luke, and whispered, "Thank you, Luke. I'll take her in and clean up these scrapes." Then she left the two alone.

Luke looked down at the ground, then back up to his aunt, and slid his hands into his pockets. "It's been a long time," he said. "You look good."

"And so do you," Margaret said, not making any attempt to retreat to the sanctuary of her house. "I heard you'd been vindicated," she said. "I was glad."

"I'll bet you were." The bitterness in Luke's voice made him angry, and he looked past her to his bike, and wished he'd never driven down this street today.

"No, Luke. I mean it."

He saw the beginning of tears in Aunt Margaret's eyes, and frowned in confusion. "Well...thank you," he said.

She swallowed, and he watched as she fidgeted with her hands, unable to hide her tension. "I...I'm glad you came by today," she said, lifting her chin to offset the weakness in her voice. "I know you didn't come to see me, but I wonder if you could come over for a few minutes. There are some things I need to say to you."

Luke checked his watch, wishing he had some excuse to avoid this confrontation, but came up empty. Strangely, he discovered that some part of him needed to hear whatever she had to say. The other part, the part that wrapped itself in that protective armor he'd always worn, told him to get on his bike and ride away. "I don't know, Aunt Margaret. I really need to go...."

"Please." The word got caught in her throat, and Luke suddenly found that he couldn't refuse.

"All right," he said, shrugging. "Just for a minute."

He followed her quietly back to her house, and stepping inside, breathed in the scent that meant sterile cleanliness and extreme neatness. He remembered having been almost afraid of that house, as if it held the power to get him banished permanently. He walked behind her into the kitchen and glanced around.

"It looks nice," he said awkwardly. "I guess it's easier to keep up without some snotty-nosed kid running around knocking things over."

She almost smiled, but couldn't quite manage it. Instead, she went to the coffeepot, poured him a cup and handed it to him. Luke pulled out a chair, careful not to scrape the shine on the floor, and sat down.

"I heard that you buried your friend this morning," she said quietly. "I'm sorry."

Luke sipped the coffee but didn't answer. Margaret wouldn't have approved of Sherry, the Las Vegas show girl, any more than she approved of him, he thought.

"And I heard about how her husband framed you, and how you were charged with crimes you didn't commit."

Luke set the cup down and looked up at her, anxious to hear what she was getting at. He could see from the way her eyes shifted to and from him, that she was having trouble expressing herself.

"I felt terrible that I was so...so sure you had done it," she said. She pulled out a chair and sat down to face him, folding her hands on the table in front of her but keeping her eyes downcast. "The other day Kristen came to see me, and she accused me of slighting you all these years, of always thinking the worst. I suppose she was right."

Luke shook his head, and held out a hand to stem the rest of her words and make the moment easier. "Don't worry about it. I gave you plenty of trouble when I was a kid. You had every right—"

"No," she cut in. "I had no right. You were different from my own kids, just like your mother was different from me. I should have given you more of a chance. I should have had a little more faith."

Luke leaned back wearily in his chair. "It doesn't matter now, Aunt Margaret. I'm an adult now. You're not responsible."

"But I feel responsible," she said. "I can't help it." She got to her feet and went to the counter, busied herself moving the canisters around. "I saw what your friend did to you, and how it's going to ruin your business and your reputation, and I realized that— maybe that's what I'd been doing to you all these years. Setting you up to be the bad boy, the one who was going to make trouble."

She turned back to him, met his eyes and inclined her head poignantly. "But you did rather well after you left us, didn't you, Luke?"

Luke couldn't answer, for he knew she was aware of all of his accomplishments. He figured it helped her gauge his failures.

"The Army, the medals, the business that was growing and becoming respected—"

"I'm closing the business," Luke said, as if offering her another prize to hold on to.

"But that's what I've been trying to get to," Aunt Margaret said, sitting down and fixing him with eyes becoming more alive. "You've built your business from scratch, into something to be proud of. It shouldn't be snatched from you like that."

Luke shook his head. "I don't understand."

Margaret reached across the table and grabbed his hand. He couldn't remember if she had ever touched him before. "You may not be aware of this," she said, "but my Michael is the president of his bank in Marietta."

Luke withdrew his hand, dreading the comparison to the successful firstborn son, and wondered if she was about to launch into a rundown of the successes of each of her children in turn.

"He needs a security system in the bank," she said, her eyebrows arching. "And he wants you to design it."

Luke's eyes flashed up, meeting hers in surprise, and that deep frown cleaved his brow again. "Come on, Aunt Margaret. Don't play games with me."

"It's true," she said. "He called me this morning. He told me that he had planned to hire you before you were arrested, and that now that you're vindicated, he sees no reason to wait."

Luke got to his feet, turned away from Margaret and raked his hand through his hair. After a moment, he turned around and stared down at her. "But...isn't he worried about the publicity? The reputation?"

"Well, he isn't hiring Hank," his aunt said. "He's hiring you. Luke, this might be just what you need to get you back on your feet. If the president of a bank would employ you, maybe others will."

"But why?" he asked. "Why would he do that?"

"Because he knows you and he trusts you," Margaret said. She got up, just feet from Luke, gazing sadly at him. "If Michael had still been at home when you moved in with us, maybe he would have kept us from being so hard on you. He always liked you, Luke."

Luke felt a lump lodge in his throat, and he gulped it back. "Tell him...tell him I'll call him this afternoon," he said, trying to control the waver in his voice. "And thank you. I really appreciate it."

He left Aunt Margaret with no display of emotion, for the two had never been affectionate in the past. But this time when he said goodbye to her, he saw a certain measure of respect in her eyes, as if the events of the past few days had changed her view of him, and she no longer saw him as the bad boy who was going to bring her family down. Now she saw him as he really was. Just another human being, struggling to make it in a mixed-up world.

Luke crossed the street and knocked on Kristen's mother's door. When she called, "Come in," he opened the door and stepped into the kitchen.

Courtney was sitting on the counter as Edith bandaged her hands and knees with enough bandages to outfit an entire army squad in wartime.

"How are you feeling, kiddo?" he asked, leaning on the counter next to her.

Courtney brandished the palms of her hands. "Fine. Grandma's putting bandages on my sores."

He grinned. "I see."

He leaned closer, reaching for her hand, but Courtney recoiled. "No, you can't look," she told him. "I'm mad at you."

"Courtney!" Her grandmother looked up from her work on the other hand. "Don't talk like that to Luke."

"That's okay, Edith," he said, moving his sobering eyes back to Courtney. "What did I do?"

"You lied," Courtney said. "You told me that you would never hurt my mommy. But you have."

Luke glanced at Edith, saw that she had dropped Courtney's hand and was looking at him with deep apology in her eyes.

"I never meant to," he whispered.

"Meant to doesn't matter," Courtney went on. "Last night I heard her crying in her bed when she thought I was asleep."

Something in Luke's heart burst. "She wasn't crying for me," he said lamely.

"Yes, she was," Courtney said bitterly. "She loves you, but you don't love her, do you?"

"Of course I do," he said. "I love her more than you could ever understand." His voice broke, and he turned away.

"Then why did you leave her?" she asked.

Luke didn't answer, and after a moment, Courtney slipped down off the counter and went to tug on Luke's sleeve.

"I wanted you to marry her," she said, her voice taking on a directness that most adults he knew hadn't mastered. "I thought you could move in with us, and be my stepdad, and read me a book every night."

Luke's sight of her suddenly went blurry, and he gazed at her through misty eyes. "You wouldn't mind that?" he asked.

Courtney frowned at the absurdity of such a question. "No, we have lots of room!"

Luke stooped down and picked up Courtney, holding her face next to his as he hugged her. Over her little shoulder, he met Edith's eyes. "And what do you think about all this, Edith? Are you mad at me, too?"

Edith set down her box of bandages, knowing that Luke's hug provided all the healing power Courtney needed. "I think that Kristen's life won't ever be really happy unless you're in it, Luke," she said. "And if you're too stubborn to see that, then I guess that does make me mad."

Luke smiled as a sudden sense of peace watched over him, for the decision didn't seem as tough anymore as it had last night, now that it was couched and cushioned in love.

"Where is she?" he asked.

Edith offered him a half smile. "Oh, probably at the law firm turning in her resignation. They weren't too keen on her representing Hank, and she wasn't too keen on letting anyone else do it."

Luke sobered. "She's resigning? What will she do?"

"Open her own office, I guess," she said. "I convinced her to use the money her father left her, now that she got your bond money back."

Carefully, Luke set Courtney down and messed up her hair distractedly. "Really? She's going to do that?"

"Yes, Luke. She said she told you that the firm was—"

Not bothering to hear the rest, Luke started backing toward the door.

"Where are you going?" Courtney asked as he reached it.

"To find your mommy," Luke called over his shoulder as he started out. "I'm going to ask her to marry me!"

"All right!" Courtney's whoops could be heard all the way out to Luke's bike, and smiling, he pulled on his helmet and headed for Kristen's house.

KRISTEN TRIED NOT TO CRY as she drove into her neighborhood toward her house. So she didn't have a job, and she didn't have Luke. She still had a client to defend, she thought, and she had a daughter who loved her. For now, that would keep her going.

She wiped her eyes and told herself that she should get excited about the prospect of opening her own law office. She should have done so earlier, she thought. Now she could stop trying so hard to conform to the image that Broussard, Street and Devereaux cared so much about. Now she could be on her own, and concentrate on her work instead.

If only thoughts of Luke didn't keep breaking that concentration.

She pulled into her driveway, turned off the engine and wiped her eyes again. She'd have to pull herself together, she thought. It had just been a bad day. First the funeral, and then the resignation . . .

She glanced up and saw Luke's motorcycle, and drawing in a sharp breath, she looked toward the front porch.

Luke sat on her steps, elbows propped on his knees, watching her get out of the car.

"Luke?" she asked apprehensively. "What are you doing here?"

He stood up, his eyes misty soft as he looked at her. "I was in the neighborhood and had a hellacious craving for a cigarette, and I thought I'd stop by and see if you might have any."

She offered him a cautious smile. "You know I haven't."

"Well, then," he said with a sigh. "I guess I'll have to scratch this itch some other way."

He reached out and touched her face and stroked a thumb across the dampness there. The teasing spark left his eyes, and a poignant seriousness replaced it.

"How?" she whispered, her expression an offering in itself.

"I don't know," he said, pulling her into his arms. "Maybe by marrying you."

She gasped, but the gasp was lost in their kiss as his lips claimed hers. And suddenly, Kristen knew that everything that had happened in her life had happened for a reason. All the pain, all the loneliness, all the heartbreaks, had brought her to this one moment. This moment when Luke surrendered.

"I love you," she whispered against his lips as he took the key from her hand and lifted her in his arms.

"I love you, too," he said, taking her through the door and into the house. "I'll never leave you again.

We'll get married as soon as we can, and I'll sell my house and move in here."

"No."

Luke stopped and let her slide down his legs until her feet supported her. "What?" he asked, alarm in his eyes.

"No, I don't want us to live here," she said. "I want to sell both houses, and buy a new one. One that belongs to both of us. One where we can both belong, so that neither of us feels like a guest in the other's home."

"What about Courtney?" he asked. "Will she go for that?"

"She'll love it," Kristen said, "because she loves you."

And as she melted in his kiss once more, cherishing the love and joy that she could feel in every inch of Luke's embrace, she knew that Luke wouldn't walk out on her again.

Because, finally, he knew where he belonged.

Harlequin Superromance®

COMING NEXT MONTH

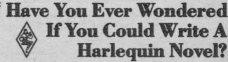

Have You Ever Wondered If You Could Write A Harlequin Novel?

Here's great news—Harlequin is offering a series of cassette tapes to help you do just that. Written by Harlequin editors, these tapes give practical advice on how to make your characters—and your story—come alive. There's a tape for each contemporary romance series Harlequin publishes.

Mail order only

All sales final

This April, don't miss Harlequin's new Award of
Excellence title from

CAROLE MORTIMER

elusive as the unicorn

*When Eve Eden discovered that Adam
Gardener, successful art entrepreneur, was
searching for the legendary English artist, The
Unicorn, she nervously shied away. The Unicorn's
true identity hit too close to home....*

*Besides, Eve was rattled by Adam's
mesmerizing presence, especially in the light
of the ridiculous coincidence of their names—
and his determination to take advantage of it!
But Eve was already engaged to marry her
longtime friend, Paul.*

*Yet Eve found herself troubled by the different
choices Adam and Paul presented. If only the
answer to her dilemma didn't keep eluding her....*

HP1258-1

H A R L E Q U I N
American Romance®

Live the

Rocky Mountain Magic

Become a part of the magical events at The Stanley Hotel in the Colorado Rockies, and be sure to catch its final act in April 1990 with #337 RETURN TO SUMMER by Emma Merritt.

Three women friends touched by magic find love in a very special way, the way of enchantment. Hayley Austin was gifted with a magic apple that gave her three wishes in BEST WISHES (#329). Nicki Chandler was visited by psychic visions in SIGHT UNSEEN (#333). Now travel into the past with Kate Douglas as she meets her soul mate in RETURN TO SUMMER #337.

ROCKY MOUNTAIN MAGIC—All it takes is an open heart.